LINE UP

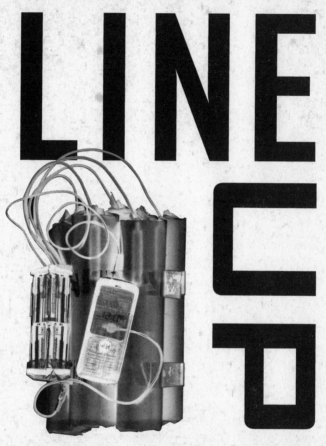

LIAD SHOHAM

Translated from the Hebrew by Sara Kitai

BOURBON
STREET
BOOKS

www.harpercollins.com

Originally published in a different form as *Misdar Zihuy* in Israel in 2011 by Kinneret Zmora-Bitan.

First U.S. hardcover published in 2013 by HarperCollins Publishers.

HarperCollins books may be purchased for educational, business, or sales promotional use. For information please e-mail the Special Markets Department at SPsales@harpercollins.com.

FIRST BOURBON STREET BOOKS EDITION PUBLISHED 2014.

Designed by William Ruoto

Library of Congress Cataloging-in-Publication Data has been applied for.

ISBN 978-0-06-223745-3 (pbk.)

14 15 16 17 18 OV/RRD 10 9 8 7 6 5 4 3 2 1

To Rona and Uri

LINE
UP

Chapter 1

SARAH Glazer raised the binoculars to her eyes and followed the movements of the young man and his dog walking down the street. He'd moved in as the third housemate in the fourth-floor apartment at 56 Louis Marshall Street a week ago, and every night since, at 12:45, he went out to walk his dog. He made his way back and forth along the block between De Haas and Brandeis until the dog had done its business, and then picked up the poo with a plastic bag. But yesterday she noticed that he didn't clean up after the dog. She'd focused on the man's face, waiting to see if it registered surprise at the absence of a bag, annoyance with himself for having forgotten it, or at least a modicum of embarrassment, but his expression remained blank. He continued on his way as if nothing out of the ordinary had happened. He didn't seem to be bothered by the fact that the dog poo was still lying there on the sidewalk. Despite her conviction that such behavior was barbaric, a sign of the moral decline of the country's younger generation, she had decided not to do anything about it for the moment. Everyone is entitled to one mistake. So now she was waiting anxiously to see what he would do tonight. If he didn't clean up after the dog again, she would no longer remain silent. Tomorrow, first thing in the morning, she'd send a strongly worded complaint to the city, anonymously, of course.

The dog stopped. She adjusted the binoculars. She'd bought them on the Internet a month ago, paying more than ten thousand shekels for what the company website guaranteed was "the latest technology." But as a woman who always kept an eye on the street, who made sure she was aware of everything going on in the neighborhood, she couldn't resist. She told no one about her purchase as she waited impatiently for the package to arrive. A few days later it did. Inside was a shiny new pair of binoculars with the finest lenses and a special button. When she pressed it she could see almost as well at night as she could in broad daylight.

Her oldest grandson had come to visit two days ago and asked if she used the computer he'd bought her for her birthday, if she remembered what he'd taught her about how to use the Internet. She almost told him about the lovely present she had got herself with all those impressive features. But she changed her mind at the last minute. She knew tongues would start wagging in the family, and she'd have to explain why, at the age of eighty-two, she had decided to buy binoculars, of all things, and such expensive ones to boot. She and Sefi, may he rest in peace, had always lived frugally, saving their money "for the children." Squandering it like this would undoubtedly raise an eyebrow or two among her children and give her two daughters-in-law good reason to mutter behind her back. And so she held her tongue. It was better they didn't know. She deserved to pamper herself now and then. And at her age she had the right to a few secrets.

The man from the fourth floor at 56 Louis Marshall Street bent down and picked up the dog poo with a bag. Yesterday had apparently been an isolated incident. But maybe not. Just to be on the safe side, she'd continue to keep an eye on him. With things like this, you had to keep your finger on the pulse.

She lowered the binoculars to her lap and yawned. She had to admit to herself that she was a little disappointed he'd cleaned up after the dog. In her head she'd already started phrasing the letter she'd write to the city about the shamelessness of the younger generation, the lack of consideration and basic human decency in the world today. This never used to happen. In the old days, everybody knew everybody. People would not have allowed themselves to behave that way. This was a neighborhood built for the workers of the Tel Aviv harbor. They were all Socialists. The four-story-high row houses, nicknamed "railroad cars," were assigned by lottery. They were all small and identical, but the tenants cared for them. They invested money and effort in the neighborhood. It was always clean and tidy, and on holidays, they would go down to plant flowers in the garden with the kids. Today, all the new tenants were well off, or the children of people with money. Sure, inside it's beautiful, but outside? Ha! Nobody cared anymore, to say nothing of planting gardens. That's why this guy didn't care about the mess his dog made.

She got up from the chair slowly. Lately, she found her head would spin for a few minutes if she stood up too quickly. She looked over at the second floor of 54 Louis Marshall Street. The apartment was dark. The day before yesterday she'd seen the couple arguing, and the man hadn't been home since. Every night the woman sat crying at the kitchen table. Her heart went out to them, especially that nice lady who always greeted her with a broad smile when they passed each other in the street.

She dragged herself through the apartment to the bathroom. Dr. Shaham had instructed her to take Nurofen four times a day for her arthritis, and like a good soldier, she always followed doctor's orders. That was why she'd been forcing herself to stay up until one o'clock the last few days. She took the first pill at seven in the morning when she got up, the second at one in the afternoon with her lunch, the third at seven in the evening, an hour before the news, and the fourth at one at night. If it weren't for that fourth pill, she'd go to bed at ten, just as she and Sefi had done every night for the past twenty years. Her daughter, Ruthie, had suggested she set the alarm, but she didn't trust clocks. And what did Ruthie know about pain anyway?

She placed the pill on her tongue and washed it down with a sip of water. Suddenly, she stopped what she was doing and straightened up. A noise was coming from outside. Something was moving around in the yard. It must be the cats, she thought. She went downstairs every morning to give them milk and brought them bones at lunchtime. They were probably fighting again, too, she thought gloomily, shaking her head. She raised the binoculars to her eyes and pressed the night-vision button.

For a moment she thought she was imagining things. But it wasn't her imagination. It wasn't cats she heard down there; it was people, two of them. A man and a woman. Like animals, she muttered to herself. Why "like"? They *were* animals. She grimaced in disgust. The man had a large tattoo on his arm, maybe a dragon, which only added to her repulsion. Barbarians and thugs were everywhere these days. Even in her own neighborhood. It was utterly repugnant. Nevertheless, she kept her eyes glued to the binoculars, unable to look away.

What she was looking at wasn't immediately clear to her. Her mind didn't work as quickly as it used to. It took a while for all the details to come together in her head to form a coherent picture. And then all at once she realized: they weren't lovers. The man was raping the woman right before her eyes, in the yard of the building she had lived in for more than forty years, just a few feet from the Indian ficus tree that her Sefi planted when they moved in. One hand was over the girl's mouth and the other was holding a knife to her throat. His buttocks rose and fell rapidly, beating at her in a monotonous rhythm. She understood now that the howling she'd heard before hadn't come from the cats.

Her skin bristled. She could almost feel the weight of the rapist bearing down on her, pressing on her windpipe and preventing her from breathing. She wanted to do something, to scream, to run to the phone and call the police, to help the poor girl lying there in the yard. But she did none of those things. She only stood by the window, frozen, paralyzed by fear.

All of a sudden the man stopped and twisted his head around, staring in her direction. Quickly, she took a few steps back, moving deeper into the apartment, letting her figure be swallowed up in the darkness. A chill ran through her body. If she called the police now and they caught him, he or his gangster friends would come back to settle the score with her. They weren't the kind of people you ought to mess with. There was no compassion in the underworld they lived in. Certainly not for a woman her age. What would she do if they showed up at her door? She was too old, too frail for such things.

No. She had to play it smart. Keep out of it.

She went into the bedroom and opened the top drawer of the nightstand with a trembling hand. Her heart was racing. She took out the nitroglycerin pills Dr. Shaham had prescribed for her heart, placed one under her tongue, and got into bed, the binoculars still around her neck. Everyone is entitled to one mistake. Besides, maybe someone else heard them, she thought, trying to comfort herself as sleep gathered her up in its arms. A lot of people live here. People who are younger and stronger than me.

Chapter 2

ADI Regev was on top of the world. Her light dress danced around her legs in the warm air. She'd just left the pub near her house where she'd been out with the girls from yoga class. They had drinks (too many), chatted (about nothing), gossiped a little (a little too much), and told each other date-from-hell stories that made them double up with laughter. And if that wasn't enough, a guy who looked great even though he was wearing a suit, which to her mind wasn't the way to go, exchanged glances with her when she went to the ladies' room, and just before they left, he came over to her, introduced himself as Kobi, and asked for her phone number. Hers! Not Efrat's or Michal's, who looked sensational, but hers. He had a nice voice, a cute smile, and, best of all, she could see the envy on Michal's face.

She loved Tel Aviv, its fast pace, all it had to offer, especially the old northern part where she lived, because even though it was close to the center of town, it still felt like a real community. She especially liked Saturday mornings, when all the young people her age crowded the coffee shops or rode their bikes to the park. When she moved out of her parents' house in Hadera to Tel Aviv two years earlier, she was afraid of being lonely in the big city, or even worse, that everyone would think she was provincial. But she found she had nothing to fear. She had tons of friends, and went out almost every night. She was working her ass off, slaving overtime as a secretary in an accountant's office in the Azrieli Towers, but she was enjoying every minute and didn't have to account to anyone for anything. Her parents (particularly her father) weren't happy about it. They wanted her to go to college, to do something with her life, to be like her big brother, who studied engineering at the Technion, or like the rest of her friends from high school, who were buried under a pile of books cramming for some exam. Meanwhile, she managed to put it out of her mind and ignore their aspirations for her. It wasn't easy, especially because they were still paying her rent. But she was making a determined effort to revel in her freedom.

She walked toward the door of her building, humming to herself. The alcohol in her bloodstream made her feel even more upbeat and lighthearted. Thursday night—a weekend of fun awaited her. Something might even come out of that encounter with Kobi at the pub.

A sound from behind the hedge broke the silence of the night, giving her a fright. It's just cats, she reassured herself, the ones that flaky old lady in the next building is always feeding.

"Do you live here?" she heard a man behind her ask politely.

She spun around, looking for the source of the voice.

A tall, thin man stepped out from behind the darkness of the thorny bushes. He had on a baseball cap and sunglasses. Sunglasses? In the middle of the night? Her body tensed up.

"You startled me," she mumbled, moving back.

He came closer, but she couldn't make out his face under the shadow cast by the brim of his cap.

"Hold on a minute, sweetheart. I just want to ask you something. Where're you going?" he said genially. Too genially. Her instincts were telling her it was time to run, but she just froze where she was, like a deer in the headlights.

"Good. That's much better." He moved toward her, reducing the distance between them. "Don't be scared. I just want to ask you something, that's all."

The words were soothing, but his voice made her nervous. There was something taunting about it, a trace of contempt.

"Sorry . . . I'm late," she answered, her voice trembling despite her efforts to keep it steady. She turned her back on him and started to draw away.

An arm pinned her around the neck, making it hard for her to breathe. A hand clutched at her long hair close to the roots, hurting her. She fell hard to the ground, landing on her side. He dragged her by the hair behind the tall hedge, her face scraping through the dirt. She kicked at him, trying to make him stop, to free herself from his grasp and get her hand into her purse where she kept the canister of pepper spray she took with her everywhere. But he was too strong.

He sat on her, grabbed her by the throat, and tightened his grip, bringing his face close to hers. He reeked of a mixture of alcohol, sweat, and aftershave, and it made her sick to her stomach. "Scream and you're dead," he hissed.

He loosened his hold on her just a little. She tried to get up, to shout, but he reacted instantly, pushing her head sharply to the ground and covering her mouth. Now she could see he had a serrated knife in the other hand. "Don't play games with me. I mean it. One move and you're dead," he warned, passing the cold steel along her cheek until the tip of the blade was against her neck. He pricked her under the chin.

It stung.

"Do we understand each other?" he asked, pushing the knife deeper into her flesh.

She tried to look away, but he grabbed her jaw and turned her face to him. There was a taste of sand and salt in her mouth.

"Do we understand each other," he repeated, "or am I gonna have to rip you apart with this knife?"

She tried to say she understood, to nod, but no sound came out and she couldn't move a muscle. It was just like the time she was sixteen, in the car with her mother, when she watched her drive straight into another vehicle. She tried to scream then too, to shout at her to stop, to keep her eyes on the road, but the words wouldn't come out of her mouth.

"You hear me, bitch? You wanna die today?" he said, jerking her head back and forth.

The shaking released her from the state of paralysis. She nodded.

"That's better. You got nowhere to run, right? You gonna be a good girl and behave nice?" he said hoarsely.

As she nodded again, the puke rose in her throat, nearly choking her.

"If you don't wanna die, you gotta beg for your life," he said, removing his hand from over her mouth. Tears were running down her cheeks.

"Beg," he spat angrily, leaning on the knife again.

"Don't, please, no, let me go . . . just . . . let me go . . ." She was crying so hard she could barely speak.

"More!" he commanded.

"Please! No, please! I'll do whatever you want . . . just don't hurt me . . ." Her face was wet with tears.

Rising slightly, he pulled up her dress, tore off her panties, and hunched over her, pushing her legs apart with his knee.

"Beg or you're dead," he repeated. His face was only a few inches from hers. She could feel his hot breath on her cheek.

"I'm begging you . . . ," she began, and then fell silent as another wave of nausea washed over her when she felt his penis tear into her, hurting her deep inside.

"More! Beg!" he commanded again, slapping her across the face.

"Please stop . . . no . . . please . . . don't . . . ," she stuttered as he thrust himself into her again and again, his movements violent and painful.

"More," he whispered in her ear, slapping her again. She shuddered in revulsion.

THE boiling hot water scalded her skin and made the cuts burn, but she ignored the pain. She had to scour herself clean, to cleanse her body of the filth, to rid it of the odor he had left on her. She scrubbed herself meticulously, making sure to reach every single spot, not to miss an inch of skin anywhere. Then she did it again. And again. And again.

SHE couldn't tell how long it lasted. Maybe forever. She prayed for it to stop, to be over, but time seemed to stand still. She lay there under him, choked by her tears, begging, while he hammered at her. Again. And again. And again.

Finally, he got off, pulled up his pants, and disappeared, leaving her lying on the ground. As soon as she was sure he wasn't coming back, she started to puke. She retched until her throat hurt.

Why hadn't she followed her instincts? She'd heard the noise behind the hedge, so how could she have let herself walk into a trap? Why didn't she scream when he took his hand off her mouth, when she had the chance? She'd read somewhere that rapists choose their victims carefully. What had she done to make him choose her?

She lay there for a long time, the tears flowing down her face. The sour odor of puke burned her nose. The cut on her chin was bleeding. She knew she should cry out for help, run away, but she felt too weak to move, numb, still under his control. Finally she pulled herself up and made her way slowly toward the door of her building and into her apartment.

THE shower kept on running, the water washing over her, scalding her skin. She sat hunched up in the corner, sobbing and shaking, still feeling him on top of her, inside her.

HER cell phone beeped with a text message from Kobi, the guy she'd met at the pub. "Want to get together?" he'd written, adding a smiley face. He'd already called earlier in the day. She didn't answer the phone. She didn't answer any of the other calls she got that weekend either. She spent the whole time in bed, sleeping, staring into space, sobbing, blaming herself—why hadn't she said she had her period, that she was pregnant, that she had a disease? Why hadn't she tried to talk him out of it? She only got out of bed to change the Band-Aid she'd put on the cut on her chin and to scrub herself raw, again and again. She took care not to catch sight of her face in the mirror, not to see what he'd done to her.

She stared at the phone. What could she say to him, to Kobi? That she was sorry but it was hard for her to go out at the moment because she kept bursting into tears? That even the thought that he might touch her made her sick?

Yesterday afternoon she'd decided that she would put it behind her, get over it, get on with her life. She'd even managed to get out of bed with a burst of energy, to convince herself it was possible. But a minute later she'd collapsed back onto the sheets, wrapping herself in the blanket. What if he'd infected her with something? Gotten her pregnant?

With trembling fingers she texted Kobi that she was sorry but it wouldn't work out; it's not you, it's me. He responded immediately with a sad face. Again she burst out crying. Then she fell asleep, exhausted.

THE cell phone woke her up. It was her parents. It was the fifth time they'd called and she didn't answer. The day before she'd texted them that she wouldn't be coming home for Friday-night dinner as usual. She decided not to tell them. She didn't want to upset them. And, besides, she knew if they saw her like this, they'd insist on taking her to the hospital and going to the police. She wasn't ready. She wanted to be left alone, to lick her wounds in solitude, not to be surrounded by cops questioning her and doctors poking at her body.

Her parents rang again. She cut off the call and set the phone to silent mode.

AT first she thought it was part of a dream. But she wasn't dreaming. Someone was really knocking on the door. Insistently. Gently to start with, and then harder. She shook in terror. Had he come back?

She looked at the clock. Ten thirty. Saturday night.

Who could it be?

She stayed huddled in bed, petrified, afraid to move. Maybe he'd give up and go away, leave her alone. All she wanted was to be left alone.

But the knocking didn't stop. It just got louder and more emphatic. What would she do if he broke down the door?

She heard someone call her name. She tried to focus, to force herself to listen.

She wasn't mistaken. She recognized the voice.

Chapter 3

AMIT Giladi looked over the titles of the latest porn films uploaded onto his favorite site. From time to time he clicked on one that caught his interest, but it didn't take more than a minute before he stopped the film and began trawling for another one. He was finding it hard to concentrate. He kept glancing over at the cell phone sitting on his desk, waiting impatiently for it to ring. His source—he had secretly dubbed him "Deep Throat" in homage to the two investigative reporters who were his idols—had promised to call that night and tell him where he was leaving the envelope.

He hadn't yet told anyone about their conversations. The story, if he could prove it, would be his and his alone. He'd been covering crime and education for the local Tel Aviv paper for seven and a half months. They'd stuck him with education a month and a half ago after they fired the reporter who used to cover the beat as part of the "streamlining" measures they were instituting. He'd learned a lot at the paper, especially from the editor Dori Engel, but he was ready for the major leagues, aching to be a real investigative journalist who reported more than merely local stories.

"Deep Throat" had contacted him claiming to have information about police corruption. He alleged that senior officers close to the police chief were being sent abroad for bogus training courses and being put up at five-star hotels at the taxpayers' expense. He even supplied the names of some of those officers and the hotels they stayed at.

Amit had tried to wheedle out of him the source of his information. Was he a cop himself? What was his rank? But "Deep Throat" threatened never to talk to him again if he kept asking questions. Still, he insisted on knowing why, of all the reporters in the country, he'd picked him. After all, this was a story for a national paper. "Deep Throat's" answer, that most of the officers were from the Tel Aviv district and that his paper had "balls," wasn't very convincing. He demanded documents in writing, hard evidence, before he'd agree to run with the story. Journalists more seasoned than he had ruined their careers by rushing into print without checking the facts first. Here, "Deep Throat" showed a little more understanding. On Sunday night, he'd promised, he'd call back and tell him where he was leaving the incriminating documents.

He'd been waiting anxiously since the afternoon, wondering when his source would call and what he had for him. But so far, nothing. It was already eleven o'clock, and the call hadn't come. Maybe he'd changed his mind, or worse—taken the story to another paper.

He threw himself on the bed and stared at the peeling paint on the ceiling. He would've been thrilled to rent an apartment somewhere else in the city, but with what they were paying him, that was all he could afford—a measly 270 square feet, a room and a half on the first floor, facing the noise and stench of busy Allenby Street. The smell of fresh falafel from the stand outside tugged at his stomach, but, no, he'd better save his money and eat his mother's stuffed peppers.

The sound of the ringtone caught him in mid-thought. Hurriedly, he reached out for the phone, almost dropping it in his excitement.

"Tell me, Giladi, why the fuck do I keep you around?" To his huge disappointment, it was Dori's angry voice on the other end.

He didn't answer. Dori might have a filthy mouth, but he also had a nose for news and very keen senses.

"Stop jerking off. There's a world out there and things're happening in it," Dori went on when he got no response.

"I hear you, Dori. What's going on?" he said in a contrite tone. Within no more than a month or two at the paper he'd learned the wisdom of not reacting to Dori's taunts. He vowed that one day he'd pay him back for all the shit he'd taken. Just as soon as he had his scoop and he could walk away from that rag and slam the door behind him. But meanwhile, he had to grit his teeth and hold his tongue. He needed Dori more than Dori needed him.

"You know what I'm hearing? There was a rape on Louis Marshall, half the cops in the city are there, all the media, with the single exception of my fucking crime reporter who's sitting at home playing with himself," he bellowed.

Amit's face went red. What a fuckup. No wonder Dori was furious. He checked his police scanner. He'd turned it off at noontime when he crashed for a while and had been so preoccupied with "Deep Throat" that he'd forgotten to switch it on again.

"I'm sorry . . . I didn't hear . . . ," he mumbled. Wonderful. Just great. He could fantasize all he liked about quitting to go over to a national paper, but if he wasn't careful he'd get himself fired before he got the chance. Dori was merciless. One mistake and you're out. The professionalism of his little paper was his top priority. Only a few days ago he'd canned their health reporter, Naama, for a couple of errors in the copy she filed. "Moron, get the fuck out of my sight," he'd yelled at her in front of everyone. Amit could suffer the same fate. Despite all his grumblings, he knew there were hundreds of people who'd jump at the chance to take over his job.

"No fucking excuses," Dori roared. "Pull your finger out of your ass and get there now. Give me five hundred words by tomorrow morning."

Amit jumped on his motorbike and sped to the old north,

running what he liked to call "pink" lights on the way. Shit like this wasn't supposed to happen. He could understand why Dori was so mad. Rape cases sell papers, especially when they occur in a safe, respectable neighborhood, the last place you expect to find violent crime. It was a shame people didn't know that "the last place" was a cliché with no basis in fact. As a crime reporter, he knew only too well that no neighborhood was safe from criminals.

Dozens of people were already milling around the scene. He caught sight of Yael Gilboa from *Haaretz* and Sefi Reshef from the army radio station. They were talking to a tall cop he didn't know. In his job, the name of the game was to get there first, to get the jump on the competition. That wasn't going to happen this time, goddamn it.

His phone rang. Dori again.

"What'd you find out?" He could actually feel his impatience through the phone.

"I just got here," he shouted to make himself heard over the commotion.

"Get me a scoop. You know what a scoop is, don't you, Giladi?" Dori snapped before hanging up abruptly. Amit let out a sigh. Their budget was constantly being slashed and questions had even been raised as to the very need for the paper. A lot of journalists had found themselves out of work recently, including some who'd been in the profession for a long time and had an impressive résumé. He knew Dori had very good reason to demand a scoop.

He started toward the two reporters, trying to overhear what the cop was telling them. Last week he'd published a story about a local high-ranking officer who verbally abused his son's principal. The police had been called. The district spokesman had asked him to bury the story, hinting that he'd find an opportunity to return the favor, but Dori had refused. "If we don't print the story, someone else will. We can't do favors in our business," he'd replied adamantly. After that incident, would he be able to find anyone on the force who was still willing to talk to him? Where would he get his scoop? With any luck, the police would ask for a gag order, and then none of the papers would be able to print the story, even if the competition knew something about the rape that he didn't.

His phone rang again. What does he want this time, he groaned to himself. The screen showed "number withheld." Could it be the call from "Deep Throat" he'd been waiting for all day? He looked around for somewhere quiet, but there was nowhere to go.

"Hello," he screamed into the phone.

A siren was wailing behind him.

"Hello," he shouted again.

He heard the sound of the call being disconnected.

Chapter 4

YARON Regev sat in his car, his eyes glued to his daughter's house. He didn't care how long it took. He'd sit there night after night for months, for years if he had to, until he was sure she was safe. He thought of the times when she was sick as a little girl and he'd sat at her bedside for nights on end. Nothing had changed. As far as he was concerned, she was still his little girl.

He pulled off the lid of the plastic box and looked at the sandwiches Irit had made. She thought he was crossing the line, that they should respect Adi's decision to move back into her own apartment. Still, the box of sandwiches was waiting for him on the kitchen counter every evening.

He unwrapped a sandwich and tossed the paper onto the passenger seat. When he got home tomorrow he'd have to clean out all the sandwich wrappers, empty potato chip bags, and Styrofoam coffee cups.

Lately, his mind kept going back to memories of Adi as a child. He summoned up pictures of her taking her first steps, saying her first words, saw himself walking her to preschool in the morning and sometimes home again in the afternoon, remembered how she'd run to him and throw her little arms around his legs, refusing to let go of his pants, laughing happily. He especially remembered her infectious, bubbling laugh. It made the whole family laugh with her and filled him with a joy beyond words.

It was painful to remember those times now that Adi didn't laugh anymore. She just sat quietly, lost in her own thoughts, staring at her hands resting on her knees, sobbing. The tears never stopped coming, dripping silently, like Chinese water torture on his heart.

Ever since that night, it took an effort for him to keep from losing it. He wanted to be strong for Adi, for Irit, but he felt his control slipping away, his sanity slowly deserting him. He couldn't function. He couldn't concentrate. He couldn't sleep. He couldn't work.

If he did manage to fall asleep, he was tormented by the same recurring nightmare. He saw Adi stretched out on the ground, petrified, pleading for her life, while a strange man, a faceless beast, raped her brutally. She turned her frightened, tear-filled eyes toward him, imploring him to save her. He ran forward, desperately trying to reach out to her, to pull her away, but he never could. He'd wake up covered in cold sweat. He wanted to shout, to scream, but he couldn't get any sound out. Not even the sound of weeping. If only he could cry.

HE was awakened by pulsating music on the radio. Despite what he'd told Irit, it was hard for him to keep a nightlong vigil. His whole body ached. Time and again he dozed off and then came awake with a start. Momentary sleep that provided no rest. Night after night. For three weeks. No time off. He tried to nap during the day, at home or at the office, when Adi was at work, at the skyscrapers of the Azrieli Center, where she was safe. Or so he hoped.

He raised his head to get a look at the time. His neck was stiff. The clock showed 1:30 a.m. Adi must be asleep. Maybe he should go home and get some sleep too. That would certainly make Irit happy.

He pulled the back of the seat upright and was reaching out to turn the key in the ignition when he stopped himself. What if she woke up and needed him?

He leaned back and yawned cavernously. He'd go get himself a cup of coffee from the shop around the corner. It was open twenty-four hours a day. There were things like that in Tel Aviv that you couldn't find anywhere else. Definitely not in Hadera. But he wouldn't want to live here. Hadera might not be the sleepy little town it used to be when the kids were little and everyone knew everyone else, but it still hadn't started to suffer from the anonymity of the big city.

He felt his eyes closing again. He'd rest for five minutes and then go get that cup of coffee. All of a sudden he tensed and sat up straight. A tall, thin man in a baseball cap was passing by the car.

The street lay in utter silence. The man was walking slowly, staring intently left and right, scouting the area as if he were trying to spot something. He stopped about thirty yards away and hastily ducked behind a car. Yaron stretched forward, trying to see what he was doing. Finally, he caught a glimpse of the top of his head between two parked cars. He looked down the street. Not far away, a girl with long hair was walking on the other side of the road.

Could this be him? Could the man he just saw be the rapist? Was he out here stalking another victim? Was he following the long-haired girl just like he'd followed his Adi a month ago? Was it he hiding in the dark between the cars?

What in hell was he supposed to do now? This was an opportunity he couldn't afford to miss. He could rescue the girl and catch the rapist at the same time. It all came down to him.

Yaron stepped out of the car. He did his best not to make any noise, but the click of the car door closing broke the stillness. He started in the direction of the man's hiding place. His target didn't move. He drew closer. Suddenly the man stood up, turned his head around, and looked straight at him. His heart missed a beat. Their eyes locked for no more than a few seconds, but Yaron was certain he would remember every detail of his face—the long chin, the aquiline nose, the thin lips, and especially the fear in his eyes.

The girl turned and looked their way for a moment before picking up her pace and heading quickly into a building. The man glanced apprehensively at Yaron again. Yaron looked directly into his eyes and knew for sure. This was the man who had raped his little girl. It all fit: his build, the cap, the hour, the way he tried to hide, the girl, the frightened look on his face when he realized he'd been caught red-handed.

Yaron could feel the rage roiling up inside him, threatening to burst out. That monster had attacked Adi in the dark, molested her. Because of him she was now home alone crying, as she had been for so many days. My beautiful daughter, my sweet baby, he mouthed to himself. My Adinka. If only he had a gun, he'd put a bullet in his head right now. His hand clenched in a fist. If only he were a few years younger, he'd finish him off with his bare hands. But he wasn't young, so he had to be smart.

The man started walking away. Yaron followed. In the morning he'd get in touch with Eli Nachum, the lead detective on the case, and hand him the rapist on a silver platter.

The man turned into a side street. Yaron hurried to keep up with him. He couldn't lose him now.

By the time he reached the corner, the man was at the end of the block. How had he gotten so far ahead of him? Was he running? Did he know Yaron was tailing him?

He had to move faster. He was breathing heavily and was already covered in sweat, his shirt sticking to his back. The strain and exhaustion of the last few weeks were getting to him. "You'll give yourself a heart attack," Irit had warned, "or else you'll go crazy from lack of sleep." He wasn't a kid anymore. He was sixty years old, a grandfather with two grandkids. Adi was his middle daughter and already twenty-four. Irit might turn out to be right. In the end, his heart would give out here in the middle of Tel Aviv. So what? He wasn't ready to give up. If Adi knew that the man who raped her was behind bars, maybe she could get on with her life, maybe she could put the atrocity behind her.

By the time he made it to the end of the block, there was no one in sight, no sign of the mysterious man. Had he disappeared into one of the buildings? Did he have enough time? Yaron stood there, panting, his heart pounding. He retraced his steps a few yards to a bench he'd just passed. He sat down and leaned his head back, waiting for his heartbeat to return to normal. The smell of cat urine pounded his nose and made him sick. He was overcome by frustration. He'd been so close!

But he was wrong. It wasn't over yet. All of a sudden he saw the man come out of a yard and stand still for a minute looking in both directions. He stared at the street intently, checking it out. The location of the bench gave Yaron a clear view of the rapist, but Yaron couldn't be seen by him. Silently, he lowered himself until he was lying flat on the bench, taking advantage of the lucky hand he'd been dealt. There was no doubt in his mind that the man had seen him tailing him and had taken diversionary tactics. He'd obviously been hiding behind the bushes in the yard.

The man started in Yaron's direction. There was less than a hundred yards between them. If he sees me, it'll all be over for me, he thought, crawling off the bench as silently as possible. He had to get to the end of the block before the rapist. He could hide behind a hedge and then follow him from there. It was only two yards to the corner. You can do it, he urged himself on, envisioning his army days.

He crouched down and started moving forward, just as he'd been trained to do in the infantry. He couldn't tell if the man saw him or not, but he forced himself not to turn around. Then he slipped into the yard of the corner building and waited. The man passed right in front of him. He was striding rapidly and confidently, heading for the main road. Yaron took up a position at a safe distance and looked to see which way he had gone. He caught sight of him standing at a bus stop. Yaron remembered reading that Tel Aviv operated a late-night bus service on the weekend. What would he do if the bus came? He was going to lose him!

A minibus pulled up and the man got on. Yaron ran into the road. In less than ten seconds, a taxi stopped beside him. He had to admit the city had its advantages.

"Follow that bus," he ordered the driver, like a character in some action movie.

The driver gave him a puzzled look.

"Just go! Fast!" he commanded brusquely.

WHEN he got home the adrenaline was still rushing through his veins. He went into the kitchen and made himself a cup of coffee, and then a second, and a third. There was no chance he'd be able to get any sleep tonight in any case. He didn't wake Irit. The situation was hard enough for her as it was. Adi's rape had dealt her a heavy blow, drowning her in rivers of guilt and a numbing sense of helplessness. He had to put an end to it. For Adi. And for Irit and himself too.

He counted the minutes until dawn, until he could contact Nachum. The last time they met, the detective had told him to feel free to call at any time, but the middle of the night seemed to be taking that a little too literally.

At six o'clock he picked up the phone and then stopped before he could dial the number. It's still too early, he decided. Turning on the computer, he looked up the procedures for police lineups in rape cases. There were cops and lawyers present. It was very stressful for the victims. He read one woman's story about how traumatic it was for her, how it made her relive the rape.

He couldn't do that to Adi. He wasn't willing to have her go through such an ordeal, to have so many people examining her, documenting her reactions in minute detail. And later some slimy defense attorney would start grilling her about why she hesitated for a second or two before pointing to the rapist. He'd seen it in the movies, how they use any dirty trick to cast doubt on the victim's testimony. He couldn't allow that.

He wanted her to walk into the lineup and point directly at her attacker. No hesitation, no stress. In and out in one minute. And then it would all be over. At last, it would all be over.

Chapter 5

INSPECTOR Eli Nachum hated reporters. Especially crime reporters. And most especially assholes like Amit Giladi. If it were up to him, he'd have nothing to do with him. But it had been a month since the rape in the old north, and the investigation was going nowhere. After making headlines for a couple of days, it had soon disappeared from the pages of the national press. But the local paper kept at it. Week after week they printed a story decrying the lack of an arrest, the ineptitude of the police force, his own incompetence as the lead detective. In his opinion, the whole crusade was nothing but yellow journalism, a sleazy way to sell papers. But it was stressing out the higher-ups, and when they were stressed out, they leaned on him.

So he'd had no choice but to give in to the district spokesman's demand that he meet with Giladi. He was forced to sit opposite him for an hour, put up with his insolent questions, and do his best to convince him that although it might seem otherwise to the public, they were making progress and working the case every minute of every day. What'd the asshole know, anyway? He was just a kid, barely over twenty—a kid pretending to be a man. He sat there looking serious, waving his pen around like a sword, patronizing him. He wouldn't last more than five minutes as a cop, that idiot.

Nachum watched Giladi walk away down the corridor, and he went back to his desk, drained. They'd moved here only three years ago as part of a general face-lift for the police force. They were now in the heart of the Tel Aviv high-tech area. He preferred the old station house, the shabby, dilapidated building that was there even before the state was declared. Every one of its rooms reeked of history. He missed the small diners, where the food was so spicy it sharpened his mind. Here everything was modernized, computerized, sanitized, with plasma screens everywhere, and instead of real food, they ate sushi. The police force was trying to be something it wasn't.

He didn't think the reporter had bought his story. People thought that if they didn't make an arrest within twenty-four hours, they'd bungled the case. They didn't know what they were up against, how complicated their job was. They expect it to be like the movies where it's all tied up with a bow in just ninety minutes.

He'd been honest with Giladi about one thing, at least. Ever since he'd caught the case, it had occupied all his time and was never out of his mind. It had been that way from the very beginning.

He'd shown up at the hospital within minutes after getting the call. The right side of Adi's face was covered in bruises from being dragged on the ground, she had a cut on her chin that needed stitches, and her eyes were swollen from crying. She sat there hunched up, withdrawn, chewing on her hair like a little girl. It was hard to get the facts from her. Mostly, she just responded to his questions by nodding her head or shrugging her shoulders. She didn't want to be there. That was one of the few things she actually said. But when her parents turned up on Saturday night, worried that she hadn't answered her phone all weekend, and found out what had happened, they'd talked her into going to the hospital and reporting the rape. It had taken them half the night to convince her. Her father stood next to her bed throughout the interview, urging her to answer his questions. Her mother just held her, not saying anything.

NACHUM had a lot of years on the job. Before that he'd been a guard in a military prison. When he left the army, it seemed natural to join the police force. He started out in logistics, but all he ever wanted was to be a detective. He'd put in one application after another, undeterred by repeated rejections. He never gave up, even though everyone else gave up on him. Finally, after making sergeant, they let him take the detective test and he got his gold shield.

He'd seen almost everything in his long career: homicide, rape, domestic violence, child molesters. He'd worked nearly every crime on the books. Over the years, his daily encounter with human malevolence and atrocious acts of violence had blunted his sensitivity. But there were still cases that broke through the wall he'd been forced to build around himself in order to do his job, cases that gripped his heart and wouldn't let go. The sight of Adi Regev, barely more than a child, whose joy in life had been stolen away from her in an instant, touched him at the very core of his being. His daughter was just a year and half younger than Adi. At the moment Adi looked like the complete opposite of his strong, independent, ambitious daughter, but he couldn't help imagining his own child in the same situation, as the victim of such appalling brutality.

Adi had arrived at the hospital almost seventy-two hours after the rape. He was well aware that after so much time had elapsed, there was little chance of finding any of the attacker's DNA on her, especially when she'd scrubbed herself all over.

He thought they'd have more luck with the crime scene. It wasn't fresh, but it was so isolated that it hadn't been contaminated. However, it didn't give them much to go on. In her short struggle with the rapist, Adi hadn't drawn blood, and there were no signs of semen on the ground. Nor did they find the knife or any usable fingerprints. The only evidence the scene yielded were partial shoe prints—Nike runners, size 10.

His team had been working the case hard in the past month. They started by looking for witnesses, going from door to door, talking to all the neighbors. No one had seen or heard anything. They'd all been closed up in their apartments, sleeping or watching TV.

Even though Adi said she didn't recognize her attacker, they still questioned all her ex-boyfriends and anyone she'd dated even once. And she dated a lot, that girl. But every lead was a dead end. They had her look over mug shots of known rapists and other sex offenders, hoping she could identify him from a photo. Nothing came of that either.

Nachum rubbed his eyes in exhaustion. He had glorious achievements on his record, but some resounding failures too. In the end, he thought, it's the failures that stay with you. Even after all these years, he could still list every one of them. And he didn't need anyone to remind him. Most definitely not some slimy reporter like Amit Giladi. He knew what people were saying behind his back. They said he was getting old, that he was losing his touch, that he spent too much time on each case, that it took him too long to put his cases to bed, if he was lucky enough to solve them.

Detectives used to be applauded for solving complicated cases. Today it was all about tables, statistics, arrest rates. Fucking CompStat had taken over their lives. Detectives were assessed solely by their output, as if they worked on a production line. He knew all the gimmicks his colleagues used to sweeten their figures. They looked out for easy cases, closed cases by the truckload supposedly for lack of evidence, and persuaded people to withdraw their complaints. He could easily do the same and get a pat on the back. It might even earn him a promotion. But he was too old for that sort of thing, and maybe, like his wife said, he was too proud to play those games. In any case, at his age he wasn't going to change. And he wasn't ready to start taking shortcuts.

He closed his eyes. He had a headache. If he thought his detractors were right, he'd leave the force. But they were wrong. He still had a lot to give. And he had to solve this case. He'd do whatever it took to put the rapist behind bars.

It wouldn't be easy. Most of the time, when the victim didn't know her attacker, the sonofabitch was never caught. And a lot of incidents went unreported or were reported too late, after precious time had been lost. Throw in the fact that most rapes by strangers were carefully planned and the perps were typically clever and calculating, and it made it even harder to catch the bastards.

He looked over the files of all the recent rapes in and around Tel Aviv. None of the attackers fit the description Adi had given. It was almost impossible to draw up the profile of a rapist on the basis of one incident. He could be a loner or a man who sought out human contact, he could have a record or be a first-time offender. But since sex crimes were an addiction, there was every chance he'd do it again. If that happened, they'd have more to go on. And if they were really lucky, he might make a mistake the next time. In Nachum's experience, that's how most rapists were caught. They let someone get a look at them. It's their arrogance, their extreme narcissism, that often leads to their undoing.

So he could sit back and wait until he raped another girl, until he made a mistake. That would probably be the best tactic. There were plenty of other unsolved crimes for him to work on, and the list just kept getting longer. Some of them were no less horrendous. But he couldn't do that. He couldn't give himself time or permission to wait for the next rape before he nailed the pervert. Just the thought of another girl suffering like that drove him on and kept him from putting it aside. His job was to prevent another rape. He was here to serve and protect, like the Americans said. Not to twiddle his thumbs and invent excuses. That wasn't why he'd fought so hard for the gold shield.

To an outside observer it might look like he wasn't doing any-

thing, just sitting and staring into space. But that's how he worked—
he turned it all over in his mind, reviewing the facts of the case in his
head again and again. "You're old-school," his commander, Superintendent Moshe Navon, had said recently. He didn't know if that was
meant to be a compliment or not.

His phone rang.

"Eli . . . it's Yaron Regev, Adi's father," a trembling voice said, followed by bitter sobbing. A cold sweat broke out on Nachum's fore-
head at the sound of the man breaking down. Please, not that. The
trauma of rape led some victims to commit acts of desperation. Adi
was definitely the fragile type who was capable of such a thing. Her
parents had coddled her all her life, given her whatever she wanted.
She'd never been forced to cope with anything on her own. And
then the rapist had shown up and extinguished her spark.

"Yaron, what happened?" he asked, worried.

The sobbing continued.

"Is Adi okay?" He felt the bile rise up and form a ball in his
throat.

"I found him," Yaron moaned. "I found the rapist."

Chapter 6

THE knock on the door startled her. She was sitting in front of the computer, bursting the bright-colored bubbles that floated onto the screen. Ever since the rape she hadn't slept, just sat at the computer for hours playing mindless games. Trying to empty her head. To forget. She hadn't been outside for ages. She'd tried last Saturday. She got her bike and rode along the Yarkon River down to the sea. She loved the sea. But the sight of so many half-naked, sweaty men running along the promenade made her sick, and she quickly returned home.

"Adi, Adinka, it's Dad," she heard through the door. Just like that Saturday night after the rape, when she hadn't left her house or answered the phone for two days. It was only because of his persistence that she'd gone to the hospital and reported the crime. He'd kept at her all night and the whole of the next day, not letting up until late in the evening, when she finally gave in and agreed to go with him.

"I need to talk to you," he said, walking straight in as soon as she opened the door. Her parents' love and concern were stifling. They wouldn't leave her alone, especially her dad. They called to check up on her every hour: How are you feeling? Are you okay? Did you sleep? Did you eat? Their questions gnawed at her. She wasn't okay, she barely ate, she lay awake all night. But she answered yes to everything, hoping to allay their concern and convince them to back off a little.

"I was just about to take a nap," she lied. Maybe he would take the hint and go. It was better when she was alone. She'd see him later anyway when she went to her parents' house for Friday-night dinner. Ever since it happened, it had become a sacred ritual for the whole family to be in attendance. They'd all sit there watching her, following her every move, falling silent whenever she opened her mouth.

"Come with me a minute. I have something to show you," her father said, leading her into the living room. He was flushed, excited, almost cheerful.

She sat down opposite him in silence, listening distractedly as the words spilled out of his mouth in a torrent, his hands gesturing wildly, his voice thundering. He started by repeating once again how much he and her mother loved her, how much she meant to them. She'd heard it umpteen times since then. It was starting to wear. She waited for him to finish so she could go back to her game. She'd tried before to set boundaries, once even angrily lashing out at her mother, but nothing deterred them. They wouldn't leave her in peace.

She realized that he'd stopped talking. She smiled at him, waiting for him to get up and leave. But he stayed where he was and then suddenly handed her a camera.

Puzzled, she looked at the camera in her hand. The LCD screen showed a man crossing the street.

"That's him," her father said, looking into her eyes.

Her head ached. Who was he talking about?

"That's the man I saw hanging around here last night. He's the one . . . ," he began, and then fell silent.

"What do you mean 'last night'?" she asked. The picture she was looking at had been taken in broad daylight.

"I just told you. I went back there this morning. I waited until he left his house and then I took pictures of him. Just look at it, Adinka, look at it and tell me it's him and I'll take it to the police right now."

Now she understood. It wasn't just any picture. The man in the photograph was the rapist. They'd found him.

She threw the camera on the table and backed away from it. She didn't want to look at him, she didn't want to remember. All she wanted was to be able to forget.

Yaron leaned over, picked up the camera, and held it out to her again.

"I know it's hard, it's scary. One quick look, that's all I need, and then I can take it to the police . . . I'm sure it's him. I just need you to say so."

She shook her head. She never wanted to see that monster again.

Yaron came to sit next to her.

"One look and it's over, Adinka. I swear to you, it'll all be over," he said, gently placing his hand over hers.

She looked down at his thick fingers shielding her own shaking hand. She wanted desperately for it to be over, to be able to sleep again, to go back to being who she used to be, before. She closed her eyes and took a deep breath. One quick look. That's all. Like ripping off a Band-Aid.

Her father switched to the next picture. It was a clear shot of his face. Was he the man who raped her? It had been dark and he'd been wearing a baseball cap and sunglasses. In the picture it was daylight and she could see his face, his eyes.

"He was hanging around the building last night," she heard her father say. "He was going to rape another girl, I know it."

She brought her eyes into focus. Everything was too bright in the picture. Not like that night.

"I'll take it to the police and make sure they lock him up for life. The bastard will never see the light of day again."

She kept silent, staring at the next photograph her father showed her. The man in the picture had the same shape face and the same build as the rapist, the same as the Identi-Kit sketch they'd drawn from her description of him.

"He was here?" The meaning of what he'd just said suddenly dawned on her.

"Right here, outside your building. Who knows what he was planning, what might've happened . . ."

She returned the camera to the living room table. The idea that the rapist was hanging around her building terrified her. What if he'd seen her again?

"He's a monster, a beast with no fear. If I hadn't happened to be here, if I hadn't interfered with his plans . . . I don't even want to think about what he might've done," Yaron said feverishly, determined to persuade her.

The terrible thoughts kept spinning around in her head: Was he waiting for her? Like he was that night? She'd done what he asked. She couldn't stop thinking about how things might've turned out differently if she'd only run away when she still had the chance, if she'd fought harder, if she'd refused to beg. She'd let him have his way, let him play with her as if she were a puppet on a string. Maybe he wanted more. That's what he'd whispered in her ear that night— more!

"You can do it, sweetheart. Just say the words and you put the nightmare behind you. You'll feel better."

Tears welled up in her eyes. She was so confused, so tired. Mainly tired. It might be him. But it might not.

"I'm not sure . . . I'm not sure," she mumbled.

"It's him. Just like you described him to the police. Take a good look. Try another picture. I've got plenty here for you to look at." He kept at her, showing her one photo after another. Her eyes were drawn to the rapist's hands, the hands that had strangled her, that had held a knife to her throat.

"Just say the words, Adinka, just say the words."

She burst into tears, covering her face with her hands. She wanted it to stop. She wanted to say what her father was asking of her, but she wasn't sure.

"Talk to me, sweetheart. I'm here for you."

She raised her eyes to him. "You're right, it's him. He's the man who raped me."

Chapter 7

IT was 1:03 in the morning when the phone rang. Despite the late hour, Ziv Nevo was lying awake on the mattress, waiting. In twenty-seven minutes he'd go out and finish what he'd started last night.

The sound of the phone made him sit up with a start. Calls at this time of night never brought good news.

"Hello, who is this?" he heard an unfamiliar woman's voice asking. He didn't have the patience for this right now. "Wrong number," he barked, hanging up.

· He lay back down again. He was in a foul mood. He'd finished off the six-pack he'd bought at a nearby convenience store a few hours ago. Things weren't going well for him. They hadn't been for a long time. Too long. He knew that drinking wasn't the answer, but he needed something to give him courage.

For at least the hundredth time his mind went back to the man who'd been following him last night. His face still haunted him. Especially the look in his eyes that first time, as if he knew what he was doing there. It was lucky he'd managed to give him the slip. A chill went down his back at the thought of what could've happened if he'd been caught in the act. He'd have to be more careful tonight. Make extra sure there was no one around, no one sitting in a car somewhere. Tonight he was going to do it right. His stomach quivered in a mixture of fear and excitement.

The phone rang again.

"Is this Ziv Nevo?" the same woman's voice asked.

He hadn't been expecting that.

"Who's asking?"

No answer. The woman hung up.

He pressed *69, but the number was blocked. He didn't like that. First that man following him last night, and now this.

He grabbed his cigarettes and lighter and went out to the small balcony for a smoke. That was another nasty habit he'd lapsed back into this past month. But he never smoked in the house. For Gili's sake.

This was supposed to be his weekend with him. But when he went to pick him up this morning, he discovered that Merav had taken him to her parents' house.

"You won't see him until you start paying child support," she'd shrieked at him when he called her cell phone to find out where they were. He did his damnedest to keep his voice calm, rational. To explain that he wasn't trying to shirk his responsibility, he just didn't have the money to give her. She didn't want to hear it. A year and a half ago he'd destroyed his marriage, got himself canned from his job, and reduced himself to what he was today. He'd apologized over and over again, but Merav still wasn't ready to forgive him.

He stared despondently at the photograph on his cell phone screen—Gili at the swimming pool, grinning, happy—and pondered his life. Maybe it was a good thing Gili wasn't here. He was better off with her, he thought, looking around the miserable apartment he'd rented. Clouds of dust swirled through the air, some of it settling on the unopened IKEA cartons that held the few pieces of living room furniture he'd purchased. Even though he lay around the house all day with nothing better to do, he hadn't gotten around to assembling them yet. He slept on a mattress on the floor. So maybe it was for the best. He loved his son in a way he never believed he could love another human being, but what did he have to offer him? His life had been a cesspool for a long time, and it just kept getting worse.

He blew smoke out into the nighttime air, counting the minutes. Very soon he'd go out and finish what he'd started. When it was over, he might feel a little peace. He heard the screech of tires and looked down at the street. A patrol car had pulled up in front of the building and two cops were jumping out. It made sense now. That's what the phone call was all about. They were coming for him. First, they'd made sure he was home.

His heart was pounding wildly. He had to think fast. It was that man from last night. He'd seen him. Now they were coming to arrest him. Think! He passed his hand nervously through his hair. The thought of being locked up made him sick. He'd had enough of that to last a lifetime. Think! He was trapped. They'd found him. He still had a little time. The stairs would slow them down. There was no elevator in the building. Maybe he could make it to the roof.

He ran to the chest near the door, a decrepit piece of furniture the previous tenants hadn't bothered to take with them. He was sure the key to the roof was in one of the drawers. As he ransacked the contents, he was pulled up short by the sight of his wedding ring thrown in among the other useless items. His hands were shaking. He couldn't bring himself to take it off even when he knew it was over for good, even when the divorce was final. A couple of months ago he'd finally pulled it off in a rage and hurled it into the drawer after yet another fight with Merav on the phone over child support and custody.

But he didn't have time to worry about that now. He had to find the key. It wasn't there. Where did he put it?

He heard Fritz barking excitedly in the Bashans' first-floor apartment. They'd be here any minute. He was running out of time. He cracked open the door and heard their footsteps coming closer. He'd hide on the top floor. With any luck they'd find an empty apartment and leave.

Very gently he closed the door behind him and started up the stairs, keeping his back to the wall, making as little noise as possible. The top of a cop's head came into view. There was only one flight between them. No more. He pressed up against the wall, praying they didn't see him.

He heard them knocking on his door and a voice calling, "Mr. Nevo?"

He held his breath and froze.

"Police. Open the door, Mr. Nevo," another voice shouted as the knocking got louder.

He didn't budge an inch. Two floors below, Fritz was still barking.

"Sigi spoke to him five minutes ago. The sonofabitch is inside," a cop said. "Open up, Nevo, or we'll break the door down."

Half a flight above him a door opened. His heart jumped. One of his neighbors, a man in his sixties, poked his head out.

They stared at each other in silence. He didn't know the man's name, only that he lived there with his wife. They passed each other on the stairs from time to time, but they'd never so much as exchanged a greeting.

"Whaddya say? Should we call Nachum?" one cop asked.

The neighbor took a step forward. He was now standing outside the door of his apartment. Ziv gave him a halfhearted smile.

"Last chance, Nevo. Open up. Police!" a cop shouted, banging on the door again.

The neighbor looked at him in astonishment. Ziv put his hands together in a gesture of pleading. Don't turn me in, he begged with his eyes.

"He's up here," the neighbor called out suddenly before retreating back into his apartment and shutting the door behind him.

He heard them running up the stairs.

He knew it was a lost cause, he no longer had any chance of escape, but still he turned and started upward. All the beer he'd drunk was making him dizzy. His feet felt like blocks of cement.

He reached the top floor and stared in amazement at the door to the roof. It was open. Why had he wasted time looking for the key? If he'd run as soon as he saw the cops downstairs, he might've gotten away. Why didn't things ever go his way? Not even once!

He looked around. Could he make a running leap onto the roof next door? He dismissed that idea immediately. They'd be on the roof before he could reach the edge. They'd probably start shooting too.

"Don't move," he heard behind him.

He turned around slowly. The cop was pointing his gun at him. He raised his hands.

The other cop came through the door, breathing heavily from the climb. He moved over to him quickly. "Hands up," he ordered, even though they were already in the air.

The second cop came around to the rear, twisted his arms behind his back, and cuffed him.

"On the ground," he commanded, not letting go of his arm.

Ziv lay down on the ground. The cop slammed his foot on his back, squashing him down onto the cold roof as if he were a cigarette butt. He didn't move. Just lay there under the heavy foot, his tears dampening the filthy concrete.

Chapter 8

NACHUM sat in his room and gazed at the screen showing the interrogation room. The hidden cameras caught Ziv Nevo pacing back and forth. He kept passing his hand nervously through his hair and glancing impatiently at the door. Nachum decided to wait a little longer. Some interrogators pounce on a suspect, taking advantage of the initial shock of the arrest to get a confession out of them. He had nothing against that method, but he had a different style, preferring to let them stew in their own juice for a while. He believed they were most vulnerable when they were left on their own. That's when they started playing out in their mind all the horrible things that were going to happen to them. It was especially scary for the ones like Nevo, who weren't accustomed to police interrogations. They were sure they were in for a beating.

He'd had him put in a room with no windows. Not a drop of fresh air. There was hardly any furniture, just an ordinary office table and two simple chairs. It was nothing like you see on TV, just a room. He'd turned off the AC too. He wanted him to sweat. He wouldn't be able to tell if the sweat and the nauseating stench were coming from the hot air in the room or from his own fear. That's when Nachum would make his entrance. That's when he'd be ready to talk.

Adi's father had good intentions. There was no doubt in Nachum's mind that he thought he had done the right thing for the investigation, for his daughter. As a father himself, he could sympathize. If anything like that happened to his own daughter, heaven forbid, he'd do whatever it took to nail the bastard, probably a lot more than Yaron Regev had done.

But he also knew that Yaron had ruined their case, no matter how good his intentions were. There were legal standards for conducting a lineup. It was like baking a cake. As long as you followed the recipe, the cake came out fine, the judge would sanction the identification, and they'd get their conviction. But if you didn't follow the directions precisely, you ended up throwing the cake in the garbage.

For the results of a lineup to be admissible, they needed eight foils whose appearance was similar to that of the suspect. The suspect had the right to choose where to stand, and the police had to respect his decision. He also had the right to have his attorney present. You weren't allowed to show the witness any pictures of the suspect before the lineup. In fact, you were barely allowed to talk to them. The lineup had to be videotaped. The suspect and his attorney were entitled to question the witness. And the whole procedure had to be recorded in detail in writing.

Yaron Regev hadn't done any of those things. Even without consulting with the DA's Office, Nachum knew he'd never convince a judge that the victim's identification of the rapist was "spontaneous." There was no question she'd been coached by her father. He'd showed her the pictures, asked her directly if he was the man who had raped her, told her he'd seen him hanging around her house at night. Any defense attorney would have a field day with a story like that.

While his team was out picking up Nevo, Nachum had read up on verdicts pertaining to lineups. "Considerably doubtful," "very little evidentiary weight"—those were the sorts of expressions judges used to describe the value of the sort of identification he had in this case. Even worse, at this stage it was too late to repair the damage. There was no point in doing it again. Even if Adi picked Nevo out of a lineup conducted by the book, even if they stood a hundred men up in front of her and had fifty lawyers arguing the case, it wouldn't do any good. The cake was already in the garbage.

The situation infuriated him. He believed all the rules and regulations made up by attorneys, judges, and other bleeding hearts were making it impossible to win the war on crime. It's true they still had a pretty high conviction rate, but he'd lived and breathed the system for so long that he could feel the change. He could sense the tectonic plates moving under their feet, the winds of liberalism blowing their way.

He watched Nevo. His gut told him he was the rapist. After twenty years on the job, he could trust his gut. And common sense told him the same thing. But you couldn't take that to court. All that mattered in a trial were evidence and the law, what was admissible and what wasn't. Rules. He had an excellent understanding of them, but that didn't mean he liked them. Nothing could substitute for the gut feeling of an experienced cop, or for plain old common sense. Everything else was just words, a game played by prosecutors, defense attorneys, and judges in the courtroom.

Nevo fit Adi's description of the rapist, and she'd ID'd him. But it was much more than that. It began with his history. Even a quick glance at his record showed a history of violence. His ex-wife had filed two complaints against him. On one of those occasions he'd been held for several hours before being released. There was also a sexual harassment complaint that was filed against him by a co-worker. He knew they were only complaints, that he'd never actually been convicted of anything. So what? All that proved was how lame the system was if a repeat offender like him kept slipping through their fingers.

According to Nevo's rap sheet, ten years ago, at the age of eighteen, he totaled a bus stop with his car. The cops who arrived on the scene reported that he was intoxicated, but they let him go when they found out he'd lost his parents in a car crash the month before.

And it wasn't just his record. Yaron Regev hadn't run into Nevo at a barbershop or a concert. He'd seen him trawling his daughter's neighborhood at night, stalking another woman, hiding between parked cars. What was he doing there? He didn't live nearby. His ex-wife didn't either. Nor did any of his relatives or his wife's relatives. Nachum had checked.

Yaron said he thought Nevo knew he was being tailed, that he'd tried to lose him, had taken cover in the front yard of a building. Add to that the arrest itself. A man with nothing to hide doesn't try to elude the cops, doesn't cry when he's caught, doesn't shake like a fucking leaf.

He reviewed what they knew so far. Nevo was obviously going through a hard time. He had lost his family, his job, and now he was in danger of losing custody of his son for not paying child support. His guys said he reeked of alcohol when they took him in. Things like that push some people over the edge. With Nevo's history of violence and sexual harassment, rape wasn't such a stretch. He was looking to strike back at a world that had betrayed him, had emasculated him, and he picked a victim he could overpower easily.

It was two in the morning. He had less than twenty hours. That didn't give him a lot of time. He was going to work on him without a break until he got a confession out of him.

Tomorrow, Saturday night at eight o'clock, Nevo would have to be brought before a judge. There was no doubt in Nachum's mind that he'd be remanded into custody. That didn't worry him. What did worry him was that it wouldn't be long before an attorney showed up and started coaching Nevo on how to twist the truth. And then other gutless attorneys in the DA's Office who didn't want any trouble would be afraid to run with the case.

He wanted to tie it all up in a neat little package before he had to tell a judge about how the identification was made, before that minor detail, that one imperfection, became the main focus of the justice game. That's why he'd chosen this particular time to bring him in. There were no attorneys lining up to represent the suspect on Friday night. And if any happened to turn up, he'd have his team take Nevo on a little tour of a few other police precincts. He'd make the suits work for it.

He moved toward the door, opened it, and went in.

Now it was his turn.

Chapter 9

AS soon as Nevo saw the look in Nachum's steely eyes he knew things were about to get worse. The bald detective was short and wiry, with a thin mustache adorning his upper lip.

"You know why you're here?" Nachum asked quietly, sitting down opposite the suspect. Nevo had expected the room to be like the ones he saw in the movies, with a big two-way mirror so the cops outside could watch what was going on. But it was no more than a tiny office, with two chairs and a table, a few plastic cups and a pitcher of water. The bareness of the stifling room just made him more nervous. They took the cuffs off his hands and legs when they put him in here, but he still felt that he couldn't move.

Nevo didn't answer the detective's question. He'd been trying to work it out ever since he saw the two cops jumping out of the patrol car. He'd screened different scenarios in his head, run through the possibilities. All the cops were willing to say when he asked where they were taking him was that they were bringing him in for questioning. "What do mean bringing me in? Am I under arrest? What'd I do?" he'd asked. "They'll explain everything at the precinct" was the only answer he got.

He knew why the police wanted to question him. He just didn't know what had put them onto him. The idea that it was all over, that they knew everything, made his blood run cold. If that was true, he was going away for a very long time.

"I asked you a question," Nachum said, pinning him with his eyes.

But what if they didn't know and were just on a fishing expedition? If he confessed now, he'd lose any chance of getting out of this mess. He'd be paying a very heavy price. He had to be smart. Watch what he said. Not let himself be played. He'd seen enough TV shows and movies to know how interrogators used mind games to force a confession out of someone, even when he was innocent.

"Cat got your tongue? Answer my question," Nachum barked.

Nevo took a sip of water from the cup in front of him. His best move was to say nothing, find out what they had before he incriminated himself. Let them do their job, he thought.

"I'm still waiting for an answer!"

"No, I have no idea," he said quickly in as confident a tone as he could muster.

Nachum shook his head in disappointment, like a teacher whose student had just given the wrong answer. "It's a shame you want to do this the hard way. I thought you had more sense," he said.

The words "the hard way" sent a chill down his spine.

The two men sat facing each other in silence. Nachum stared intently at Nevo, not looking away for a second. Not even when he refilled the cup of water. His piercing eyes were like searing laser beams.

"Let's try again. Would you like to tell me why you're here?" Nachum said, breaking the silence.

"I already told you . . . I don't know . . . I have no . . . ," he stuttered, his voice cracking despite his efforts to sound self-assured. He felt like Nachum could read his mind just by staring at him, like he knew he was lying.

"Start by telling me what you were doing at one a.m. last night in north Tel Aviv," Nachum cut in.

His heart fell. They knew. The minute he saw that man tailing him, he knew things were going to go bad for him. When he came out from behind the bushes in the yard and didn't see the guy on the street, he'd let himself hope that it was all in his mind, that no one was following him. But deep down he knew it wasn't true. He knew the guy didn't just happen to be there, that he was going to take him down.

"What were you doing there last night?" Nachum screamed, his fist coming down on the table so hard that the water splashed out of the plastic cup.

"Nothing," he said, looking at the puddle in front of him to avoid meeting Nachum's eyes.

"That's only because someone got in the way. If it wasn't for him, who knows what you would've done," Nachum said.

Nevo didn't answer. Every word out of the detective's mouth was another nail in his coffin. They knew everything. The man must have kept on his tail even after he thought he'd shaken him off. He realized it was all part of a plan. The guy was waiting for him. So they must've found what he left behind and they probably had his fingerprints too.

Did they also know about Meshulam? No way he was going to rat him out. He might be locked up for years for being stupid, but at least he'd still be alive. At least he'd see his son grow up. That meant a lot. Gili was the one ray of light in his life, and he needed his father. Even if he was doing time.

Maybe Meshulam was already under arrest and this whole thing was an act. He finished off the water. If that's the case, why not look out for himself? That's how it worked: the little fish gave up a bigger fish who gave up a whale. He'd broken the law, but what he did was nothing compared to Meshulam.

"It's over for you, Nevo. Somebody saw you. He saw what you did and we've already put all the pieces together. So don't play games with me. It's not in your best interest."

He passed his hand through his hair nervously, rubbing his head as if it were Aladdin's lamp. Gili loved that movie. But no genie appeared. Just ugly reality. And in this reality, he didn't have enough facts to make the right decision. He needed more time. More information. If he opened his mouth now, there was no going back.

"I want a lawyer," he said abruptly. He knew from all those TV shows he'd watched that he was entitled to one. He was in desperate need of someone to talk to, someone with experience to tell him what to do.

Nachum leaned back in his chair and sneered. "No problem, pal. You'll get your lawyer. But what good is it gonna do you, huh? What can he do for you? We've got an ironclad case against you. The best lawyer in the world isn't gonna get you off. The more you fight me, the worse it's gonna be for you. It'll just cost you money and it won't do you any good."

Nachum was scaring him, confusing him. He sounded so sure of himself. What was he supposed to do now? How did he get into this mess? It was because he was so weak, because he couldn't resist temptation. And now he was paying the price. One stupid mistake and he was going away for a long time.

"Look at me, Nevo," Nachum ordered.

He raised his head slowly, not wanting to look into those X-ray eyes again. Maybe he was imagining it, but something in Nachum's expression seemed different, softer.

"Let me help you, Nevo," the detective said.

Chapter 10

ALL in all, Nachum was quite pleased with how the interrogation was going. The first stage had taken even less time than he'd anticipated. Now Nevo was ready for stage two. If he played his cards right, he'd be closing the Regev rape case very soon.

Actually, he thought, interrogations are more like a game of chess. Both pitted one mind against another, and both required the same two stages for a win. First comes the "check," the threat to your opponent's king, and then the "mate," when you've got him cornered, with no way out.

Nevo knew very well that he'd been made, that his arrest wasn't just some mistake he could worm his way out of. And like most rapists, he was no fool. That's why he was hunched over in his chair, agitated, drinking water like a fish, passing his hand through his hair in a gesture Nachum already recognized as a nervous tic. He wondered how he had any hair left on his head the way he kept pulling at it. The detective reached up and touched his own bald pate.

The only question in his mind was exactly how to go about the next phase of the interrogation. He had enough experience to know you can drag a confession out of practically anybody. He'd witnessed it over and over in his long career. Time and again he'd seen how weak and fragile people are. Apply pressure in the right places, and they break. Some hold out longer than others, but ultimately the outcome is the same.

He could go at it like many other detectives would and spend hours with Nevo, confusing him with endless questions, threatening, shouting, switching interrogation teams, and making him start all over from the beginning each time, not letting up on him for a minute, driving him crazy, wearing him down until he confessed. But his instincts were telling him to use a different tactic here. He knew how much defense lawyers loved to get their claws into confessions they could claim were obtained under duress. But it was more than that. He sensed that Nevo was already teetering, that all it would take was one more nudge to push him over the edge, to get him to tell the truth, to make a confession no one could poke holes in. If he tried to intimidate him or tire him out, he might shut down. No. He was going to take the positive approach; he'd be the "good cop," empathetic and understanding. He'd set him a honey trap.

"LET me help you," he repeated.

There was a look of surprise on Nevo's face. Nachum knew that very soon that look would turn suspicious, that he had to work fast, to use what he'd learned when he did his homework before coming in.

"It may be hard for you to believe, but I'm serious," he went on in a quiet, confident tone. "I wanna help you. I checked you out earlier. That's just normal procedure before we start questioning anyone. You were a demolition officer in the army, an officer in the 605, right?"

Nevo nodded. A good sign, Nachum thought to himself, refilling Nevo's cup yet again. It was an old trick of his, making the suspect suffer the physical discomfort of a full bladder.

"My brother was an officer in the same unit. He was killed in Lebanon, five days into the first war."

Nachum paused, studying Nevo's face. The pressure he'd been feeling was starting to lift. The story about his dead brother was a lie, but it had affected him. Now he had to gain his trust, to make him forget the role each of them was playing in this room, the fact that he was being interrogated, that he'd been arrested on a rape charge.

"When I saw that you served in that unit, it made me think twice about you," he continued. "I know what kind of guys you are, especially the ones who get picked to be officers. So I know you're not a bad person, Nevo. You're like a lot of good people who get into trouble; you're just a good person who made a mistake."

For the first time, Nevo looked Nachum in the eye without being ordered to. Knowing he was on the right track, he took a deep breath before going on. It was time for the last little nudge.

"You made a mistake, didn't you, Nevo?" he asked gently.

Nevo took a sip of water but didn't answer. Nachum kept to his game plan. He waited for him to put the cup down and then repeated the question. This time, Nevo nodded.

"I saw you got a divorce not long ago," he went on, encouraged by Nevo's response. "It must be a hard time for you. Your ex-wife is out to get you. She filed a complaint against you for an assault that never happened, right? What was that all about? She get mad at you for hooking up with the girl at work?"

Nevo nodded again. "Something like that," he said.

"And that girl screwed you too, didn't she? You can't imagine how many cases like that I've seen. They ask for it, and then when you give it to 'em they change their minds and start screaming 'sexual harassment' and call the cops. Is that what happened? Tell me I'm wrong."

"You got it right," Nevo agreed, looking down.

"That's what I'm saying. It's only natural for a guy like you, a guy who gave so much to his country, it's only natural to get mad when women treat you like that. They can ruin your life. Those two broads ruined yours, didn't they?"

Nevo kept silent. Nachum examined his face. For a minute he thought he'd lost him.

"Forget it, it doesn't matter," he said. "Look, I wanna help you. I've dealt with a lot of scum in my career, and I can tell who's a scumbag and who isn't. And you're not. I saw it right away. The fact that you were in my brother's unit is just a bonus; it just tells me I wasn't wrong about you."

Nevo made eye contact with him again. Nachum could see that he'd regained the trust he'd started to build with him, the trust he'd lost for a second when he talked about Nevo's ex-wife and the woman he'd harassed at work. Maybe he still had feelings for one of them. Maybe that's why he did it.

"I'm not gonna kid you, Nevo. What you did was really bad. It's gonna cost you a long time behind bars. But if you cooperate now, if you tell me exactly how it went down and why, I'll do what I can to make things easier for you. I've been on the job for a long time, people listen to me, and that's good for someone like you who I wanna help out. You cooperate and I'll go to the DA and put in a good word for you. It won't be easy. All the prosecutors are women. A case like yours, they ask for the maximum, and they usually get it. They got the judges by the short hairs, too scared not to give them what they want."

He could see that Nevo was starting to panic, that his tactic was getting to him. He'd go gentle with him, stroke his ego a little more, and then scare him shitless again.

"Just don't lose it, kid," Nachum went on, holding out the carrot. "Like I said, you be straight with me, you tell me everything, and I'll do what I can to help you. My brother, may he rest in peace, for him the guys in his unit were like family. I know it sounds strange, but helping you out, it's like I'm doing it for him. All you gotta do is trust me. You trust me, don't you, Nevo?"

Nevo nodded.

"So let's talk about Adi Regev," Nachum said, refilling the cup again. He knew from experience how important it was to make the victim a real person in the perp's eyes, to give her a name, an identity.

Nevo stared at him in confusion.

"Yeah, that's her name. You didn't know her name, did you?"

Again Nevo passed his hand through his hair, making it stick out in odd directions.

"You didn't know her, did you?" Nachum went on, keeping his eyes on Nevo. This was the delicate part, when he actually started talking about the crime. He was walking on eggshells here. One false move and the whole structure he'd erected so meticulously could collapse.

Nevo didn't respond. He couldn't rush him. He had to keep his impatience in check.

"If you did know her, they'll go harder on you. But you didn't know her, did you?" he asked after a few minutes of silence, treading carefully.

Nevo shook his head.

Another stage successfully completed. Was it time to ask for a written confession now, or was it still too soon? He was definitely on the right track. The only question was how to proceed from here.

"Is she okay, that Adi woman?" Nevo asked suddenly, interrupting his thoughts.

Nachum stared at him, caught totally off guard by the question. He hadn't anticipated anything like that. Was Nevo sorry for what he did or was he playing games with him? Was it possible that it'd all been an act? After all, rapists were typically liars, manipulators. Was he just scamming him?

"Yes, she's okay, she's doing better," he said, deciding to continue to play his own game.

"Good, I'm glad to hear it," Nevo said, the relief telling on his face.

Nachum managed to keep a poker face despite the storm raging inside him. What the hell was going on here? Where was this coming from? What was this display of sympathy for his victim, the girl he'd raped so brutally?

"I could speak to her, you know," he said, keeping to his original plan. "I could ask her to forgive you, tell her you know you made a mistake and you're sorry. They have this thing these days in court where the victims get to say how they feel."

"Thank you," Nevo muttered with a half smile. Nachum focused on the smile. He couldn't see a trace of cynicism or maliciousness.

"What do you want me to say to her?" he asked.

"Tell her I'm sorry if I hurt her . . . that I didn't mean to . . ."

"You can count on me," Nachum replied gently.

He took a pad and pen from his bag and placed them on the table in front of Nevo. He was ready. Checkmate.

Nevo looked at him, mystified.

"If I'm gonna help you, you have to write down everything just like it happened. You understand?" he said, his eyes fixed on Nevo.

Nevo looked down at the plastic cup, unwilling to meet the detective's eyes. He took a sip, barely able to swallow, as if his throat were bone dry.

"I know it's hard, you're scared," Nachum said, leaning in closer to force Nevo to look up, to create a sense of intimacy.

"But that's the only way for you to end this, the only way I can help you. And I really wanna help you, Nevo."

He considered saying something about Nevo's late parents, assuming the role of a father figure, but decided he'd leave that for later. He was so close he could taste it. Too much pressure could be counterproductive.

Nevo's eyes filled with tears. Nachum breathed a sigh of relief. He had nothing to worry about. Nevo wasn't putting on an act.

He was genuinely sorry for what he'd done. Police work was full of surprises, and Nevo was a big one. Not only was he already feeling remorse, but the detective had managed to maneuver him into that state in record time.

"I understand . . . I understand."

"Write it all down, how you raped Adi Regev . . . ," Nachum said, pushing the pad closer to Nevo.

Chapter 11

ZIV thought he must've misunderstood. He was so tired, maybe his mind was playing tricks on him. "Raped?" he said, echoing the detective's words. What was he talking about?

"Forget it. It's just a legal term. Write it however you want. You don't have to use the word if it makes you uncomfortable," Nachum said in his nice-guy voice.

His mind wasn't playing tricks. All this time Nachum had been talking about some girl who got raped. He'd got it all wrong. They were looking for a rapist. A rapist!

He took a deep breath. His arrest was just a case of mistaken identity. It had nothing to do with Meshulam and what he'd done last night. They thought he was a rapist. He was so relieved, he nearly jumped up and kissed Nachum.

"You're not writing," the detective said.

"No, you don't understand. You got it wrong. I'm no rapist. I didn't rape anybody. You made a mistake. It's some other guy, not me. I'd never do anything like that." The words were coming out rapidly and confidently now. And to think he was just about to tell the truth, to tell them about Meshulam, about what he was doing in north Tel Aviv last night. How lucky can you get!

Nachum kept silent.

"I'm really sorry. I didn't get it. Rape? No way. I swear on my life, on my son's life, on anything you want, I'm not a rapist." Nevo continued in the same animated manner.

Nachum's expression was frozen. Does he realize he made a mistake, Nevo wondered.

"I see you've decided to play games with me," Nachum said. "Okay, you're not a rapist. I believe you. You're just here by accident."

Nevo couldn't tell if the detective was mocking him or not.

"So if you didn't rape Adi Regev, what were you doing in north Tel Aviv last night? What was all this about the crime, the victim? Explain it to me, Mr. Nevo, starting with what you were doing last night."

By the end, Nachum was almost screaming.

Nevo felt like a balloon with all the air sucked out of it. His relief had been premature. But no matter what happened to him now, there was no way he was going to tell the cop about last night. He didn't want to end up with a bullet in the head.

"I'm waiting, Nevo. I'm all ears. Go on, I'm listening." Nachum crossed his arms over his chest and leaned back in his chair.

What could he tell him? How could he answer his questions? Rape? The detective didn't have the slightest idea what kind of trouble he was in, how deep in shit he was.

"Let me explain something to you, Nevo," Nachum said, breaking the silence. "The case against you is ironclad. You already told me enough. What you said about Adi Regev, about how you chose your victim. I don't need to sit here and listen to you anymore. I can go home to my family. I can take my son out for a bike ride like I promised. I'm done here. Whether or not you write down what happened, it makes no difference to me. But I want you to know I'm not like you. I wasn't playing games. I meant it when I said I wanna help you. So it's up to you to decide if you wanna spend the next twenty years in jail. All you gotta do is write it all down, the rape, the knife, the whole thing."

"But I didn't do anything." Nevo could hear his voice trembling, but he was no longer able to summon the confidence he'd felt only moments before.

"You're not hearing me, kid. I'm offering you a once-in-a-lifetime deal. You tell me what happened and I make sure they go easy on you. If I were you, I'd grab it with both hands. But it's up to you. You can decide to pass, and I'll go home and you'll never see me again. But then you're gonna rot in jail, and believe me, you're gonna be very sorry you missed your chance. You're gonna curse yourself for being such an asshole you refused to take the only help you're ever gonna get."

Nevo stared at him in silence. Whatever he did now, it wasn't going to end well for him. He was trapped. Suddenly he had to pee so bad he thought he would burst.

"I need to take a leak," he said.

Nachum gave him a nasty laugh. "It doesn't work like that. You piss when I say you can piss. You better get used to it. That's how it's gonna be for the next twenty years."

He sure changed colors fast, Nevo thought. A minute ago he was saying how much he wants to help me.

"I'm gonna give you two minutes to make up your mind. Either you pick up that pen or I'm outta here."

Nevo squirmed uncomfortably in the chair. Nachum drummed his fingers on the table, tapping out a rhythmical beat. The second hand on the clock was counting down. Time was running out for him. Nachum tapped faster.

The silence was broken by the sound of a phone ringing. Nachum glanced at his cell phone and smiled at Nevo.

"You know what?" he said.

Nevo shook his head. He really had to go. Urgently.

"That's the crime reporter from Channel Two," he said. "He got word we made an arrest. He wants a name, a photo. Whaddya say, should we give the guy what he wants? Should we make you famous so everybody in the whole country knows what kinda man you are? You want your family, your son, to see your face on the news?"

Nevo could picture Merav and Gili watching the news in the living room. What would she think? Would she believe he could do such a thing? How would Gili feel when he saw his face on the screen? He was all the family he had now that his parents were dead and he'd split from Merav. He hardly ever heard from his own brother, Itai. He didn't have any friends either. The friends he used to have when he was married all went with Merav after the divorce. The image of his parents sent a knife through his heart. A day didn't go by when he didn't think of them. He felt their absence so intensely, especially in the good times when he thought about what they were missing out on. He'd learned to deal with the bad times on his own. Even when they were alive, he never told them anything he knew they didn't want to hear. His arrest would've broken their hearts.

"This's crazy," he said, whether to himself or Nachum. "I didn't do anything. I didn't rape anyone."

Nachum just gave him a cold stare, not saying a word.

"It wasn't me . . . You got it wrong," he muttered.

"I'm still waiting for you to make up your mind. You've got forty-five seconds. Then I'm outta here," Nachum said, standing up.

He paced back and forth in the interrogation room, looking at the clock every few seconds to remind him that his time was running out. The pacing made Nevo even more nervous. His bladder pressed down harder. It really hurt. He hadn't been thinking straight when he drank all that water Nachum poured him. And after he'd downed the six-pack, his bladder was already full when he got here.

"But you got it wrong," he said, nearly shouting. "It's not like you said . . . I didn't rape anyone."

Nachum threw him a look of disgust, picked up the phone, and said dispassionately, "Arrange for a transfer to Abu Kabir.

"You ever been in Abu Kabir, Nevo?" he asked.

Nevo shook his head.

Nachum snickered maliciously.

"You're gonna regret your decision, you can't even imagine how much you're gonna regret it. I already got your confession. Not writing it down for me, that's your mistake. You know what an asshole you are? You're leaving here a confessed rapist without my help. I haven't seen a loser like you in a long time."

Chapter 12

NACHUM wasn't happy. Something had gone wrong at the last minute. Nevo was broken, consumed by remorse, ready to make a full confession, and then for some reason he'd backed off. How had he fucked up? He was so sure he had Nevo right where he wanted him that he'd taken the bait, swallowed the hook, and all he had to do was reel him in. Secretly, he was even hoping that once he confessed to raping Adi Regev, he could get him to confess to prior acts as well. There was a good chance this wasn't the first time he did it. Adi's father had seen him stalking another victim.

Had he been too eager to hand him the pen and paper? Timing is everything. Maybe he should've waited a little longer, or written it down himself instead of telling Nevo to do it. If he'd done it that way, he might be sitting here now with a signed confession in his hand.

He looked at the feed from the surveillance camera that continued to show Nevo in the interrogation room, hunched up in his chair, hardly moving a muscle. An hour had gone by since he'd walked out and left him there alone. He'd told his assistant, Ohad, to escort him to the toilet. Pain made some people even more recalcitrant. So he'd let Nevo relieve the pressure in his bladder, but it didn't get him anywhere.

Something had changed right before the end. Then again, maybe nothing had changed and it'd been an act from the beginning.

Nachum got up and walked to the window. It was four thirty in the afternoon. He was exhausted. He hadn't had a break since he got the call from Yaron Regev yesterday morning. He hadn't made it to Friday-night dinner with his family. At least one thing he said to Nevo was the honest truth: he'd promised Omer, his fifteen-year-old, a bike ride through the Jerusalem hills. He knew how much Omer had been looking forward to it, knew he'd let him down. And he'd been looking forward to it too. But this was his job, and sometimes it had to come first.

The first rain of the season began coming down, chasing the cluster of cops who'd gone outside for a smoke back into the building.

He'd gotten a lot out of Nevo, but it wasn't enough to make a case against him. His lawyers would argue that it was worthless, and someone in the DA's Office would get cold feet and go for a plea bargain. They might even decide not to charge him at all.

Adi's identification wouldn't have the slightest merit for them. They wouldn't even consider the possibility that she was telling the truth. The whole thing would fall apart as soon as they found out it wasn't conducted by the book. And they wouldn't put much stock in the cap they found in Nevo's apartment, no matter how similar it was to the one Adi described. Or the sunglasses, or the shoes, even though they were the right size and style. He could already hear the DA: "It's a common size, it's a popular style, lotsa people have baseball caps and sunglasses." There was no end to it. People can talk their way out of anything. Little kids did it in school, suspects did it in the interrogation room, defendants did it in court.

It was still raining. He stared out the window, mesmerized by the falling drops. Nevo was the rapist, there was no question in his mind, but he couldn't figure out why he'd denied it at the very last minute, why he'd refused to confess. There could be a million reasons. Maybe he suddenly realized he was sealing his own fate and panicked, maybe he got scared when Nachum said the word "rape," maybe he hadn't even admitted it to himself before. Who knows?

But that wasn't what mattered. What mattered was whether he was guilty or not, and Nachum had no doubt about the answer to that one.

He'd even asked Ohad and the other members of the unit. He wasn't the type who'd never admit he could be wrong. But everyone's gut was saying the same thing. They had the right man.

Ohad tapped lightly on the door and walked in. Nachum made an effort to shake off the thoughts gnawing at him. Ohad was a good cop. A little too political for his taste, a little too concerned with what other people would say, but all in all he did good work and got results.

"We gotta get a move on," Ohad said, gesturing with his head toward the clock on the wall. In a few short hours Nevo would have to be brought before a judge. That was the law. They couldn't hold him for more than twenty-four hours without an initial arraignment.

That didn't worry him. He was confident the judge would remand Nevo into custody as soon as he saw the evidence they had against him and the procedures they still needed to perform to move the investigation along. And the judge was the only one who'd get a look at that material. Not Nevo and not his attorney. As usual, they'd list procedures from here to Timbuktu, all of them requiring that Nevo remain in custody. Most judges didn't even bother to read it. They had too many arrests to handle and very little patience for them, so they were very generous with remand orders. Especially at this early stage in the investigation of a serious crime.

No, it wasn't the arraignment that was weighing on Nachum's mind, it was what would happen afterward, when all their investigation reports and warrant applications were no longer confidential. Nevo and his attorney would get copies of every piece of paper pertaining to his arrest. Nachum knew only too well that if he revealed that Adi had seen pictures of Nevo before the lineup, it would eventually be thrown out. It didn't conform with any of the legal requirements, and they didn't get a do-over. So he'd just have to risk keeping that information to himself. There was a good chance that if they kept at Nevo for a few more days, they'd either get their confession or find new evidence. But there was also a chance they wouldn't.

What would happen if they didn't dig up anything new or if Nevo took his lawyer's advice and kept his mouth shut? Once Adi's identification was thrown out, they'd be left with nothing.

Ohad handed him the documents for the judge. Nachum went over and over the description of the lineup. It wasn't good enough. He had to think ahead, to consider how things were going to play out later.

With a sigh, he started rewriting the report. Ohad came to look over his shoulder, gave him a pat on the back, and left.

They had arrested Ziv Nevo, he wrote, in the wake of a phone call from the victim's father, who had seen a man answering his daughter's description of the rapist loitering late the previous night on the street where she lived and displaying suspicious behavior: he was hiding between parked cars and stalking another woman. A squad car was sent to the suspect's address and he was taken into custody. A lineup in the presence of the victim had yet to be conducted and was planned for Monday morning. Since Nevo had been arrested on Friday night, at the start of the weekend, they had been unable to arrange for it earlier.

Nachum reread what he'd written. He wasn't born yesterday. He knew plenty of cops who played fast and loose with the facts. But that had never been his way. Just as he'd never doctored the numbers to improve his chances of a promotion, he'd never submitted a false report to the court. But that's precisely what he was doing now. In order to get Nevo remanded into custody, he was claiming they hadn't done a lineup even though they had, inventing a story about plans for a lineup that was never going to happen. What'd gotten into him?

It wasn't just that he was certain Nevo was guilty. There'd been enough times in the past when he was sure he had his man and he knew the perp could slip through his fingers because of some stupid technicality. But never before had he even considered doing what he was doing now.

Was the pressure to close his cases getting to him? Was he bitter about being passed over for promotion for longer than he liked to remember? The police force was his life. He'd given it his all. It ate away at him to see other guys being promoted over him, getting jobs that were rightfully his. And there was no point in denying that it was also affecting his family life. He'd married pretty late in life. Even when he was younger, he wasn't much to look at, and his reserve and serious nature made it hard for him to approach women. It probably put them off too. Leah was the younger sister of a cop he'd worked with in logistics. They'd never been equal partners in the marriage. From the beginning, she'd looked to him to make the decisions for both of them. The division of roles in the family had been comfortable for him, and he imagined for her as well. But things had been changing lately, especially since the last time he missed out on a promotion. Leah had started complaining that he didn't help her enough around the house, demanding that he do things he'd never been expected to do before.

The thoughts clogging his brain were giving him a headache. Why was he tormenting himself with this rubbish?

He read the report he'd written one last time. There were no personal motives behind it. Nevo had raped Adi Regev. Nachum was just doing what he had to do to prevent him from raping some other poor girl. No one could fault him for that, no one at all.

Chapter 13

YARON Regev didn't hesitate for a second before assuring Inspector Nachum that he had nothing to worry about, he could count on them not to breathe a word about the first lineup. He was surprised to get the call from Nachum, and even more surprised by the detective's disapproving tone. He had no idea he'd done something wrong. And he certainly hadn't meant to do anything illegal or cause trouble for the police. All he wanted was to protect his daughter, to save her from another ordeal, to do what any normal father would do. He made only one request concerning the "proper" lineup Nachum was planning: "Just get it over with as fast as possible."

The psychologist had explained that Adi would have good days and bad days, that they shouldn't regard every little thing she did or said as a sign of improvement or decline. Still, he felt that her spirits were a bit lighter now that they'd caught the bastard. It seemed to give her some relief. He could tell. Despite everything she'd been through on Friday, when the family was sitting around the dinner table that night she'd laughed along with the rest of them at one of Adam's funny army stories. It lasted only a brief moment. Irit was so relieved to see her laughing at her brother's anecdote that she burst into tears, and then Adi started crying, and her little sister Michal joined in. He had to admit that even his own eyes were wet. But still, she *had* laughed.

He debated telling Irit what Nachum was planning. She had enough to deal with at the moment and he didn't want to add to her burden. But he decided he had no choice—he needed her help.

Her response caught him off guard. He knew Irit hated what she called "dirty tricks and half-truths," but he was sure this time she'd see things his way. After all, it was their daughter they were talking about.

"You want me to tell her to lie?" she asked incredulously.

It had obviously been a mistake to tell her. They'd been married for thirty years. He should've known better.

"Calm down. Why do you have to make such a big deal about everything? It's only if his attorney asks her directly. No one's telling her to lie. You're making a mountain out of molehill," he said in a lame attempt at damage control.

"I don't like this, Yaron. It doesn't smell right. I won't have either of you lying about anything. I think you should call that detective back and tell him that if they question you about it, you're going to tell the truth." She wasn't budging. He hated that self-righteous tone of hers that implied she was the only one who knew right from wrong.

"Do you hear yourself?" he shouted. "Who exactly are we lying to? The rapist? The scum who agreed to represent him? That's who you're standing up for? What about your own daughter? Who's standing up for her? Am I the only one who's thinking about Adi?"

"That's a cheap shot, and you know it." His words didn't seem to be having any effect. "I'm thinking about Adi just as much as you are, even if I'm not playing at being an undercover agent and lurking around outside her house. I want to see him behind bars just like you do. All I'm asking is to do it honestly, without getting Adi messed up in any underhanded schemes the cops are plotting. She's suffered enough."

Irit's holier-than-thou attitude infuriated him. He sympathized with Nachum. He'd been the manager of a high-tech company for a long time. Five years ago they'd gone public, and ever since then he'd been plagued by an army of interfering fools: quality control-lers, safety officers, comptrollers, accountants, lawyers, directors who did nothing but rake in money. If they'd just leave him alone to do his job, he'd get things done much faster, and much better too. Sometimes you had to take shortcuts to keep on moving forward, to get to where you really wanted to go. He'd done it often enough. That's just how it was in the real world.

Trying to talk Irit into changing her mind was a waste of time. He stood up.

"We're not done here," she said, getting up and waving a finger in front of his face. "At the very least I want to talk to Adi and see what she thinks about it."

"What do you mean, 'Talk to Adi'? Are you crazy?" he shouted. "No way. For three weeks I sat outside her house until I finally nabbed that animal. I'm not going to let you screw this up, Irit. He's going to rot in prison like he deserves, you hear me? Save your lectures for your bleeding-heart friends. This is the real world. You're not going to get in the way and you're not going to talk to anyone. You hear me, Irit? Don't fuck this up!"

Not waiting for a reply, he strode quickly out of the living room and into the study, slamming the door behind him. Why had he ever imagined he could enlist her help?

ADI was in front of the computer bursting bright-colored bubbles again. He watched her for a while, wondering why she found this game so fascinating and trying to find the words to explain to her what was going to happen at the lineup tomorrow. He and Irit hadn't exchanged a word since their fight. The silence had been broken only once, when he asked her again last night to keep out of it, and she promised not to interfere, but not before repeating that she didn't like it at all.

"I heard that monster got himself a sleazy lawyer who twists everything the police say. He's a lying bastard," he began.

Adi barely looked up before returning her attention to the game.

"You don't need to have anything to do with him. You don't even have to talk to him. But if he asks you if you ever saw a picture of his client, it's best if you say no. That way it'll all be over quickly, no questions asked."

He stared at her intently, waiting for her reaction. She didn't give the slightest indication that she'd even heard what he said.

"I don't know, Dad. I don't think I want to do that," she suddenly blurted out without taking her eyes off the screen.

"There's nothing to it, Adinka. The lawyer doesn't matter. It's not a courtroom." He wondered if Irit had broken her promise and spoken to her.

"I'm not sure it's him."

Her voice was so soft, he wasn't certain he'd heard her properly. His face registered astonishment. "What do you mean you're not sure it's him?"

"It was dark," she went on in the same quiet tone. "And I didn't get a good look at his face because of the cap. I'm not sure."

"But Friday you said it was him. We were sitting in the living room and I showed you the pictures. You said it was him, you said you recognized him." Yaron couldn't get his head around it. He'd come here today convinced that the only problem he had to deal with was the little white lie Nachum had asked them to tell. He'd never expected this.

Silently, Adi went on playing, rapidly moving the mouse and clicking incessantly.

"Look at me, Adi." He couldn't keep the irritation out of his voice. Why did everyone in the family have to be so difficult?

She turned her head and he could see the tears in her eyes. He felt his heart seize up.

"I understand, baby. This whole lineup thing is hard for you. You're nervous about it," he said, his voice almost as soft as hers. "I know it's messing with your head. But don't let that confuse you. It's him. Believe me, Adi, he's the man who did it."

"How do you know that?" Now she was the one who sounded irritated. She turned back to the screen. "I was there."

"He confessed," he said. "The police . . . they told me he confessed to raping you. The judge even remanded him for seven days."

"So what do they need me for if they've got his confession? I don't . . . I don't want to see him. What do they need me for?" she repeated, suddenly sounding like a little girl.

"I don't know why they need you, honey, but they do," her father replied, trying to comfort her just as he did when she was a baby. "I guess it's routine procedure, something they have to do to get a conviction."

Adi continued to focus on her game, ignoring him.

"Talk to me, Adinka," he pleaded with her. "They need you there tomorrow."

"But I already told you, I'm not sure."

"I understand, you're upset, that's perfectly normal." He started to remind her of the pictures, of how she'd recognized him when he showed them to her, but she cut him off. Pushing her chair back, she stood up and faced him, shouting accusingly, "You're not listening. I'm sick of it. You never listen to me!"

He stared at her in shock, powerless to respond. The Adi he knew never raised her voice. She'd never been rebellious. His friends had rebellious children who caused them all sorts of heartache, but not Adi. She'd always been such a pliant child. "What do you want me to do? Tell me, what are you asking me to do?" he said finally, speaking gently to avoid another outburst.

She didn't answer.

"Adi, sweetheart," he began, and then he didn't know how to go on. When they'd arrested the rapist he'd felt a huge weight lifted from him. And it made him very happy to know he'd played such an important role in catching the creep, that he'd fulfilled his duty as a father to protect his child. But ever since, the obstacles had been piling up, preventing him from moving forward.

"I'm just not sure," she repeated, bursting into tears.

He gathered her in his arms. To his surprise, she didn't resist. In fact, she almost fell into his embrace. He could feel her body trembling. "It's okay, Adinka," he whispered in her ear. "Everything's going to be okay. I'll take care of you. Don't worry about it. It'll all be over very soon."

Chapter 14

ZIV Nevo's spirits rose when he saw the seven other men waiting to be led into the lineup with him. He'd spent the past two nights locked up in Abu Kabir in a long, narrow cell that reeked of urine, feces, Lysol, and fear. One of his eleven cell mates had been arrested on suspicion of homicide, one was facing charges of grand theft, and the rest were junkies and petty thieves. He did his best to look tough, but he was shaking inside. He sat in the corner apart from the others, didn't talk to anyone, didn't make eye contact, and kept out of their fights and shouting matches. Despite his exhaustion, he got almost no sleep.

On Saturday night he'd been remanded for seven days. The whole procedure took less than five minutes. The judge merely approved the terms his attorney had agreed on with the prosecution, with little more than a glance in his direction.

He wasn't even allowed time to talk to the lawyer. Fifteen minutes before the hearing a man had appeared, introduced himself as Assaf Rosen, and announced that he was the public defender appointed to represent him. Ziv stared at him in confusion. "That means you don't have to pay me," Rosen explained. He apologized for not meeting with him sooner, claiming the police had deliberately sent him to the wrong precinct. "Never mind," Ziv said, "at least you're here now." Rosen asked him a few questions that didn't seem relevant and then said that, given the circumstances, he would advise agreeing to a remand for seven to ten days.

"In cases like yours, the police usually get whatever they ask for. The best move is to close a deal. They'll ask for fifteen days,

I'll say five, and we'll meet in the middle." He sounded very sure of himself.

"But I'm not guilty, I didn't do it . . . I'm innocent . . . ," Ziv protested.

Rosen interrupted. "That doesn't make any difference at this stage. If you want to fight it, I'll do it. But you've got to understand that it won't do you any good. In the end you'll just get fifteen days. Especially with Judge Luzon on the bench."

Rosen eventually got the prosecution to agree to seven days. He flashed Ziv a big smile, very pleased with himself. "Be thankful," he whispered to Ziv before they took him away, "it could've been much worse."

Ziv had seen Rosen again a few minutes ago. He'd explained that the suspect had the right to have his attorney present during the lineup, and that's why he was here. "This is critical to our case," he said. Ziv had already figured that out for himself. They'd sat side by side, waiting for the lineup to begin. He wanted to tell Rosen the whole story, prove to him that he was innocent, but the lawyer cut him off. "We'll talk afterward," he said. "No point in wasting your breath now."

"It'll go okay. I didn't rape anyone," Ziv told Rosen, more for his own benefit than for the lawyer's.

"Let's wait and see," Rosen answered, giving him another broad smile. He was only a few years older than Nevo and didn't look anything like the flashy lawyers you see on TV. But Ziv knew he didn't have the money to hire someone like that.

He'd used his one phone call to contact his older brother. "Asshole, how did you get yourself mixed up in something like that?" Itai had shrieked at him when he told him where he was calling from. "You've been going from bad to worse ever since you and Merav split up." Ziv didn't reply. "I need money for a lawyer," he said quietly. "I don't trust the guy they gave me." Itai didn't promise anything. "The mortgage payments are killing us," he said. Ziv kept silent, choosing not to remind his brother that he'd signed over to him most of his share in their parents' life insurance settlement because of his upcoming marriage to Nurit. They used to be best friends. Some people even mistook them for twins. But they'd grown apart since their parents' death. His divorce didn't help either. Like the rest of the world, Itai and Nurit took Merav's side, blaming him for the breakup. It was only after he hung up that he realized that Itai hadn't said he believed him, that he knew he didn't commit rape.

THE door opened and in walked Ohad, Nachum's second-in-command.

"Come on, let's get this show on the road," he said drily.

Rosen shook his hand. "I'll be in the other room with the victim and the cops. I'll be watching everything. Good luck."

Ziv stood up and followed Ohad down the hall, his heart pounding. What if it isn't okay? What if something goes wrong? It suddenly occurred to him that the cops could pick guys for the lineup that didn't look anything like him. What if they did it to confuse her, and then she pointed to him? He was sorry he hadn't thought of that before, when Rosen was there.

But then he'd seen the guys waiting to go in with him and he felt a little better. They were all more or less his height and build. He counted seven. That made eight altogether. Listening in on their conversations, he learned that five of them were cops and the other two were detainees like him.

It had to be okay, no question about it. he comforted himself, secure in the knowledge that he didn't rape anyone. He'd never even met Adi Regev.

Ohad led them into a narrow room with the numbers one to eight on one wall and a mirror on the other. Just like in the movies.

Ohad asked him what number he wanted. "Anything but five," one of the detainees told him. "They always pick five."

"Four," he said. "I'll be number four."

The men lined up and waited. What should he do? How should he stand? What kind of expression should he have on his face? Serious? Calm? Amused? If he'd ever seen a real rapist, he could try to look different, but how should he know what a rapist looked like?

He was having trouble standing still. He kept shifting his weight nervously, until he caught himself doing it and stopped fidgeting. The last thing he needed was to draw attention to himself.

He looked at the mirror. What was going on back there? It was taking a long time. Maybe that was a good sign. Maybe the girl couldn't make up her mind. Or the cops could've told her the man who raped her was in the lineup and she desperately wanted to pick the right one, but she didn't recognize any of them.

The door opened, startling him, and Ohad walked in.

"That's it. We're done here," he said evenly.

Ziv followed Ohad back down the corridor in silence. If he was off the hook, Ohad would probably tell him, maybe even let him go. On the other hand, if the girl didn't ID him, that meant the cops got it wrong, and maybe that's why he wasn't in a talking mood. He ran his hand through his hair. He'd never been so nervous in his life.

Assaf Rosen was sitting at a table in a tiny room. He rose when Ziv was led in.

"What did she say?" he blurted out immediately.

"I'm sorry. She picked you out of the lineup."

"What? What are you talking about?" He felt like someone had punched him in the gut. His face was burning. How could that happen? He was innocent! He didn't rape her, he didn't rape anyone.

"Was she positive?" he asked, looking in desperation for some tiny ray of light to hang his hopes on, something that would help him make sense out of the craziness.

Rosen nodded. "She pointed to you right away, didn't wait more than a second or two. Not enough for us to make anything of it."

Ziv collapsed onto the chair.

"What am I supposed to do now?"

Rosen didn't answer.

"I didn't do it, I didn't rape her. You believe me, don't you?" he asked, his voice breaking.

Rosen got up. "I'll be back tomorrow and we can talk then."

"Can't we talk now?" Ziv pleaded. He needed someone to tell him what to do, someone to be on his side.

"Sorry, I can't stay. I have to be in court in an hour and a half and I'm already running late," Rosen said, reaching out his hand as if they'd just closed a deal.

"The only thing you have to remember is to keep your mouth shut. Don't talk to the cops. Don't talk to anyone. There's a good chance they'll stick you in with a guy who'll pretend to give you advice, act like your best friend, try to get you to pour your heart out to him," he went on. "No matter how much you want to, don't say anything. The guy'll be a plant, an undercover cop or a punk who thinks the judge will go easy on him if he does the cops' dirty work for them. Just remember to keep your mouth shut. Got it?"

Ziv nodded.

"Okay, then. Tomorrow," Rosen said as he walked out of the room, leaving Ziv all alone. I'm not guilty, I didn't rape her, he wanted to shout after him, to shout to the whole world. But he kept silent. What was the point? Who'd listen to him?

Chapter 15

DAVID Meshulam made another pass through the streets near her house to be certain he hadn't missed it. This was his fifth time around, but he didn't see the car anywhere. It was gone. Swallowed up.

The radio promised that the autumn heat wave would break by the evening, but it was still hot and humid. He was sweating profusely, and not only from the heat. He'd dialed her number an hour ago to check if she was home, disconnecting as soon as she picked up. If she was in her apartment, where was the car? She didn't have a husband or kids, so who could've taken it? Where did it go? Could his biggest fear be coming true?

He glanced at the clock on the dashboard. It was midnight. If he didn't find the car, he'd have to wait here all night, wait until she left for work in the morning and follow her. He didn't have that much time to waste. It might already be too late. Nevo might've spilled his guts to save his own neck.

He'd tried frantically to get hold of him all day Saturday. The fact that Nevo wasn't answering his phone drove him up the wall. He knew it wasn't the smartest move, but he had no choice but to go talk to him in person. He wasn't home. His instincts were telling him it was bad. Maybe they caught him. He considered telling Faro but decided against it. He didn't know how he'd react, and the last thing he wanted was to upset him. It was his job to be a man Faro could count on, not to make trouble for him.

He couldn't believe it when he heard Nevo had been picked up on suspicion of rape. The cops must be out of their minds. He knew better than anyone what Nevo was doing on Louis Marshall Street

Thursday night. It was a big relief that they were holding him for rape. Even the dumbass detectives would figure out sooner or later that they'd got the wrong man. But a day and half went by and Nevo still wasn't out. He started to get worried. What'd they really want from him? What if the whole rape thing was just a trick to get to Faro? What if they knew?

He decided not to risk it. He managed to get a message to Meir, who was being held for assaulting that bouncer. He'd find Nevo and make sure he knew to keep his mouth shut if his life, and the life of his little kid, meant anything to him. Even a pinhead like Nevo would get the picture.

But Meir hadn't been able to make contact with Nevo yet, and Meshulam didn't want to take any chances. He had to get rid of the car with the explosives underneath. He knew how the cops could work a guy over, especially someone like Nevo. And if Nevo broke and told them about the bomb, he had to be certain they didn't find anything when they came looking. All the way here he'd been thinking about what it was going to feel like driving around with a bomb under him, knowing it could go off at any second, but he didn't have a lot of options left.

All his plans were going up in smoke. The car was gone. Vanished into thin air. Maybe Nevo had already blabbed and the cops came and towed it away. But then why was she alone in the house without police protection?

He cursed her, Nevo, and the whole fucking mess he'd gotten himself into. Why did he have to decide to play the hero? He knew the rules.

His cell phone rang. Faro's number flashed on the screen. His whole body tensed. What if he'd already heard? He forced himself to remain calm. Faro would never say anything incriminating over the phone. The cops could be listening in.

He'd been working for Shimon Faro for thirteen years. He'd dropped out of school at the age of fifteen and gone to work in Shlomo's corner grocery. Whenever Faro came in, he used to talk to him. He'd ask Meshulam questions about himself and the boy did his best to make a good impression. He knew very well who Faro was, and he knew he was supposed to show him respect. Once he delivered a big load of groceries to his house, and he could see Faro was surprised by how strong he was. A few days later he came into the store and offered him a job as a courier.

He'd been a total loser until Faro got hold of him and made a man out of him. He owed him his life. If Faro hadn't taken him under his wing when he was sixteen, he probably wouldn't be alive today, or else he would've turned out like a lot of the kids he grew up with—homeless, a junkie, a wino, a nobody.

Faro had saved him. All his life he'd been told he was a loser, that he had no future. He didn't have a dad. Or a mom, for that matter. She was a hopped-up hooker who didn't think about anyone but herself. He grew up looking out for himself like a stray cat, with no one in the world who gave a rat's ass what happened to him.

Faro gave him a job, respect, a home. For the first time in his life, there was someone who took notice of him, someone who treated him like a human being and made him feel he mattered.

He started out as a courier and gradually rose in the ranks. Faro saw his potential, his blind loyalty. He knew Meshulam would go through fire for him. If he didn't have such a short fuse, if he could just manage to control his temper, he knew he could rise even higher in the organization.

He'd gotten the dumbass idea to get Nevo to plant the bomb two weeks ago when he was celebrating his birthday in the Black Sabbath Club. He was thrilled when Faro showed up. He'd been hoping he'd come, but he never really believed he would. Faro is a very busy man, he kept reminding himself. When he saw him in the doorway, his heart swelled. He'd never let it show, but inside he was over the moon. Faro made him feel like part of the family. Meshulam fawned over him all night, bringing him drinks and making sure he was comfortable and was having a good time. But it didn't improve Faro's mood. He'd worked for the boss long enough to know when something was wrong. When the party was winding down and most of his friends had left, Meshulam went up to Faro and asked if there was any way he could help him out. "This business with Yariv is eating at me," Faro said, sighing deeply. He was talking about Yariv Cohen, another soldier in the organization. He'd been arrested for murder. "The bitch won't let up," Faro went on. Meshulam could see the sadness in his eyes. The boss cared about his soldiers like they were his sons.

He hadn't been able to get that conversation out of his head. The bitch deserved to be punished for what she did. That's what Faro would want. It was his idea to use Nevo, the guy who chauffeured Faro around. He knew he'd been a demolition officer in the army. In fact, he figured that's why Faro brought him into the organization in the first place, not just for his driving skills. But you could never tell with Faro. The press made him out to be a monster, but he had a big heart. He was always ready to help a guy out, give him cash when he needed it, solve problems for him. And not important people either, just ordinary guys. The kind the important people don't see, don't even bother to piss in their direction. Little guys, like him.

He was sure Faro would give him a pat on the back when he heard what he'd done. He'd be proud of him, pleased to see he'd understood what he wanted from him. What could go wrong?

He'd told Nevo to make it a small charge, only enough to hurt her, not kill her. Just to get the message across. He never dreamed the shit would hit the fan like this.

"WHAT'S up?" he asked casually. He and Faro had their own code. They understood each other without having to spell things out.

"You're not gonna believe what I just heard. The clowns picked Nevo up for rape."

Meshulam tensed. What was Faro trying to say? What was he hinting at?

"He's a good guy, that Nevo. He was my nephew's commander in the army. Every now and then he does me a favor, takes me to family events." Meshulam knew the boss wasn't really talking to him. Everything he was saying was for the benefit of the cops who were probably listening in. He wanted to make it clear that Nevo didn't know anything about anything.

He made his standard reply. "The cops are fucking assholes."

"Shuki Borochov will be back in the country the day after to-morrow. I'll send him to Nevo. He'll be out in an hour," Faro said.

"Yeah, he'll show 'em."

Faro hung up and Meshulam wiped the sweat off his brow. It was all blowing up in his face. Shuki Borochov was one of the law-yers Faro used to get the cops or the DA off his back when necessary. As soon as Nevo heard he'd been sent by Faro, he'd spill, and then Faro would know about the bomb, that it'd all been Meshulam's idea, that he'd fucked up. In all the years he'd worked for Faro, he'd almost never fucked up before. He didn't want to disappoint him now.

He could feel his face going red. He was in deep shit because of Nevo. He'd asked him to do one simple thing and the loser couldn't even get that right. One thing he knew for sure—he couldn't let

Nevo meet with Borochov. His best option was to take him out while he was still in detention. But it wasn't easy to arrange a hit in twenty-four hours, especially in Abu Kabir, where the inmates were packed in like sardines. He'd have to find some other way, some creative solution to his problem.

Chapter 16

ELI Nachum looked up. Adi Regev was standing at the door to his office. Something in her body language, in the way she was chewing nervously on a lock of hair, had him worried. He could sense she was upset, maybe even angry.

She'd called him last night and said she had to meet with him urgently. He'd tried to get her to tell him what it was about and why it couldn't wait, but she'd refused to say. He'd considered putting her off but decided against it. If there was a problem, it was best to deal with it immediately, before it got any worse.

"Thank you for yesterday," he said. Starting the conversation on his terms would give him control over the situation. "Thanks to you, a very dangerous man is going to go away for a very long time. If you hadn't helped us nail him, he would've done it again. There's no doubt in my mind."

Adi squirmed in her chair. She was still chewing on her hair. She was doing the same thing in the hospital the first time he saw her, and during yesterday's lineup too. He could understand why she was nervous then, but why now? What was bothering her? Thankfully, Nevo's attorney hadn't asked her if it was the first time she'd ID'd Nevo, and she hadn't volunteered the information. The possibility that she'd say something damaging had kept him up at night, even though her father had assured him he had nothing to worry about, that he'd spoken to her and she knew what was expected of her.

"You know," he said, giving her a paternal smile, "I have a daughter around your age. A little younger. She lives on Horkanos Street, not far from you. You know it?"

Adi nodded.

In a minute or two she'd tell him why she was here. Until she was ready to do that, he'd draw her in as much as he could, talk about his daughter so she'd see him as a father and not just a cop. But he couldn't help thinking how different his daughter was from Adi. She might be younger, but she was much more mature.

"As a father, I have to say I've been sleeping much better the past couple of days, thanks to you and your dad."

Adi cut him off.

"I want to retract what I said at the lineup."

He stared at her in silence. This wasn't the first time he'd heard something like this. Witnesses were unreliable. They'd give a version of events and then retract it or give a different one. Some people did it on purpose to throw the cops off the scent. Others were just confused. And of course, sometimes they received threats. It was his job to figure out why they decided to back down, to calm their fears, and, if necessary, to rethink the case.

"I made a mistake and I want to fix it," she insisted when he didn't respond.

"Are you sure it was a mistake? Is it possible you're making a mistake now?" Nachum asked quietly. He couldn't let her see what he was feeling. He had to keep her calm and find out what was behind this.

"Stop it," she said coldly.

"Stop what?" he asked, although he knew perfectly well what she meant.

"Stop trying to confuse me, to manipulate me into saying what you want me to say."

He didn't reply. Better not to intervene, to let her vent her anger and deliver the speech she must've prepared on her way here. After that, he'd be able to talk to her with less tension in the air.

"I . . . I wasn't certain from the beginning," she went on, "but my dad was so positive it was him and he wanted so much for me to say it, that I did. It was the same thing at the lineup . . . Everyone was waiting for me to point to him, like it was some test I had to pass."

"No one's asking you to say anything you're not comfortable with," Nachum said soothingly, in an effort to pacify her. "You and I share the same goal. We both want to catch the right guy, the bastard who raped you. We're on the same side, you and me."

She looked at him in silence. He could see that some of the tension was gone from her face. "If you thought any different, I want to apologize. That certainly wasn't my intention," he continued in the same tone.

"So what do you want me to do now?" she asked. "Like I told you . . . I'm not sure."

She was like a little girl with no experience of the real world. He was a bit disappointed by her reaction.

"Whatever you feel is right," he answered. "You know he confessed. You identified the right guy. From the start you weren't mistaken. Not you and not your dad. Remember, he caught him loitering near your house. All he wanted to do was protect you."

He held back for a moment to see what effect his words were having. The fact that she didn't try to refute what he was saying encouraged him to go on. "It's natural for you to be worried, to have doubts. It happens to a lot of rape victims. But I've been doing this job for a very long time, and I can assure you, you didn't make a mistake. There's no reason at all for you to be afraid your testimony will put the wrong man behind bars."

"That's wonderful. I'm so glad to hear it," she said.

She'd gone from anger to acquiescence too fast, too abruptly. She sounded too pleased, as if she'd gotten what she wanted. It made him wary.

"So you won't mind if I say in court that I'm not one hundred percent sure it was him, that I was never sure," she asked with seemingly artless innocence.

He examined her closely, trying to understand what was going through her mind. What had changed since Friday? At the lineup he'd seen that she was nervous, uncomfortable, but that was only natural. And when it came down to it, she'd fingered Nevo. So what had changed? What had he missed?

"Think about it for a minute, Adi. I know it's confusing, upsetting."

"I know what you did," she said quietly but firmly.

"I don't understand."

"My little sister, Michal. She heard our parents fighting and she told me what you asked my dad to do, how you tried to manipulate me behind my back like I was your puppet."

Nachum took a deep breath. He couldn't afford to lose patience with her now. She was angry. She was hurt that they hadn't confided in her. It had nothing to do with whether she could or couldn't identify the man who raped her. She needed to vent her anger, and he and her father were easy targets.

"Why were you afraid his attorney would ask me if it was the first time I'd seen him? Why did you need me to lie?"

"I think you're jumping to conclusions. I never asked your dad to tell you to lie. That would be wrong. All I wanted, all your dad wanted, was to protect you. The perp's attorney doesn't care about you, he doesn't see . . ."

She jumped up impatiently, her fury showing on her face. Nachum stood up.

"Why are you doing this, Adi?" he asked, looking straight at her.

"I'm sick of being used, lied to. You're raping me again, making me do things I don't want to do," she shouted, her eyes filling with tears.

She seemed to be taken aback by her own outburst, surprised by the sound of the word "rape" issuing from her own mouth.

"There's no reason for you to feel that way. You . . . ," he started, still trying to calm her, coax her, even though he could see from her expression that he'd already lost her.

"You didn't even have the common decency to talk to me directly!"

"We've got the right man," Nachum said gently, attempting to shift the conversation. He knew he couldn't do anything about the way she was feeling. "Your testimony will put him away. We'll be sure that what happened to you will never happen to another woman. Think how you'll feel if he gets off and does it again. If you told me he wasn't the guy, it'd be a different matter. I'd tell you to withdraw your statement. But you said you're not one hundred percent certain, and that's something else. You're just under stress. It'll get better, you'll see."

She picked up her purse and slung it on her shoulder, indicating that their meeting was over.

"I told you to stop it, didn't I?" she said angrily.

Nachum kept silent.

"You know why I agreed to play along? You want to know the real reason? You, my dad, everyone, you all told me that all I had to do was point to him and this whole nightmare would be over. And I believed you. I believed that if I said it was him, if I picked him out of the lineup, I'd finally be able to sleep. But you know what? It didn't happen that way. I still can't sleep. I still lie awake all night and see him standing right there, in front of me."

THE headache that had started during his meeting with Adi now felt like a sledgehammer in his head. He could hold on to it, pretend they never had this conversation. The DA would file charges, and they'd have a while, a few months at least, before the trial. There might not even be a trial. There was a good chance Nevo would plead out. And even if he didn't, Adi would have time to calm down, to forgive her father, to realize she was just being childish. She kept saying she wasn't sure she'd identified the right man, but he knew that wasn't the reason for her anger. It was the sense of violation and helplessness all rape victims suffer.

He was sorely tempted to forget it, but he knew he wouldn't be able to let it go. There were lines he couldn't cross, and keeping this information to himself was one of them. In any case, this sort of thing always came out in the end, and the results could be catastrophic. He could already see the headline: "Police Conceal Crucial Evidence." It'd destroy whatever credibility the police force still had and would have serious implications for other cases that were no less important.

He sat down, closing his eyes. He'd thought he'd put the case to bed. Tomorrow morning the DA was supposed to inform the court that they were planning to charge Nevo with one count of rape. He'd been hoping his success with this case would finally prove to everyone that he knew what he was doing, that he wasn't ready to be put out to pasture. But when the brass heard about what he'd done with the lineup, they wouldn't look the other way. They'd come gunning for him, and he'd have a lot of apologizing and explaining to do.

He picked up the phone and dialed the number. He almost hung up after three rings. Was he making the right decision? Maybe he should wait and see how things panned out. He let it ring twice more. Why rush into anything?

"Hello?" ADA Galit Lavie finally picked up.

No. There were some things he couldn't keep to himself. Adi Regev had left him no choice. She'd forced his hand. If the victim withdrew her statement, the whole case collapsed. The cake was ruined.

"Hello?"

"Hey, Galit, it's Eli Nachum. We have to meet. It's urgent," he said.

Chapter 17

AT first he thought it was just fear messing with his head. But as the minutes ticked by, Ziv realized he wasn't being paranoid. The thug with the beefy arms covered in tattoos who'd been thrown into the cell two hours ago hadn't taken his eyes off him for a second. He did his best to ignore him, to make himself invisible, but every time he raised his eyes for an instant, he saw him staring at him threateningly.

He wondered if it was like in the movies, where the sex offenders are the lowest of the low on the prison totem pole and regularly get gang-raped. He was strong enough to take care of himself. He'd kept himself fit. But right now he didn't have much physical strength to call on. It'd been drained out of him by all the pressure and sleepless nights.

He made an effort not to think about the man glaring at him and concentrate instead on his conversation with the lawyer that morning. Rosen wasn't very optimistic, to put it mildly. He said a trial was like a game, and at the moment the scoreboard read 2–0 in favor of the cops. They had his confession (Ziv had decided not to tell Rosen that it was just a misunderstanding), and they had the victim picking him out of a lineup. The only way he was going to get out of this was if he could change the score to 3–2. If he had an alibi for the time of the rape, for instance, that would be a game changer. But what alibi could he give? Since the divorce, he'd hardly ever left the house, certainly not at night, unless Faro called him, and there was no way he was going to tell them that.

The other option was to prove that the girl was mistaken. But

Rosen was skeptical of their chances. He'd been present at the lineup and seen that everything was done by the book.

Bottom line, Rosen thought his best bet was a plea bargain. The prosecution was swamped with cases. They'd probably be willing to be generous if he saved them the headache of a trial. And a few years less in prison was nothing to sneeze at.

Rosen rubbed him the wrong way. All he talked about were the problems they had, but he never offered a single worthwhile solution. Ziv knew Rosen was bothered by the difficulties they were facing, but that didn't mean he had to throw in the towel, did it? Ziv wasn't ready to give up. Assaf Rosen might be a good lawyer, but he didn't believe him, and that was the real problem. How could he win if his own lawyer didn't believe him? If he was convinced he was guilty? What kind of chance did he have?

Tattoo stood up and walked over to him. He was a head taller than Nevo, maybe more. Ziv tensed and moved back, trying to keep some distance between them.

"You got a smoke?" Tattoo asked. Despite the reek of piss and shit from the primitive toilet, which was making Ziv sick to his stomach, he could still smell the sweaty stench of the man who sat down next to him.

He shook his head and moved back even farther, until his back was flat against the wall. The man didn't budge, just sat there training his eyes on one of their other cell mates who was sitting on the bunk opposite them. A guy in his fifties, he looked like a seasoned junkie. Within a second or two, he got up and moved away. Ziv wished he could do the same.

Tattoo turned to him and held out his hand. "Meir." Ziv reached out his hand. He knew something bad was about to go down.

Meir grabbed his hand and squeezed it painfully. "You're Nevo, right?"

He wanted to ask how he knew his name, but he decided the less he said, the better. He just nodded.

"What're you in for? What'd they charge you with?" Meir asked. Something in his tone made it clear to Ziv that his companion already knew the answer.

"They say I raped a girl," he said quickly.

"And what do you say?"

"I didn't do it . . . she got it wrong . . . she's confusing me with someone else," he stuttered.

Meir laughed. "That's what they all say, right?"

They sat side by side in uncomfortable silence. If he could, he'd get up and move to a different bunk, but he knew he had to stay there, that their conversation wouldn't be over until Meir said it was. He looked down at the floor, avoiding Meir's eyes.

"What does your lawyer say? You got a lawyer, don't you?" Meir said, breaking the silence.

Ziv nodded, ignoring the question. Meir didn't take his eyes from him. He was waiting for an answer.

"Who understands lawyers, right? They say one thing, then something different." Ziv tried hard to put a smile on his face.

"I hear they got the goods on you, that you're screwed."

"Where'd you hear that?" Ziv asked, unable to restrain himself.

Tattoo didn't answer. Who was this guy, anyway? How did he know these things? What did he want? The questions were racing through Ziv's mind.

"You ask me, you oughta confess. It's best for everyone. Get it?" Meir said after another minute of tense silence.

Ziv was about to ask who "everyone" was, but he stopped himself in time. Meir kept his eyes fixed on him as if he were waiting for him to agree. What the hell does he want from me? Nevo wondered.

Then he realized what was going on. Tattoo was working with

the cops! Just like Rosen warned him. He was probably an under-cover cop himself. The realization filled Ziv with confidence. He had nothing to fear from him. Meir was nothing, just hot air. He stood up.

"We're not done here," Meir snarled.

"I am," Ziv declared.

It happened very quickly. He'd barely taken a step when Meir seized him from behind and threw him onto the bunk on the op-posite wall. He lay on top of him, squashing Ziv under his enormous weight and squeezing his throat so he couldn't breathe. Ziv gasped for breath, trying to push his attacker off, but he was too strong and just tightened his grip.

"We're done when I say we're done. Get it?" he said, putting even more pressure on Ziv's neck.

He nodded in submission, but Meir didn't loosen his grip. His head was spinning and he felt himself losing consciousness. He nod-ded weakly again in case Meir hadn't seen it the first time, but the man didn't let up. He tried kicking at him, but it didn't make the slightest impression. He's going to kill me, right here and now, Ziv thought.

All of a sudden, Meir released his hold. Ziv sat up, coughing. His throat was on fire, his ribs ached, and his head was pounding.

The other prisoners were lying on their bunks, keeping their dis-tance, pretending to be blind.

Meir gave him a cruel smile. "I've got a message for you from Shimon."

Ziv froze.

Meir put his face next to his. The foul stench from his mouth was sickening. "People are talking. They say they nabbed you be-cause of the father. He saw you on his daughter's street that night," he whispered in Ziv's ear.

"I didn't tell a soul what I was doing there!" he whispered back in terror. "Tell Shimon he's got nothing to worry about . . . He can count on me." Ziv did his best to sound confident.

"Not good enough," Meir snarled. "He wants you to confess."

"What?" He couldn't believe what he was hearing.

"Confess to the rape," Meir said drily.

"B-but . . . I swear I won't say anything . . . I didn't say anything till now . . . not the rape . . . I didn't do it . . ."

"Tomorrow you tell your lawyer you wanna confess. Tell him to cut a deal. Get it?" Meir said, ignoring Ziv's pleas.

"You can't ask me to do that!" he said, nearly shouting.

"Save your breath. It's a done deal." Meir started to get up.

"Wait!"

Meir turned around, his face expressionless.

"What happens if . . . I mean if I decide not . . . ," Ziv stammered, unable to complete the sentence, to say the words out loud, to entertain the possibility.

Meir gave him another smile. "Then Gili'll have to pay the price," he whispered.

A tremor went through Ziv's body at the sound of his son's name. Meir looked him in the eye.

"We understand each other?"

How did he get himself into this? And what was he supposed to do now?

"We understand each other?" Meir repeated.

Ziv nodded.

"One more thing," Meir said, getting up and dusting off his pants, "after you confess, you don't meet with anyone and you don't talk to anyone. Even if someone shows up and says Shimon sent him, even if it's a lawyer. They're lying. You don't talk to anyone at all, get it? You confess and then you keep your mouth shut."

Chapter 18

GALIT Lavie was sitting in her office, wondering if the day could get any worse. It had started with a hearing in the Tel Aviv District Court at nine o'clock in the morning. A man was accused of stabbing his wife to death with a kitchen knife. The judge tried to pressure her to agree to a plea bargain and avoid a trial. "Without prejudice to either party, I would suggest you reduce the charge to manslaughter," Judge Brill instructed. When she refused, he started threatening her with the possibility of an acquittal, talking about how the case wasn't airtight, how some of the evidence was problematic.

When Galit was just starting out, she might have given in to that kind of pressure from the bench. But nowadays she was more immune to it. She understood that judges had a vested interest in plea bargains because they lightened their heavy caseload. So she countered the barrage from the bench by stating respectfully that the prosecution believed the evidence justified the charge of homicide.

By the time she finally got back to the office at eleven thirty, she felt like she'd been run over by a steamroller. She considered going out for coffee before attacking the pile of work waiting on her desk, but then Nachum showed up. She'd almost forgotten about his call yesterday when he asked to meet with her urgently.

She listened in silence while he told her about the phony lineup and the false report he'd filed with the court at the remand hearing. When he got to the part about the pressure he'd applied on the suspect during the interrogation and how he'd tried to get him to confess even after he'd asked for a lawyer, her head started throbbing. By the time he got to Adi's visit to his office, she was suicidal.

Galit was furious. She was used to the cops' screwups, but she expected more from Nachum, much more. He knew the rules and what it meant to flout them. What was he thinking? How could an old warhorse like him make those kinds of mistakes? She wanted to reprimand him, but she kept silent. She'd worked with Nachum on other cases and had learned to respect him. And he looked so morose, so upset and depressed by the whole story, that she knew anything she said would be superfluous. She also knew that whatever happened, his actions would have personal consequences for him, that there were plenty of people on the force who would be happy to use this against him. And she knew he knew it too.

Now it was up to her to decide what to do with the information, how to go forward with the case. This morning they had informed the court of the intent to press charges against Nevo and requested that he be held in remand until formal charges were filed. That gave her five days. If they didn't issue an indictment by then, they'd have to let him go. Of course, she couldn't do anything without the consent of the DA, Rachel Zuriel. Galit was a disciplined soldier, not the sort to provoke her superiors or overstep her authority. And the years she'd worked with Rachel had taught her it would be best to go to her with a firm recommendation on how to proceed based on careful consideration of all the facts.

Days like this made her nostalgic for the early years of her career, when everything seemed so straightforward. She'd imagined that by dissecting every case with the precision of a surgeon, all the answers she was seeking would be spread out before her with utter clarity. She'd been at it for ten years now, and during that time she'd seen a lot. She'd matured enough to realize that nothing was all black or all white. There were many shades of gray in her job, just like there were in life.

She looked around her office. A tiny cubicle overflowing with files, it looked more like a storeroom than a respectable office. She had college friends who had gone to work for large law firms and had already made partner, earning five times her salary. Still, she wasn't sorry she'd stayed in the DA's Office. She loved her work. It gave her a sense of mission, the feeling that what she was doing was important. She had her parents to thank for that. They'd brought her up to believe there were things in life that mattered more than money. She got up and looked out the window at the gray city. She'd waited a long time for an office with a window.

Galit looked back at the file on her desk. In legal terms, there was only one conclusion she could reach: they had no hard evidence. The confession Nachum had gotten from Nevo wasn't worth much, and as for the lineup, the less said, the better. If Assaf Rosen knew even half the truth, Nevo would be a free man by now.

Strictly speaking, she ought to pick up the phone and tell Rosen they wouldn't be filing charges. But things were never that simple. The last thing Nachum had said before leaving was that he was convinced Nevo was guilty. Despite all the screwups and the legal ramifications, he knew they had the right guy. Was she supposed to ignore that?

Any beginning law student would say yes without a moment's hesitation. She was obligated to ignore the cop's gut feeling and act only on objective evidence. But she'd been doing this long enough to know that evidence wasn't everything, that sometimes it distorted the truth, misrepresented the facts, or clouded the issue. And sometimes, it was simply incomplete.

Nevo had linked himself to Adi Regev, had said he'd picked her at random, and had even expressed remorse. And he matched the description Adi had given not long after she was attacked. Galit agreed with Nachum that she'd withdrawn her identification not because she thought she'd fingered the wrong man, but because she was confused, frightened, and upset by being kept in the dark.

What was she going to do? Turn a blind eye to all their suspicions? Let a man who was most likely a rapist go free just because the cops botched the interrogation? And what if he did it again? How would she feel then? What would all the rules and regulations matter if she opened a new file and found photographs of another girl who'd been raped by Nevo?

She herself lived only a few houses down from Adi. The first time she saw her picture, she thought she looked vaguely familiar, like someone she might have seen around the neighborhood. She had a clear memory of the patrol car closing off the street, of the frightened whispers exchanged among the neighbors. The news had spread like wildfire: a woman had been brutally raped on their street, in the front yard of her own home; the villain had escaped.

Ever since, she pinned her hair up in a severe bun before she left the office, made sure not to get home too late, not to walk down unlit streets, to have her pepper spray within easy reach. It'd been a great relief to hear they'd nabbed the guy.

She opened the file and leafed through the documents. Nachum believed the case was still salvageable. He suggested she talk to Adi and try to bring her around. She hadn't been involved in the investigation up to now and she wasn't a cop, so maybe she could succeed where he had failed.

She didn't know if he was right or not. What she did know was that he'd put a time bomb on her desk and asked her to disarm it. It was her choice. It was up to her to decide what to do now, how to proceed. But what kind of choice was it? All she had were bad options, and there'd be a heavy price to pay for whichever one she chose.

Chapter 19

ZIV knew right away that something had happened. Rosen didn't have a broad smile on his face just because he was happy to see him. The last time they'd spoken, here in this same room, he'd been very somber, without even the trace of a smile the whole time.

Now it was Ziv who wasn't smiling. He felt as if he'd swallowed a lead ball. His encounter with Meir was still very fresh in his mind. The gun he was holding to his head, to Gili's head, left him with no choice, no room to maneuver.

"I got a call from the ADA on the way here," Rosen said with obvious satisfaction.

Ziv still didn't know where Rosen's sudden optimism was coming from. He'd lain awake all night, tossing and turning on the narrow metal bunk with its thin green grease-stained mattress. Whenever he looked over at Meir, he saw him watching him, keeping a close eye on him.

"I think they're having trouble making their case against you," Rosen explained. "They never give a lot away at this stage, before they issue an indictment. Especially not Galit Lavie, who thinks 'plea bargain' is a dirty word. She likes to take her cases to trial. But that's the sense I get."

He gazed at the attorney chattering away, planning strategies, mapping out their next move. He knew it was all meaningless. His fate was already sealed.

Ziv remembered a TV program he'd seen a few years ago. A slick American journalist was interviewing some homeless man who told him how his life had gone downhill until he reached rock bottom,

how because of a series of unfortunate circumstances and bad decisions he'd gone from being a husband and father with a good job
to living on the streets. He recalled thinking the guy was hiding
something, some big secret, because things didn't go sour so quickly,
it didn't happen like that. Now he'd be happy to trade places with
him.

If he could only turn back the clock, he'd go back to that Tuesday when Gili was around two and a half. He and Merav had been
married for almost four years and, all things considered, he had a
pretty good life. He loved his wife and son, he was happy in his job
as sales manager at IrrTech, a manufacturer of automatic irrigation
systems. He'd only intended for it to be a temporary job, a way to
pay his tuition while he got a degree in economics. He'd had bigger
dreams than selling sprinklers. But he'd been surprised to find that
he really enjoyed the work, and he started putting his heart and soul
in it. He liked the negotiations, the satisfaction of closing a deal.
And the company was pleased with him as well. Customers asked
for him by name, complimented him on his thoroughness, amiabil-
ity, and professionalism. And then when his boss retired, the CEO,
Dov Shore, offered him the position of sales manager.

There wasn't anything unusual about that week. Gili had a cold
and wasn't sleeping well. As usual, whenever there was even the
slightest problem with Gili, things became tense between him and
Merav. They were fighting all the time. Gili's birth had brought a
joy into his life he'd never known before. He was constantly torn
between the demands of work and family, but he didn't complain.
He'd been alone for a long time. The death of his parents had taught
him to appreciate the value of family.

But something changed when Gili turned two. Maybe it was just
the endless routine, all the baths, bedtimes, and feedings that started
getting on his nerves. Or maybe it was Gili himself. Their plump,

cheerful infant had been transformed into a defiant toddler who fought him and Merav over every little thing, who answered any request with a "no," who had become a whiny, spoiled brat. Or maybe it was Merav, who was always exhausted and couldn't handle Gili. She complained constantly, demanding that he spend more time at home. Everyone told him it was a phase, it would pass, every kid went through it. But he was losing patience with Gili's screaming and Merav's nagging and inability to cope. Of course, he didn't tell her that and he didn't do anything about it, but he longed for a taste of freedom, for a little time for himself, a brief interlude when he didn't have to be someone's father, husband, or sales manager, when he could just be Ziv.

That Tuesday he'd stayed late at work. Edva came into his office as he was hanging up the phone after another fight with Merav. Edva was one of his team members, a part-time saleswoman. She was dedicated, hardworking, and bright. But they didn't have any sort of special relationship.

"Something wrong?" she asked with a smile.

"Everything's fine," he said. He had no intention of sharing his marital problems with her.

She'd come in to consult with him about a quote she'd given a customer. Their conversation should've taken no more than five minutes, but he kept it going. He wasn't in a hurry to get home, and perhaps unconsciously he wanted to punish Merav.

Edva listened attentively, showed interest, asked questions, and Ziv suddenly found himself telling her about the death of his parents, about his time in the army, about how he'd started working for the company as soon as he finished his tour of duty. She was easy to talk to, laid back, and made him laugh with stories that had nothing to do with diapers, feeding times, and how to keep a two-year-old occupied. He couldn't help thinking how different their lives were, although they were about the same age. Since Gili was born, he and Merav hardly ever went out. The routine of everyday life was wearing them down. Most days he wandered around half-asleep. And he'd had to drop out of college, unable to juggle work, a new baby, and school.

He didn't like to admit it to himself, especially now that he had everything he'd thought he ever wanted, but he envied Edva's exciting life of clubs he'd never heard of, singers whose songs he didn't know, restaurants he'd never eaten in, dating and sex.

When she told him about the man she'd started seeing, he felt an inexplicable stab of jealousy, and when she said she wasn't sure he was right for her, he couldn't stop himself from saying he thought she should break up with him, that she deserved better. With a laugh she said she wished she could find someone like him. He blushed. His embarrassment seemed to please her because she added, "Your wife must be on cloud nine. Not only good-looking, but a real man. Believe me, there aren't a lot like you on the market today."

They went to the break room and he noticed it was already very late. There was almost no one else in the office. Only Aviva, the accountant, was still bent over her desk working on the semiannual report. As he poured milk into her cup, he couldn't resist a quick peek down her blouse. The sight of her voluptuous breasts cupped in a push-up bra excited him. He felt himself getting hard.

He was ashamed of his reaction. Sex with Merav had become increasingly rare since Gili, and he'd taken to filling the gap by jacking off with the help of porn sites. And now here he was with a hard-on because of nothing more than the low-cut blouse of a woman he'd never given a second thought to before tonight. Edva laughed—had she seen?—and he felt himself going red again and quickly turned his back to her.

When they returned to his office, she closed the door behind her and started moving toward him. Was he reading her signals right? This sort of thing didn't happen in real life, at least not to him. But then he saw the look on her face and knew he wasn't mistaken. They did it right there, in his office, on the stained carpet, trying to make as little noise as possible so as not to attract Aviva's attention.

The sight of Merav asleep next to Gili when he got home filled him with excruciating guilt. He swore to himself that he'd never do it again. But he did. For the next month, he seized every opportunity, fucking Edva in his office, in her apartment, in the car. He was astounded by her unbounded sexual energy and by the way she released his. She made him feel young and wanted, agreed to do things Merav would never even consider. He jumped on the chance to give free rein to all the sexual fantasies he'd never shared with anyone else. Time and again he swore he'd tell her it was over, and time and again he gave in to her next proposition.

As time went by, they began to get careless. One night, when they thought everyone else had gone home, the CEO walked in on them. They were going at it on his desk. He was bare-chested and she was naked except for her panties. "I want you both in my office tomorrow morning," Dov shrieked once he had recovered from the shock. Then he marched out, slamming the door behind him.

Ziv prayed he'd be able to persuade Dov that it was a one-off indiscretion, that it would never happen again, but as soon as he walked into his boss's office he knew he was in too deep. It wasn't just the expression on the CEO's face but the fact that the company lawyer, Roy Warman, was there.

"You can't imagine the kind of shit you've gotten us into," Dov spat.

"Your girlfriend has filed a complaint against you with the cops," the lawyer stated drily.

"For what?" he asked incredulously. Last night he'd assured her it would be all right, that he would talk to Dov and make certain she didn't suffer any repercussions.

"According to the law, you're guilty of sexual harassment," Warman explained.

"What're you talking about? It was completely consensual. I never harassed her! If anything, she hit on me!"

"It doesn't matter. You're her boss. You're in a position of authority over her. That makes it sexual harassment. That's what she says in her complaint."

"Why would she do such a thing? It's crazy!"

"This is why, you moron," Dov said, hurling a sheet of paper in his direction. "Don't you have a brain in your head? You want to screw around, go ahead. But how could you be so stupid as to hit on an employee of yours?"

Ziv picked the paper up from the floor and started reading, but the words were spinning in front of his eyes. He couldn't make any sense of it.

"It's from her attorney," Warman said. "She's suing the company for half a million shekels."

"You get it now, you asshole?" Dov burst out. "It isn't enough that I can't fire her, I have to shell out to her too!"

Ziv was speechless, in shock. The hand holding the attorney's letter was shaking. He ran his other hand through his hair over and over again. It was all happening too fast. There must be a way out. It was just casual sex between two consenting adults. Sexual harassment, my ass!

"I'll talk to her. I don't understand how this happened, but I'll talk to her and work it out. Trust me, Dov. I know I made a big mistake, but I'll fix it," he said standing up.

"Sit down," Dov barked. "I'm not done with you yet."

"If you ask me," Warman said softly, "she played us all. I bet someone put her up to it, told her how to turn a handicap into an advantage. Meanwhile, there's a complaint against you and a lawsuit against us. I'm guessing in a couple of days we'll reach an agreement and she'll drop both of them. But let me give you some friendly advice—talking to her won't help. It'll just make matters worse."

The lawyer's assurance was soothing. There *was* a way out, a solution to the problem. It wasn't as bad as he thought. But Ziv's relief was short-lived. "Given the circumstances," Dov said, "I assume you understand we can't keep you on here."

He was fired on the spot. What was he going to tell Merav? What could he say? That he'd cheated on her with one of his employees, that they'd caught him and he'd been canned? That what he had with Edva was only sex? He loved Merav and he didn't want to lose her. He let himself hope that everything would work out like the lawyer said and then Dov would calm down and give him his job back. In the end, he was half-right: they cut a deal with Edva and she withdrew her complaint against him, but Dov wouldn't even agree to see him.

Every morning he got up early, showered, shaved, kissed Merav and Gili good-bye, and left the house as if he was going to work as usual, as if everything was normal. He spent the day roaming the streets aimlessly or sitting on a park bench reading the sports page. He was desperate to be working again, but he didn't bother to look for a job. The irrigation market was a small one. There were only six manufacturers, all vying for the same limited number of customers. He was ashamed to apply to any of the other companies. He assumed they'd all heard what had happened, why he'd been fired. Who'd hire him? No one wanted a man who couldn't keep his dick in his pants, who put his employer at risk for lawsuits and scandals.

The first month when there was no salary in the bank he told Merav it was just a minor delay, a cash flow problem that would be worked out soon. She didn't say anything, but she looked surprised. Not long ago he'd told her how well the firm was doing and how much they valued him.

Then another month passed, and another. Every day he left the house without a word. Merav started asking questions: What's going on with the company? How come you're not getting your salary? Did they stop paying all the employees or is it just you? Their meager savings were dwindling. How would they make the mortgage payments? He realized he couldn't keep lying to her, that his back was against the wall. Finally, he told her he'd lost his job.

He was planning to tell her the whole truth, but he couldn't do it. When she asked why he'd been fired, he said the firm was in bad shape because of the water shortage, that they had to downsize. "How many people did they fire?" she asked. "What difference does it make," he said, hoping she'd let it go.

He felt better once he'd told her, and for the first time he started looking for a new job. But time after time he was turned away. One irrigation company showed an interest in him, but it didn't take him long to figure out that all they really wanted was to get trade secrets from his former employer. He couldn't go along with that. Even though he thought Dov had treated him unfairly and should've given him a second chance, he felt he owed him for seeing his potential and promoting him to sales manager. And he felt guilty for letting him down.

He tried expanding his search to other fields, but he had no luck with that either. There was a recession on, and he didn't have a recommendation from his last employer or any special qualifications.

Merav began losing patience. She couldn't understand why no one wanted to hire him. After all, he wasn't fired because of anything he did. He wasn't to blame for the state of the economy. "Can't Dov help you? Why don't you ask him for a recommendation?" she asked repeatedly. And each time he just shrugged his shoulders and changed the subject. He wanted to tell her the truth, even phrased in his mind exactly what he'd say, but he couldn't bring himself to do it. He knew that if she found out the real reason he lost his job, it would destroy her, destroy their marriage. Instead, he started to resent her nagging.

They tightened their belt even more. They took Gili out of pre-school and Merav worked overtime, sometimes bringing work home with her. But without another source of income, there was no way they could make the mortgage payments. Delinquency notices from the bank were piling up. Merav pressured him to let her ask her parents for a loan, but he refused and yelled at her for telling them about their financial problems. He also dismissed her suggestion that he ask her uncle for a job. He lived in Strasbourg, where he had a plant that made flowerpots. Ziv didn't want any favors from her family, thank you very much. Besides, it didn't make any sense to move to France. He didn't speak a word of French. And just to sell flowerpots?!

And then one day it all blew up in his face. It began with another interrogation by Merav: What'd you do all day? What'd you say in the last job interview? What'd they ask you? It continued with a story about her sister and his brother-in-law Motti, a claims adjustor, who was, naturally, the world's greatest husband. And it ended with another attempt to persuade him to ask her parents for help when they went to their house for dinner on Friday. "They're just waiting for you to ask," she said. Her badgering was doing his head in. He begged her to stop, said that Gili would hear them, that she was tormenting him, but she kept at him. She shouted that he wasn't doing enough to find a job, that he was content to stay home all day and do nothing, that he wasn't the man she married. She accused him of not even being able to get it up anymore, so it was no wonder they couldn't get pregnant. Gili hurled the toy truck he'd been playing with across the room and started bawling. Merav hurried over to comfort him. "You see this? You see what you're doing to your son?"

Her words cut through him like a knife. All of a sudden he despised her. And then, without thinking, everything he'd been keeping so tightly locked up inside him for months came spilling out of his mouth. He wanted to hurt her as much as she'd hurt him. "I'm not a man, huh? While you lie in bed like a frigid bitch all night, I'm out fucking my brains out," he spat. Unable to hold back, he told her about Edva, the real reason he'd lost his job, and everything else he'd been hiding from her. For months he'd been planning how to tell her and couldn't do it, and now he'd done it in a fit of rage just to get back at her for constantly putting him down.

He was sorry the instant the words were out of his mouth, but they were already there, hovering between them in the air of the living room. She stared at him, stunned. He wanted her to scream or cry, but she just stood there. In chilling silence she put Gili down and came toward him. "You don't deserve to be a father," she said. Instinctively, he pushed her away, and she stumbled backward and fell. No one spoke. He'd never raised a hand to her, never even been tempted to. He turned to look at Gili and saw the fear in his eyes.

Sobbing, Merav went to Gili and held him tight. Ziv froze, not knowing what to do. He wanted to go to them and hug his family tight, bring them back to him, say he was sorry, that it wouldn't happen again, that he was ashamed of what he'd done. But he couldn't move. Finally, when he could no longer bear the pain, he turned around and walked out.

HE hadn't been home since. Merav hired a lawyer who made it very clear to him that their marriage was over. She even filed a complaint against him for assault. He was picked up and held for several hours until a temporary restraining order was issued, forbidding him to go anywhere near her for three months.

He crashed with his brother for a while, but Itai soon informed him that he'd outstayed his welcome. "Nurit doesn't feel comfortable with you sleeping on our couch," he said. Ziv got up, packed his few belongings, and left the same day. He rented a shabby apartment in south Tel Aviv and spent his days drinking cheap beer.

He still hoped that Merav would come to her senses and agree to take him back, that she'd remember how much he loved her and understand he'd only tried to protect her, to prevent her from suffering because of his mistakes. No matter how many times she rejected his plea for forgiveness, he kept on hoping. For months after their divorce was final (he'd agreed to whatever she asked), he was still wearing his wedding ring. He couldn't bring himself to take it off.

And then one day he'd gone down to the convenience store to buy another six-pack and run into Noam. Noam had been one of his soldiers in the army. They'd never been close, but Ziv was very happy to see him. Talking to him eased the terrible loneliness of his current life. That night they went out to a pub together and he told him about Edva and Merav, about how he was broke and couldn't find a job, couldn't pay child support, couldn't do anything to help Merav and Gili. And then suddenly, he started sobbing. He never cried, not even at his parents' funeral. Embarrassed at letting Noam see him break down, see how weak he'd become, he wanted to get out of there fast, but his friend put his hand on his shoulder and said he understood what he was going through. He wanted to help. He even had an idea that might work.

Two days later he met with Shimon, Noam's uncle. Shimon told him he sometimes needed a chauffeur, and if Ziv was interested, he'd be happy to let him drive him around from time to time. Ziv recognized Uncle Shimon immediately. He was the infamous Shimon Faro, the man the papers said was the head of a crime syndicate. But he took the job anyway. He owed money, Merav's lawyer was leaning on him, and there was nothing illegal about chauffeuring someone around. And maybe if Merav saw that he was getting himself together, that he had a steady job and was making the child support payments, she'd forgive him a little.

But Shimon hardly ever called on him. Now and then he asked him to take him to a family function, and rewarded him very generously each time. But Ziv still had no money to speak of, no real job, and no family.

A few weeks ago, Meshulam had knocked on Ziv's door. "I work for Shimon," he said, adding, "which means you work for me. You get my drift?" Nevo nodded warily. Meshulam ordered him to come with him, Shimon wanted to see him.

But he didn't take him to see Shimon. Instead, he took him to an abandoned warehouse in the Petach Tikva industrial zone. Once they were inside, Meshulam said Shimon wanted him to make a car bomb. Ziv balked. "Sorry," he said guardedly, "that's not my thing." Meshulam just laughed. "It isn't a request," he said. "You really thought Shimon Faro needed a driver? He wanted you because of what you know about bombs, from the army."

Seeing that Nevo was still not convinced, Meshulam pulled out a gun. Ziv realized he didn't have a choice.

"Just something that'll hurt a little, that'll send a message," Meshulam said when Ziv asked exactly what Shimon wanted from him.

But making the bomb wasn't enough. Once he'd finished putting a charge together from the materials waiting for him in the warehouse, Meshulam told him he'd also have to place the device under the car. On Wednesday night he took him to north Tel Aviv for a trial run. "We'll be watching you," he said, handing him a baseball cap, "just to be sure nothing goes wrong."

Ziv panicked when he saw the car. He didn't want to know anything about the target. He figured he was in the middle of a gang war—they kill one of yours, and then you kill one of theirs. But when he saw the bathing suit on the backseat, he realized the target was a woman. Stunned, he returned to the pickup point and tried to persuade Meshulam to find someone else for the job. He told him he wasn't cut out for this kind of thing, that his hands would shake, that he was too scared. Meshulam looked at him with contempt. "Cut the bullshit," he said, "and just make very sure your hands don't shake. You better not fuck this up."

And so, on Thursday night, Meshulam drove him back to north Tel Aviv. And this time he brought the bomb along.

"Good luck," Meshulam said chillingly before he let him off, handing him the baseball cap again.

The street was empty. He spotted the little red car, walked over to it slowly, and ducked down. With a trembling hand, he reached into his pocket for the small charge constructed from two military hand grenades. Why was he doing this? What if he'd made the bomb too big and it killed her? He was no murderer.

But he didn't want them to kill him either. Meshulam's gun had made it very clear that he didn't have a lot of options. He held the bomb to the exhaust pipe, just below the gas tank.

All of a sudden he heard a door click shut behind him. Someone had gotten out of a car not far away. A cold sweat broke out on his brow. He'd made sure there was no one around! How had he missed him? He knew he had to hurry; he had no time to waste. He worked like a robot, attaching the charge to the exhaust pipe with duct tape.

Then he heard footsteps coming toward him. From the sound they made, he could tell it was a man. Quickly, he removed the pin from one grenade and then the other, stuck them in his pocket, and began to wire the detonator to the ignition. It had been years since he'd worked with explosives, but he knew he couldn't screw up. He moved as rapidly as possible.

The man was very close. He couldn't afford to get caught. Meshulam didn't seem the type who believed in second chances.

He took a last look at the bomb and realized he'd wrapped it too tightly. He ought to loosen the duct tape. But he didn't have time. The stranger was almost there.

He stood up quickly and saw a man in his sixties a few feet away. The man stared at him suspiciously, as if he knew what he was doing there. Ziv started down the street, walking at a fast pace. To his astonishment, he heard the footsteps hurrying after him. He glanced behind him, trying to do it as casually as possible. The man looked straight at him. Was he following him?

He turned into the first side street and started running. When he got to the end of the block, he stood still and considered going back the way he'd come, but then he caught sight of the older man again. He hadn't been mistaken—he was definitely following him.

He made another turn at the corner and began running again. His ears were ringing with the sound of his feet on the pavement and his heavy breathing. He was seized by a fear he'd never known before, not even when Meshulam pulled out the gun. He kept turning his head to look behind him, but there was no one there. The man hadn't caught up to him.

At the end of the block he raced into the yard of a building and hid behind the bushes. He crouched down, his whole body tense, waiting to get his breath back, struggling to keep calm. He might still be able to get away. After a while he straightened up and started moving toward the street. He didn't see anyone. The man must've given up, he said to himself, hoping desperately it was true.

He considered going back to the car and finishing the job but decided against it. The man might be waiting for him. Besides, there was a good chance the bomb would go off anyway. And if it didn't, it might be a sign that he shouldn't have put it there in the first place, that the owner of the car deserved to go on with her life, uninjured.

Ziv walked rapidly toward the bus stop on Pinkas Street, following Meshulam's instructions. He looked in all directions, but there was no one in sight. He breathed a sigh of relief. Maybe he'd just panicked and imagined it all.

"ARE you listening to me?" his lawyer repeated. "I'm telling you I've got a hunch the ADA wants to meet with me because they're having trouble making the charges stick. We're back in the game."

He'd known from the start that he couldn't say a word about what he was really doing that night. Not only had he committed a crime no less serious than rape, but Shimon Faro and his little army of soldiers would never let him get away with it. He knew he was paying a heavy price for his silence, and would continue to do so. The main reason he was Nachum's prime suspect was because he didn't provide any explanation for his presence on the girl's street that night.

He'd thought that would be enough for Shimon, but it turned out it wasn't. They wanted more. Not just his silence, but his confession as well. That's what happens when you sell your soul to the devil.

He looked up at Rosen without a word. The last time they'd met, when he told him he didn't do it, he could tell the lawyer didn't believe him. All it took was one phone call from the prosecutor, one request for a meeting whose purpose was still unknown, and the attorney thought they were "back in the game," that everything was fine and he had good reason to smile.

"Now it becomes a mind game," Rosen said, "like poker. The longer we play, the sooner they'll fold. You just continue to keep your mouth shut. Don't open up to anyone. I'll handle the negotiations, and naturally, I'll keep you informed of what's going on."

Meir had made himself very clear. He'd even specified the price he'd have to pay if he didn't cooperate. And those guys had plenty of ways to exact that price.

"Tell them I confess," he said to Rosen, his voice breaking.

"What'd you say?" The smile vanished from the lawyer's face.

"I want you to go to the meeting and tell the ADA that I raped Adi Regev," Ziv repeated, struggling to keep his voice steady.

"Why? Why on earth do you want me to do that?"

"Because I raped her, because everything she said is the truth," he answered heavily, "because that's what I want, because I told you last time, you're my lawyer and you have to say what I tell you to say, and that's what I'm telling you to say."

Rosen drummed his fingers on the table in obvious irritation.

"I'm sorry, but I really don't understand where this crap is coming from. Last time you sat right there and told me you didn't do it, that you want me to fight the charges. And now I bring you good news, maybe even the best news, and you want to confess? Can you explain it to me? What's going on?"

Ziv didn't answer. What could he say? Gili's face floated up before his eyes, a ball of sweetness. "He's a carbon copy of his father," people always said. He loved him so much. Gili was the most precious thing in the world to him. He'd give his life for him. He couldn't expose him to any risk, no matter how high the price. He'd already hurt him enough.

Rosen leaned toward him. "Did someone threaten you?" he whispered, fixing him with his eyes.

Ziv stared back at him. Something had changed in the lawyer's voice, in the expression on his face. For the first time he felt he was seeing him as a human being, not just a case number or a pawn in a legal game.

"Like I told you last time, anything you tell me is covered by lawyer-client confidentiality. If someone is threatening you, there are steps we can take. We can go to the police, we can tell them . . ."

Ziv shook his head.

"Please don't be an idiot. Think about what you're doing. Let's wait awhile. They'll issue an indictment in a few days and then we can see what they've got. But I'm telling you from experience, if they want to meet with me now, their case is falling apart. Just hold on a few more days, that's all. Trust me," Rosen pleaded.

The breakfast Ziv had eaten that morning rose in his throat, threatening to gush out of him. He didn't want to be there anymore; he had to get out of the room. His fate was sealed and there was nothing he could do about it. The price was too high.

He got up, walked to the door, and banged on it loudly. Silently, Rosen followed him with his eyes.

The guard opened the door. "Is there a problem here?" he asked.

Ziv shook his head. "No problem," he heard Rosen say behind him.

He turned to look back at him. "Just do what I said and do it right away. When you meet with the ADA, you tell her. No horse trading, no tricks. Everything they're saying is true. It was me. I raped her."

Chapter 20

WHEN Assaf Rosen walked into Galit Lavie's office, he suddenly remembered the erotic dream he'd had about her after they'd faced off in court a few months ago. She'd been a tough adversary that day. In fact, she was known to attack all her cases with flinty determination. But in his dream, their lovemaking was extraordinarily gentle and tender.

The memory disconcerted him. She smiled graciously as he came in. He lowered his eyes, unable to get the picture of her naked body out of his head. She'd prosecuted a number of his cases, and he'd always found himself attracted to her. He wondered how she'd react if he asked her out.

They chatted for a few minutes, gossiping about mutual acquaintances in their professional world. Each of them was well aware that this was merely foreplay, a prelude to the negotiations that would determine Nevo's fate.

Rosen still had no idea where he was going with the case, what his position would be, and, more to the point, what it should be. Nevo confounded him. He was used to hearing his clients protest their innocence, claim they were being set up, that someone was out to get them. But there was something genuine about Nevo, some poignant quality that resonated with Rosen. Naturally, he kept his feelings to himself. He'd learned long ago that the best way to protect himself was to maintain a certain distance. Whenever he got emotionally involved, he took a loss too much to heart. And if the legal system didn't let him down, the client did. After the trial was over, it would turn out that his client had been lying to him the whole time or was too much of a sleazebag to have any intention of cleaning up his or her act.

Nevertheless, when he got the call from Galit he was happy for Nevo. He even gave himself a pat on the back for still having sharp enough senses to pick out the one innocent man among all his clients. He hoped this might be the type of case he'd dreamed of, the reason he'd become a defense attorney in the first place: against all odds, he'd procure the release of an innocent man. But then he'd met with Nevo again and everything changed. Now Nevo was saying he'd committed the rape and he wanted to plead guilty.

Who was he supposed to believe, the first Nevo or the second? It doesn't make a bit of difference, he chided himself. His job was to serve as Nevo's mouthpiece. If he wanted to fight the charges, he'd fight them, if he wanted to confess, he'd inform the prosecution. He had to follow the client's wishes. Since when did the truth matter? What role did it really play in his profession? Like every other defense attorney he knew, he never asked clients if they were guilty or not. He was used to pleading cases, arguing passionately and fighting like a tiger, without ever knowing the truth.

But this one was gnawing at him. Something had obviously happened between his two meetings with Nevo, something that had nothing to do with whether Nevo raped Adi Regev or not. He groused regularly about the high conviction rate in the country, complaining that the cards were stacked against the defense, and now that he had a client who was probably innocent, he didn't know what to do. What was wrong with him? A few years ago he would've gotten his teeth into a case like this and never let go until he'd figured out what was going on. He would even have fought the request to extend Nevo's remand. He was still young, only thirty-three, but apparently he was already burned out. His job was wearing him down. He couldn't believe he'd become his father so soon.

"HOW does your client want to proceed with the case?" Galit asked, putting a serious expression on her face to indicate it was time to get down to business.

"If I'm not mistaken, you called this meeting, not me," Rosen answered, returning the ball to her court. She might not be willing to admit it, but he was pretty sure the prosecution was in hot water with this case. Why else would Galit ask to see him? If they weren't in trouble, they'd file an indictment and go straight to court, certainly with someone like Galit in charge.

The ADA merely smiled.

"So what's going on, Galit. Is there a problem with the evidence? Did the victim change her story? Did some unexpected DNA results come back from the lab?" Rosen decided not to beat around the bush.

"We're offering two years," she said, evading the question.

Rosen was confused. Such a light sentence for a rape charge? And he noticed she didn't answer his question. With any other case, he'd get up and walk out. It was worth the risk. If that was their opening bid, he could expect better offers down the line. As soon as they filed the indictment, they'd have to show him what they had and all their secrets would be out in the open. He'd find out everything they were trying to hide from him. But his client had given him specific instructions. He wanted to confess, and he'd ordered Rosen to tell that to the ADA without any delay.

Galit was watching him intently. With every second he continued to hesitate, her expression grew more incredulous. What did she know? What was missing in order for her to make the case? When he was just starting out, he'd believed that as an officer of the court, the prosecution was a straight shooter, that all that mattered was the truth, not conviction rates. He wasn't so naive anymore. By now he knew that prosecutors sometimes played dirty, just like defense attorneys. An ADA's conviction rate mattered very much. No one liked to lose, no one liked to go back to the office and report to their colleagues, and their boss, that they'd been outplayed.

"Six months' probation."

"For rape?" Galit replied, raising an eyebrow. "You can't be serious."

"Reduce the charge to assault."

"But he raped her!"

"If you were so sure of that, I wouldn't be here, would I?"

"If your client was so sure he was innocent, you'd tell me where to shove my offer and you'd go to trial, wouldn't you?" she shot back.

They sat facing each other in silence, like two poker players just before they reveal their hands. But there were no chips or bills on the table. Here they were playing for a man's freedom.

"You go jogging in the middle of the day?" Rosen asked, gesturing with his head at a pair of red sneakers sitting under a file cabinet. He was hoping to ease the tension in the room.

"No, I've been walking to work. I lent my car to my brother. He and his wife flew in for a visit." She had a captivating smile. He remembered his dream again.

"So what now?" he asked, pulling himself back down to the real world.

"Aggravated assault. Two years' probation with time served."

He was right. They were in serious trouble with this case. He debated taking the offer to Nevo but decided there was no need. Even if he was innocent and was being threatened, it wasn't relevant. His instructions were clear. Rosen had told him it would be a mistake to confess, but Nevo hadn't budged an inch. On the other hand, he hadn't forbidden him to strike a deal for a reduced sentence either.

"What do you say, Assaf?" Galit was waiting for an answer.

Chapter 21

GALIT hated what she was being forced to do. If Nevo was guilty, her offer was scandalous. If he wasn't, she was making an innocent man confess to a crime he hadn't committed, a crime that would leave a stain on him for the rest of his life. But what choice did she have? The lineup was useless, she didn't have any hard evidence, and the victim had withdrawn her identification. All she had was the gut feeling of a longtime cop, who might be right and might be wrong.

"Deal, aggravated assault, two years' probation with time served," Rosen said finally.

Galit detested most of the defense attorneys she had to bargain with. They were unprincipled liars who'd use any dirty trick to get their clients off. But she had a fondness for Assaf Rosen, and not just because he was good-looking (a fact all the women in the office agreed on). She had the feeling he liked her too. Several times she'd been tempted to see if their relationship could go beyond the professional, but she decided it wouldn't be proper. She was a good girl who always did the right thing. If Alon hadn't announced just before the wedding, after they'd been together for ten years, that he wanted a different life that didn't include her, she'd probably be married by now. She might even be a mother.

"We're going to have to sell it to the press. The case got a lot of media attention. To the man in the street, probation is the same as acquittal. And the local paper's been running a story about it every week," Rosen said, merely stating out loud what she already knew. In fact, she was much more worried about how she'd sell it to the press than about how she'd sell it to her boss.

"No problem. We'll just explain that Nevo had this ace lawyer who made the DA's Office look like a bunch of clowns," she said with a smile. Seeing he wasn't amused, she added seriously, "The victim and her family agreed to the deal. There won't be any human interest stories about how the DA sold her down the river, didn't believe her, didn't take it seriously. No op-eds about lack of consideration for the victim's feelings."

At Nachum's request, she'd met with Adi yesterday. What she saw was a girl who was confused, hurt, and angry, and immediately agreed with Nachum's assessment that she'd changed her story for reasons that had nothing to do with whether or not she could honestly ID Nevo. Even if she could coax Adi to change her mind, there was no telling what she'd say under cross-examination. It'd be better for her to close the case with a plea bargain that was hard to swallow than to hear the victim testify on the stand that the police and the prosecution had forced her to point the finger at the defendant against her will.

Rosen was staring at her in silence. She knew exactly what he was thinking. How come the DA was willing to reduce the charges from rape to assault? What were they hiding from him? He was smart enough to know that something was going on. But Galit was no fool herself, and she sensed there was a reason Rosen didn't want the case to go to court either. She'd come up against him before and she knew he didn't scare easily. The smart thing for him to do would be to wait for the indictment when he could see the holes in their case. But here he was, ready to plead out.

"You'll still have to explain what happened to the rape charge, why you only indicted him for assault with no mention of any indecent acts," he insisted.

"We're used to getting fried by the press. We can take it. It isn't pleasant, but we'll get over it," Galit said, getting up to put an end to the discussion. The deeper he dug, the more questions he asked, the harder it would be for her to close the deal. In the end, he might back out and she'd lose the little she'd managed to salvage.

Rosen rose and held out his hand. She noted how firm and warm his grip was. She nearly suggested they go out for coffee but stopped herself in time.

"You'll send me a draft of the indictment?" he asked, without letting go of her hand. It seemed to her he was holding on to it a little longer than necessary.

"Naturally," she replied with a smile, withdrawing her hand. "Tomorrow. Maybe even later today."

Neither of them mentioned that they still had to go before a judge. Plea bargains in criminal cases weren't the same as settlement agreements in civil suits. The judge didn't have to sign off on them. But they'd been doing this for quite a few years, and they both anticipated the same scenario: the court would grant its approval. The judge might raise an eyebrow, ask a question or two. Some liked to make background noise first, to bully the prosecution and the defense and remind them that the judge wasn't just a rubber stamp. But in the end they all accepted what was placed in front of them.

A large percentage of criminal cases ended in plea bargains. No witnesses ever testified, no defendants ever told their story, no juries ever got to deliver a verdict on the basis of the evidence. Galit found it depressing. She was infuriated by the statistics her office gave out showing their high conviction rate. Most of those convictions were achieved through plea bargains, which meant negotiating and handing out reduced sentences. As a result, most offenders got a lot less than was coming to them.

But that was life. Without plea bargains, the system would collapse. The court would sign off on her deal with Rosen without any complications and no one would ever know what had gone on here today. To be honest, no one would even care.

In a little while, Nevo would be a free man. She remembered what Nachum had said to her: "At least get probation for when he rapes the next woman." Had she just helped to put a rapist back on the street?

Chapter 22

WHEN Amit Giladi heard about the plea bargain, he was outraged. It was ludicrous. "Aggravated assault?" Adi Regev had been raped! He used all his contacts to try to get more information, but no one was talking. Not the cops, not the DA, not the defense attorney—no one. He couldn't get a word out of anyone. This vow of silence only made him more suspicious. In his short career as a reporter, he'd learned that people love to talk, gossip, criticize. But this time there was nothing.

He hadn't been eager to stay on the rape story. It wasn't the sort of thing he'd become a journalist for. He wanted to be an investigative reporter, but Dori told him to keep leaning on the cops.

Amit was no idiot. He knew very well why Dori wanted him to keep the story alive. It sold papers. It played on the fear of women that it could happen to them. But with all due respect, he wasn't here to terrify women. That wasn't his goal in life.

Still, the inexplicable plea bargain changed the picture. He had a feeling something big was behind it, that it was part of some larger conspiracy.

Ever since the call from "Deep Throat," with his claims of explosive information about police corruption that reached to the highest echelons, all his time had been taken up by drivel. That was the lot of a reporter in charge of the crime and education beats for a local paper. But this might be his big chance. It was because of the rape that he'd missed the call from "Deep Throat." Maybe the plea bargain would give him the opportunity to make up for it.

He went to ask for Dori's advice on how to attack the story, but to his surprise, the editor displayed little interest in it. "Who gives a fuck? They make lousy deals all the time. The rape story is dead, at least till the next one," he said, waving Amit away. He'd given up trying to understand what made Dori tick a long time ago. He'd been a senior editor at a major national paper until he was booted out for some reason no one seemed to know, and ever since he'd been stuck at the local rag. It was rumored he'd had an affair with the wife of the editor in chief, although some people claimed he'd fabricated a story. Bottom line: nobody knew what had really happened.

Screw Dori, he wasn't going to let it slide. His gut was telling him to keep digging, that the plea bargain was a cover for something that could turn out to be a gold mine for him. The only question was where he would get the information he needed, how he was going to find out why they agreed to this outlandish deal.

And then it came to him. Why hadn't he thought of it sooner? From the beginning, Dori had pushed him to interview Adi Regev. He'd used every trick in the book to get out of it. What journalistic value would it have? She'd been through enough without having him harass her just so a few readers could shed a sympathetic tear and mutter "poor dear."

He kept coming up with excuses. He was busy with another story: the principal of a prestigious high school who tweaked students' grades in exchange for donations from their parents; the son of a city counselor who got wasted and was caught naked in the fountain outside his father's office. Dori had even provided him with a list of questions for Adi: What went through your mind when you saw the rapist? Do you still have nightmares? Tell me about the moment you realized what was happening. The questions only strengthened Amit's determination not to do the interview.

But the situation had changed. Now there might be real value in talking to Adi. It was no longer just an excuse for a soap opera disguised as news.

HE tensed when he saw her leaving the building. He'd considered going upstairs, knocking on her door, and introducing himself like a gentleman, but decided it would be best to wait for her to come out. After everything that'd happened to her, there was no chance she'd let a strange man into her apartment. Even when Dori had been urging him to interview her, he'd told him to wait for her outside, take her by surprise.

He chewed on his lips. He wasn't happy about what he was doing, but he had a good reason. Something bigger than both of them was going on, and it was his job as a reporter to find out what it was.

As he started toward her, he realized he'd never actually seen her in person. The detective, Nachum, had shown him pictures of her injured face for the shock value, but that was it. Now he saw she was definitely worth a second look. She had beautiful eyes, long flowing hair, and a cute butt. Under any other circumstances, he might've hit on her. He was twenty-six and single. Every now and then he met a girl on Facebook, and even managed to get some of them into bed, but that was as far as it went. Dori once said that real journalists could never have a serious relationship because they were committed to the truth and relationships were inevitably based on lies. Who knows, maybe he was right.

Adi was walking rapidly. She was about to turn into Pinkas Street, which was busy at this time of day. With so many people around, it would be hard to get anything out of her.

"Excuse me," he called after her.

She turned to look at him, alarmed. He had to be careful. In her fragile state, she could shatter as easily as a piece of glass.

"Don't be scared," he said, trying to calm her fears. But his words had the opposite effect.

"I'm late," she said, turning around quickly and walking away.

"I don't want to hurt you," Amit insisted. "I'm a reporter. I just have a few questions . . . ," he said, running to catch up with her.

Adi didn't stop. What was it with this girl?

"I don't know if they told you, but the DA closed a deal with the guy who raped you. He's getting out. I want to talk to you about it. I don't think it's right. I think they're selling you out." By now he was jogging alongside her, panting.

They were on Pinkas Street now. Adi kept walking swiftly toward Ibn Gvirol Street, not turning her head even once.

"I'm on your side. I want the bastard to rot in prison. He shouldn't go free because of a disgraceful plea bargain," he said, entreating her to listen.

When she reached Ibn Gvirol, she stopped and looked at him for the first time. Amit tried to read her expression. Had he finally gotten through to her? Maybe she hadn't even known about the plea bargain.

"Leave me alone," she spat. "Go away!"

He grabbed her arm to keep her from walking off, but she pulled out of his grip and yelled at him. "I told you to leave me alone."

Her shout startled him. Out of the corner of his eye he could see that passersby were watching them.

"Adi, I'm on your side. If it had happened to my sister or my girlfriend, I wouldn't want . . . ," he tried again.

She started crying. Some stranger who looked like a local version of Arnold Schwarzenegger clamped a huge hand on Amit's shoulder.

"Is this creep bothering you?" he asked Adi.

Without speaking, she turned and ran.

"Leave her alone, you hear me?" the stranger said, removing his hand.

Chapter 23

WHEN Ziv stepped out of the Tel Aviv courthouse, his eyes were blinded by the bright sunlight. The hearing had ended half an hour ago, with Judge Spiegler approving the plea bargain. Rosen had prepared him for the possibility of complications, but everything seemed to go very smoothly. The performance went off without a hitch. The charges against him told a fictitious tale about how he'd assaulted Adi, causing her bodily harm, and he and his attorney confirmed the prosecution's lie. In the courtroom, the judge asked indifferently, reciting a time-worn formula, if he admitted to the facts in the indictment, if he understood what he was confessing to, if he had anything further to add, and he'd answered, yes, yes, no, just as Rosen had instructed him. The judge barely looked at him. She convicted him of aggravated assault on the basis of his confession and then listened with undisguised boredom as the prosecution and the defense explained in pat phrases why she should accept the plea bargain they'd agreed on. Nodding mechanically the whole time, she concluded the proceedings by signifying her approval.

"That's it. You're free to go. Take care of yourself," Rosen said, shaking his hand hurriedly and turning to talk to the pretty ADA with the long brown hair and green eyes. The whole thing took less than half an hour.

Rosen warned him there might be reporters in the courtroom and cautioned him not to speak with them. "I'll do all the talking for you," he assured him. But there was only one reporter from some local paper, a guy whose face he remembered from his initial remand hearing, and both Rosen and the prosecution simply ignored his questions. Aside from him, the press no longer seemed interested in the case. The rape that had once earned banner headlines had been forgotten.

When he'd first walked into court, he'd seen a few people nodding on the long, brown benches. In response to his question, Rosen said he didn't see the victim among them. He wondered what she thought about it all, why she'd agreed to this circus. Why didn't she get up and scream that she wouldn't allow the man who raped her to be convicted of something as absurd as aggravated assault and get off with no more than two years' probation? He realized he felt sorry for her.

Turning on his cell phone as he left the building, Ziv was disappointed to see that no one had called. No one had come to any of the hearings, and no one was there to pick him up. He missed Gili terribly and was dying to see him. He hadn't asked Merav to bring him to the detention facility. The place was too frightening and depressing. Naturally, she didn't offer to bring him either.

He dialed her number. It was busy. What he wanted most in the world right now was to hug Gili close, to kiss him, hold him, and breathe in his smell. He tried again. She didn't pick up. She must be screening his calls.

He'd just been set free with a much lighter sentence than he'd expected. He should feel happy, but he didn't. All he felt was utterly alone, and angry—angry at Merav for being unwilling to forgive him for the one mistake he made in their whole marriage, angry at his brother who'd turned his back on him, angry at Shimon Faro and Meshulam for sacrificing him without a second thought, like a pawn in a chess game. If it weren't for the prosecutor's sudden change of heart, he'd be rotting in jail for years for a crime he didn't commit.

He was sick of everyone trampling him underfoot as if he didn't matter. He had to pull himself out of this slump. What he needed was some grand gesture that would turn his life around. He just didn't know what it was.

Deep in thought, Ziv didn't notice he was being followed. As he was about to cross the street, a black car pulled up alongside him. His heart missed a beat when Meir stuck his head out the window. "Get in," said the man who had almost strangled him in Abu Kabir.

It was only when he was in the car that he saw there was someone in the backseat. Meshulam. He hadn't seen him since he'd sent him off to plant the bomb. He looked burlier and more intimidating than he remembered.

"I see you got out," Meshulam said in his gravelly voice.

Ziv didn't know what to say.

"How come? They stop putting rapists behind bars?"

Now he got it. Faro must think he ratted them out, that he made a deal with the cops, squealed in exchange for a reduced sentence. How else could he have gotten out without doing time?

Ziv realized what an idiot he'd been. He hadn't even considered what Faro would think. He was thrilled when Rosen told him about the plea bargain, convinced that everything had worked out in the best possible way. They let him go with no more than probation, and he hadn't said a word. But he hadn't done the math either.

"I told my lawyer I wanted to confess," he said, looking at Meshulam in the rearview mirror, "even though you know I didn't do it. I guess the prosecution couldn't make the charges stick, so they agreed to . . . I didn't have anything to do with it . . . My lawyer arranged . . ." He was babbling. He saw the icy look on Meshulam's face and stopped talking. Meir didn't utter a word either. The silence was ominous. Don't let your fear get to you, he ordered himself, remembering his mother's favorite quote, "The only thing we have to fear is fear itself."

"Nobody knows what I was doing on Louis Marshall Street that night," he tried again. "Nobody . . . you have nothing to worry about." His companions remained silent.

He looked out the window at the streets rushing by. "What does Shimon want with me?" he asked, knowing he wouldn't get an answer.

Meshulam didn't reply. Meir only gave him a vacant look.

Suddenly he realized they were driving in the opposite direction from Faro's office. "Where're we going?" he asked.

"Enough questions," Meshulam snapped from the rear of the car.

Ziv broke out in a cold sweat. They didn't believe him. First they'd interrogate him and then they'd kill him. Maybe they wouldn't even bother with the interrogation. How could he convince them he hadn't ratted them out? He didn't even know himself what had gone on in the meeting between his lawyer and the ADA.

He was too exhausted to undergo another interrogation. And he wasn't very good at it to begin with. He almost broke when the detective questioned him, and Nachum hadn't raised a finger to him. These guys wouldn't be so gentle. They'd beat him mercilessly until he told them what they wanted to hear, and after that there'd be no judge or lawyer to protect him. They'd simply carry out his death sentence.

"Look, see for yourself," he said, pulling out of his pocket the documents Rosen had given him when he was released. "I confessed to assault. The judge sentenced me to two years' probation because the prosecution caved . . . I don't know why . . . I didn't say anything . . . not even to my lawyer."

Meshulam glanced at the wrinkled pages Ziv was waving in front of his face and snorted contemptuously.

"Take a look, see what it says," Ziv urged, trying to shove the pages into Meshulam's hand. But the big man just turned to look out the window.

If they believed me they'd be friendlier, Ziv thought to himself. But their faces remained expressionless. He realized he should've expected it. He could appeal to them, try to persuade them, throw himself on their mercy, but they'd just stare at him with their cold eyes and never believe that a man who confessed to rape got off with no more than probation.

He had to get away. If he stayed in the car, they'd kill him. Even that might not be enough for them. There was a chance they'd carry out Meir's threat and hurt Gili too. They might want to make an example of him, show other people what happens to anyone who betrays Shimon Faro. He didn't have any influential friends. It would be easy to make a scapegoat out of him. He had to warn Merav, tell her to grab Gili and run.

The car was stuck in traffic. Nothing was moving. Nevo saw a patrol car in the next lane. If he got out now, they wouldn't be able to chase him. They were probably taking him to the abandoned warehouse in Petach Tikva. They could interrogate him there, even kill him, without anyone being the wiser. It would be months before someone stumbled on the body. After all, nobody'd be looking for him. Who'd even notice he was missing?

He glanced at the patrol car again. Was it a sign? Was his luck finally turning?

How would he get out? He didn't have to try the door to know it was locked.

Think, think, he goaded himself.

He started coughing. No reaction. He coughed harder, leaned forward, and rested his head on the dashboard.

"What's up with you?" Meir finally asked.

"I'm going to be sick," he said weakly.

"Don't even think of puking in the car," Meshulam spat from the rear.

"I can't . . . I can't . . . ," he muttered, trying to sound as if he was going to vomit any second.

"You puke here and I break both your arms and both your legs," Meir warned.

Ziv didn't respond, except to continue making gagging noises. He needed a few more seconds. The idea of opening the door had to come from them.

"Unlock the door and let him puke outside," Meshulam said.

Meir turned his head to see if Meshulam would confirm the order.

"You want him to stink up the car?" Meshulam asked. Ziv emitted another gagging sound to remove any doubts his companions might have.

He heard the click of the locking mechanism.

"Do it outside, moron," Meshulam barked.

Ziv opened the door. His plan had worked. He was going to get away.

When he was halfway out the door, he turned and said in a clear voice, "I didn't say anything to anyone. Your secret's safe with me. Tell that to Shimon."

The two men stared at him in surprise. There was more he wanted to say, but he knew he didn't have time. Slamming the door behind him, he started running as fast as he could between the cars stuck in the traffic jam. He had to call Merav and warn her.

After about a hundred yards, he stopped and looked back. Meshulam was standing outside the car, watching him from a distance. As he'd hoped, they weren't chasing him.

He hopped onto the sidewalk and kept on running, letting himself be swallowed up by the crowd.

Chapter 24

ELI Nachum stepped out of the office of his commander, Superintendent Moshe Navon, and leaned on the wall in an effort to tame the storm raging inside him. Without the wall for support, he felt his knees would buckle, and he couldn't allow that to happen. He'd always been careful to keep his feelings to himself, especially when it came to work. All these years he'd built up the image of a tough cop who was as hard on himself as he was on subordinates or suspects.

A cop walking down the hall threw him a puzzled look, undoubtedly wondering what he was doing standing there like a zombie, not moving. Nachum flashed him a polite smile, gesturing for him to keep going. There's nothing to see here.

"You okay?" the cop asked, stopping anyway.

"I'm good," Nachum said, nodding with obvious impatience.

The cop gave him another curious look and went on his way. He had to get out of here. It wouldn't be long before everyone knew what had gone down in the superintendent's office. Malicious tongues would wag. At least he had to prevent them from adding a melodramatic description of him standing stock-still in the hallway as pale as a ghost.

Nachum had known he'd pay a heavy price for fucking up the Regev case. He'd been hoping Galit wouldn't reveal his role in the screwup, although he knew the chances of that happening were slim. He'd prepared himself for his commander's recriminations, an official reprimand in his file, or worse. But not this. After years of working side by side with him, Navon had informed him that he was suspended for two months, pending the decision of whether or not to convene a disciplinary hearing. "IA is in the picture, and they're not going to look the other way," Navon had said quietly.

The color had drained from his face. He'd tried to explain that he'd only been trying to save the case, to clean up the mess the victim's father had made. Navon merely nodded. From the glazed look in his eyes, Nachum could tell that he wasn't interested in hearing what he had to say. The meeting was only a matter of protocol. The decision had been made.

Nachum's mouth went dry. He was familiar enough with the system to know that this suspension meant the end of the line for him. He felt the rage building up inside him. After all these years of devoted service, he deserved better. He had no intention of going quietly, of letting them throw him to the dogs.

But before he could utter a word in his defense, the door opened, and with perfect timing that seemed highly suspect, Navon's assistant walked in and told him the district commander wanted to see him urgently. Obviously anticipating the supposed summons, Navon jumped up quickly. What a coward.

"Don't worry about it," he said, patting Nachum on the back as he ushered him out. "As long as the national press doesn't get its teeth into it, as long as it doesn't go further than that local guy Giladi, I'll do whatever I can to avoid a disciplinary hearing."

"And what if you can't?"

"We both know there are creative solutions to the problem if it comes to that," Navon said, barely above a whisper. Nachum didn't need him to spell it out: he could take early retirement.

"This isn't right, Moshe," Nachum answered angrily. "Everything I did was for the good of the case, just like always. I was put in an impossible position and I did what I had to do."

Navon remained silent, making the detective's blood boil even more. When they wanted to, the higher-ups knew very well how to turn a blind eye, to cover for a cop in order to make Internal Affairs go away. He used to enjoy that sort of immunity. Apparently, he didn't anymore.

"Everything'll be fine. Don't worry about it. I'll look out for you," Navon had muttered, virtually shoving him out the door.

Nachum moved away from the wall and started down the hall. His feet felt like lead. Despite Navon's parting words, he didn't have a good feeling about this. He was very good at reading between the lines.

What would he tell his wife? His kids? He worked long hours and brought his work home with him, but they knew they could count on him to be their rock, to provide for them. Now what? He'd be out of a job? Mope around the house all day? He had to do something.

He needed a strategy. The police force was more than just a job. He'd invested his heart and soul in it, the best years of his life. And he loved his work. Was it all over for him?

No way! He wasn't going to throw in the towel. If he had to, he'd knock on every door, and if they threw him out the door, he'd climb in through the window. There were plenty of people on the job who'd understand what he'd done, plenty of people who remembered what he'd been like in his heyday and still looked up to him. Taking encouragement from these thoughts, his mood was lighter as he went down the stairs. It wasn't over yet. He'd still have the last word.

He decided to go by his office and make sure he didn't leave anything behind. As he passed Ohad's office, he stopped. Ohad was sitting behind the desk with a big grin on his face, surrounded by the cops who'd been Nachum's subordinates until a few minutes ago. They seemed to be having a grand old time. News of his suspension had traveled fast. He didn't even get the chance to tell them himself.

He felt like he'd been punched in the gut. In a month's time they'd come and say they were sorry to inform him that they'd decided to convene a disciplinary hearing, or worse. Holding that gun to his head, they'd give him the friendly advice to take early retirement.

He moved a few steps back. He didn't want them to see him like this: angry, hurt, humiliated. He had to get out of there fast.

He was starting down the stairs to the exit when he heard Ohad behind him. "Wait up, Eli. I want to talk to you."

He took the stairs two at a time, pretending not to hear.

Chapter 25

MERAV was waiting to order a salad at the deli under her office. She glanced impatiently at the long line ahead of her that was inching forward very slowly. She had to pick Gili up from preschool at four thirty, and she couldn't be late. She was all on her own. There was no one else to do things for her, no one to share her burdens. She knew she'd be eating at her desk again today.

The first time she heard her name called, she thought she must be mistaken. He was in jail, wasn't he? Being held on suspicion of rape. She'd heard from the friend of a friend of a friend that they had a rock-solid case against him, so there was no chance he'd be getting out anytime soon. She was stunned when she learned of his arrest. It might be true that you never really know someone, not even the people closest to you, that everyone has secrets, but she didn't believe for a second that Ziv could commit rape. Despite what she thought of him, and despite the violence of their last encounter, she knew he could never do such a thing. Not Ziv. "Merav," she heard again in a soft voice. Turning around, she saw him standing right behind her in line. How could that be?

"What are you doing here?" she whispered. Alarmed, she took a step back. She hadn't been this close to him in a very long time. "They let me go," he said. "They realized it wasn't me, they made a mistake."

When he was arrested, her divorce attorney, Guy Bernstein, told her she'd be able to get whatever she wanted now: sole custody of Gili, supervised visitation once a week with no sleepovers, increased child support. His arrest was like an atom bomb in the war between them, he'd said, almost licking his chops. Still, she was glad to see that he'd been released and was no longer suspected of rape. And not just so Gili wouldn't have to bear the stain of being a rapist's son for the rest of his life. Not just for Ziv's sake either. It was also because it confirmed what her heart had always told her—Ziv wasn't a bad man. He wasn't capable of hurting anyone intentionally. She was still furious with him for cheating on her, for lying to her for months about the real reason he lost his job, for ruining the family financially and destroying their marriage. She was still paying off the debts that had piled up when he wasn't earning a salary, and child support was a joke. He hadn't been able to make regular payments since the divorce.

When a friend recommended she hire Bernstein, she hadn't hesitated for a second. He had a reputation for taking no prisoners. Bernstein told her she'd have to file for divorce with the rabbinical court, and they always favored the husband. If she didn't want to see Ziv walk away with everything despite the affair, she had to be ruthless. "You don't have a choice," he repeated whenever she showed any sign of weakness or questioned a tactic he proposed. Trusting in his sharp legal mind, and eager to get back at Ziv and hurt him as much as he'd hurt her, she agreed to do exactly as he said. That's why she'd filed a complaint against him for assault. It's true he'd pushed her, and she'd been shocked and frightened by his unaccustomed violence, but even then she'd known he hadn't meant to do her harm and he was sorry for it the minute it happened.

"WE have to talk," he said, moving nearer to close the distance she'd opened between them.

She stared at him in silence, unsure how to respond. They'd met in the army. She'd been stationed at the command post of his sapper unit. One day he came into the office to talk to the unit commander. While he was waiting, he told her he'd come to try to convince him to go easy on a soldier who'd gone AWOL. The guy's father had died, and ever since he'd disappeared from base from time to time. But he always came back. She listened without interrupting, enchanted by the handsome, charismatic officer who cared so much about his soldiers. When he came out of the meeting, he stopped by her desk to tell her he'd managed to talk the commander into looking the other way. She couldn't believe it. The colonel had a reputation for being very tough on anyone who thought the rules didn't apply to them. "How did you do that?" she asked. "I invoked the brotherhood of orphans," he said with a wink. She assumed he was teasing her and took offense. It was only later that she learned he'd lost both his parents in a car crash.

A few months later she ran into him at a party in Tel Aviv. She didn't expect him to remember her, but he did. He came over to talk to her. He was even more handsome out of uniform. Uncharacteristically, at the end of the night she found herself in his bed.

Their relationship moved fast. They spent every free moment together. He wooed her, pampered her, pleasured her. Merav was ecstatic. Very soon, he was part of the family. He'd been on his own since the death of his parents, and her family embraced him warmly. He responded in kind.

"What do you want?" she said icily.

It was because of their history that she was so angry with him. She'd loved him with all her heart and trusted him implicitly.

"I have to talk to you," he pressed.

"I have nothing to say to you," she snapped back. Time had taken the edge off her anger, but she still couldn't forgive him. The situation was becoming awkward. She didn't know how to back down from the embattled stance she'd adopted.

"Please, Merav, I'm begging you. It's important," he said gently, putting his hand on her arm. She'd gotten thinner. She'd lost at least ten pounds since the last time he saw her. And she looked tired, and worse—harried.

"Okay, so talk," she said stiffly.

"Not here," he said, nodding toward the bench outside.

She looked at her watch. If she left the line now, she wouldn't have time to come back. She'd have to skip lunch, which meant she'd be hungry and out of sorts when she picked up Gili. Nevertheless, and despite her lawyer's explicit instructions never to talk to her ex-husband without recording the conversation, she decided to follow him outside. The urgency in his voice convinced her she ought to hear what he had to say.

Merav gazed at Ziv in silence. She could barely see any resemblance between the man sitting beside her and the strong young officer who had swept her off her feet. He seemed tense and kept scanning the street as if he were looking for someone. An alarming thought flashed through her mind. Maybe they didn't release him, maybe he escaped.

"You've got to get Gili and disappear for a few days," Ziv said.

"What are you talking about?" He wasn't making any sense.

"I've made a lot of mistakes, Merav. Not only with you." She was losing patience with him. She stood up. Ziv planted himself in front of her. With a somber expression on his face, he looked her straight in the eye.

"Gili may be in danger because of something I did. There are people who may try to hurt him, bad people . . . criminals."

"What?" She didn't understand. Criminals? But he was charged with rape.

"I'm sorry," he said, looking down.

Merav felt the blood draining from her face. Her heart was pounding wildly. "What do you mean 'hurt him'?" Barely able to get the words out, she collapsed back onto the bench.

"I thought maybe you can take him to your friend Orit in the south. It's just for a few days, until I sort things out," Ziv said softly, ignoring her question.

"That's crazy," she said angrily, getting to her feet again. "Why should I do that? I'm going to the cops."

She started walking off rapidly, trying to get away from him, from what he had told her.

Ziv ran after her and grabbed her arm. "Merav . . . I'm begging you . . . It's not a matter for the cops. I'd go to them myself if I thought it would help . . . These people, they don't have any scruples. They won't stop at anything."

She looked at him in desperation. There was no doubt in her mind that Ziv loved Gili with all his heart, that his son meant the world to him and he'd never do anything to hurt him.

"What did you do, Ziv?" she asked. She heard the tremor in her voice.

He looked down at the ground.

"What did you do? Does it have to do with the rape charge?" Her voice was steadier now, louder. "How the hell did you dare put your son in danger? How could you?"

"You're right . . . I messed up," he said, raising his eyes. "I wish I could change what I did. I'm trying to fix it, but I need time. Meanwhile, Gili's in danger. The only way to protect him is for the two of you to go away for a few days."

She wanted to scream at him, but she held back. She could see the terror in his eyes. The danger to Gili was real.

"Promise me you'll take him somewhere."

Merav didn't reply. Finally she broke the silence. "I have to go," she said.

Ziv spun around and started walking away. Instinctively, she called after him. He turned to look back at her.

"Be careful," she said.

Chapter 26

INSPECTOR Eli Nachum was sitting in his car watching Adi Regev's house. Finding a parking place around here in the evening was a headache, but at this hour of the morning the street was empty. What in God's name was he doing here? It was more than likely that Adi was at work, like most of her neighbors. And even if she was home—what then? Why had he come?

He was only a few days into his suspension, but he couldn't stand to stay in the house any longer. He felt like a prisoner, wandering from room to room looking for some way to occupy himself and not finding anything to do. His rage at the way he'd been treated, at being thrown out like garbage after years of devoted service, ate away at him incessantly. Fuck them all. He'd done what he had to.

He took it out on Leah. Every word out of his wife's mouth set him off. He read into it criticism, disappointment, and humiliation. Throughout the years of their marriage, their roles had been clearly defined: he went to work to provide for the family, and she stayed home to raise the children. And now, long before he'd anticipated retiring, he was stuck at home with her from morning to night. He'd decided not to tell her anything until the situation became clearer, but the news had spread very quickly. Even before he made it home, Leah's brother the cop had called to ask her if the rumor that was going around the precinct was true.

Yesterday he'd realized that if he didn't want to lose his family along with his job, he'd better get out of the house. Luckily, they hadn't taken his car away yet. Without thinking about where he was going, he'd found himself parked outside Nevo's apartment. He'd sat there for hours, watching the entrance, waiting for him to come out, without any real purpose. He knew very well that he couldn't touch Nevo. Even if they found new evidence, it wouldn't matter. "Double jeopardy," they'd say.

After several hours with no sign of Nevo, he got bored and headed for Adi's house. He'd been sitting there for a while when he finally saw her coming home from work at six o'clock. He didn't approach her. What could he say? He walked up and down the street a few times to check if her father was still keeping an eye on her, but he didn't see him. If he had, he might've told him he'd also become obsessed with the case. When Leah called at eight to ask where he'd disappeared to, he drove home.

And now here he was again in the same place, sitting outside her apartment for no good reason. It was just an excuse to get out of the house. He didn't know what else to do with himself now that he had no job to go to. They say criminals return to the scene of the crime; apparently cops do too. Overcome by a sense of futility, he leaned his head on the steering wheel.

The sound of rapping on the window made him jump. An old woman was gesturing for him to roll down the window.

"You're a police officer?" she said, somewhere between a question and a statement.

He nodded.

"I want to make a complaint," the woman said through the half-open window.

He'd been so absorbed in his own problems that he hadn't given a thought to the impression he was making on anyone else. Did she think he was running surveillance on someone? Or maybe she imagined he was watching over the neighborhood to make sure no one stole it, he thought, chuckling ironically to himself.

"Ma'am, if you have a complaint, I suggest you go to the local police station," he said disinterestedly, moving his hand toward the key as if he were about to start the car and drive away.

"There's a man in that building," she said, ignoring him and pointing to a house across the street. "On the fourth floor. His name is Ilan Meron. He doesn't clean up after his dog. To be fair, when he moved here a month and a half ago, he did. But it's gotten very bad lately. Every night for the last ten days . . . ," she went on.

"Pardon me, ma'am, but I'm in a hurry," he said, cutting her off. "I suggest you take your complaint to the city . . ."

"That's just it. I did," she cut in. "I already sent them two letters. I even called the citizen complaint line. But nothing helped. They won't send a warden out at one in the morning, and that's when he walks his dog."

"I suggest you continue to appeal to the city. I'm sure they'll do something about it eventually." Hoping that would be enough to get rid of her, he turned the key in the ignition.

Abruptly, he stopped what he was doing and looked at the old woman again. She was seventy at least, if not eighty. What was a woman her age doing up at one in the morning for ten days straight?

Nachum switched off the engine and climbed out of the car. If it didn't help, it certainly couldn't hurt. After all, he had nothing else to do.

It was only when he was standing opposite her that he saw how short she was. Daunted by their difference in height, she took a step back.

"I'm willing to make an exception and take your complaint," he said, earning a satisfied smile in response.

ALONE in the living room, he could hear Mrs. Glazer busy in the kitchen. He'd refused her offer of something to eat or drink and insisted he didn't have much time, but he soon realized it made no difference what he said.

The faces in family pictures smiled down at him from a dark wooden credenza. Without having to ask, he could tell that the man who appeared in the older photos but was absent from the newer ones was her late husband. She was clearly a widow who lived on her own.

The apartment reminded him of his parents, who had passed away years ago. He felt an ache in his heart. Even though he assumed his parents and Mrs. Glazer came from very different backgrounds, the room he was in was very similar to the home he'd grown up in: bulky furniture, cotton throws spread over the armchairs, vacation mementos, heavy drapes, and the familiar odor of mothballs hanging in the air. His father had died of cancer while Nachum was still assigned to logistics. He never got to see his son fulfill his dream and get his gold shield. His mother, who'd never been sick a day in her life, died of a broken heart two and a half years later.

He got up and walked to the balcony. It was just like the one in his parents' house, he recalled. It even held the same kind of lounge chair. He opened the blinds slightly to check the view from the balcony and was disappointed to find that it looked out on the main street. The rape had taken place on the other side of the building. Mrs. Glazer couldn't have seen anything from here.

As soon as he'd arrived on the scene that night, he'd ordered his detectives to knock on every door and question all the neighbors. He hadn't been present during the interviews, believing it was more important for him to remain at the site and oversee the work of the crime scene investigators. The detectives came back empty-handed. No one had seen or heard anything, they reported. It had happened late at night, and as Adi Regev told him herself, the perp had covered her mouth so she couldn't scream. And like most rapes, it was all over in a few minutes.

"Officer Nachum," Mrs. Glazer called.

She was standing behind him holding a delicate glass of tea on a small matching saucer. A plate of cookies was on the table beside her. She apologized for not having anything better to offer him, saying she had not been expecting guests, but nevertheless it was clear from the expression on her face that she wouldn't agree to talk to him until he'd finished off at least one cookie.

Like a well-mannered child, he chewed the cookie, complimented her on her baking skills—the cookies were actually very good—and listened patiently while she explained they were Abigail's favorites and gave him a few choice details about her granddaughter.

"About your complaint," he said, cutting in.

"Yes, yes, of course. Like I said, his name is Ilan Meron. He's around thirty, and by the way he dresses, I think he's a lawyer . . . Are you writing this down?" she asked.

"I want to get a clear picture in my mind first. You say he walks his dog around one in the morning . . . ," he said, trying to point her in the direction that interested him.

"That's right. He takes the dog out and he doesn't clean up after it!" she declared with a note of triumph in her voice.

"How do you know?" he asked.

The look she threw at him made it obvious that she was not only surprised by his question but also rather offended that he might doubt her statement.

"My husband, Sefi, passed away two years ago. Ever since, what can I say, I have trouble sleeping," she said with a sigh after a short pause.

"So you sit there and look out on the street?" He pointed to the lounge chair on the balcony.

"You know, at my age, it's relaxing just to sit and watch what goes on outside. It helps pass the time," she said, lowering her eyes.

He looked at her in silence. He knew what she meant more than she imagined.

"Good for you, ma'am," he said, pulling himself together. "It's good you keep an eye out, that you care. Young people today, they only care about themselves."

"This neighborhood matters to me. I've lived here forty years, I raised my children here. And believe me, things are getting worse every day. It's like you said, people don't care anymore. That's why I always keep an eye on the street so I'll know what's going on," she said, eagerly agreeing with him.

"I bet you could tell me stories . . . ," Nachum replied, hoping to encourage her to go on talking, but she just gave him a sheepish grin, like a young girl.

"You keep it up . . . We policemen need people like you . . . When things happen, it's good that someone's watching." He went on stroking her ego. He debated if she was ready for him to start questioning her about the night of the rape but decided to hold off until he was sure he'd gained her trust.

"My job isn't very different from what you do," he said. "If you only knew how many hours I spend in surveillance. Maybe I should recruit you for the force." He was rewarded with another smile.

"Can I tell you something, Officer Nachum?" she asked, leaning closer.

"You can tell me anything you want," he answered, holding her gaze.

Mrs. Glazer stood up, went to the balcony, and pulled a box out from under the lounge chair.

"I haven't told anyone else about this," she said. To his astonishment, she opened the box and took out a very professional-looking pair of binoculars.

"This is how I see the scoundrel who doesn't clean up after his dog," she said, holding them out to him.

He examined them closely to be sure they were what he thought they were. He was right. These weren't ordinary binoculars. They were a highly sophisticated model with night-vision capability!

With a quick movement, Mrs. Glazer took them back and returned them to the box. He could tell she regretted having given in to the temptation to reveal to him what was undoubtedly a closely guarded secret.

"Can we get back to Ilan Meron and his dog? That's why you're here, isn't it?" she said, sitting down opposite him.

"Two months ago a woman was raped in the yard behind your building," he said gently.

She covered her mouth in shock.

"A young woman. She was brutally raped," he repeated to be sure she had heard him.

"Yes, I know," Sarah Glazer said after a pause. "Poor thing." She sighed.

"Did you see anything that night?"

"No," she answered, shaking her head firmly. "I told the policeman who came here. I was asleep. It was late. I didn't see anything."

Nachum focused his eyes on her, but she wouldn't make eye contact with him. He was about to remind her that she'd just told him she had trouble sleeping but stopped himself. He didn't want to put her on the defensive.

They sat facing each other in silence. She picked up her glass and took a sip of tea. He could see her hand trembling. Was she hiding something? If she was, he had to tread carefully. His relentless determination had already gotten him in enough trouble.

"Whatever you tell me will remain in confidence," Nachum said reassuringly. "No one else will know. You have my word."

She reached out for a tissue from a box on the credenza and wiped her eyes.

"I'm so ashamed."

He listened in silence, his fingers gripping the glass of boiling hot tea tighter and tighter as she told him about that night, how she'd watched the rape in the yard behind her house from the window of the bathroom on the other side of the apartment, how she'd stood there frozen, petrified. When she told him about the large tattoo on the man's arm, he poured the whole glass of tea down his throat, scalding himself.

"It's okay, entirely understandable," he said soothingly when she had finished her story and was again saying how sorry she was, how ashamed she felt.

Knowing the chances were slim, he opened his bag and took out a picture of Nevo. "Is this the man you saw?"

Sarah Glazer took the photograph and examined it closely. He didn't take his eyes off her.

"It's hard to say," she said finally.

"Try. It's very important," he implored.

"I don't know. Maybe it's him and maybe not."

HE sat on a bench outside the house. He needed time to gather his thoughts, to digest what Sarah Glazer had told him.

If Ohad had dug a little deeper, they might have heard her story the night it happened. Everyone knew that eyewitnesses were often too scared to talk, especially elderly women who lived on their own. And rightly so. But if he'd known about it then, he wouldn't have had to rely so heavily on Adi's identification of the rapist. And he would have been able to use her neighbor's testimony to convince her that she'd fingered the right man, that she had nothing to be concerned about.

At the time, he hadn't thought to pay attention to any distinguishing marks. Now he strained unsuccessfully to remember—did Nevo have a tattoo on his arm or didn't he?

Chapter 27

ADI dragged herself through her apartment, trying to get ready for another day at work. She used to leap out of bed, get herself together in record time, and skip down the stairs. But she couldn't get back into a routine. She felt like the world had moved on without her while she was trapped in a shell of sadness, and she'd been left behind. Everything around her seemed too fast, too loud, too bright.

She'd returned to work three weeks ago, and on the surface things were back to normal. But her life had changed completely. She almost never went out, never did anything for fun. Dating was out of the question. She couldn't even bear the thought. She came home and sat in front of the TV all night or played some dumb game on the computer. Anything else required more than she had to give. Her parents were pressuring her to leave Tel Aviv, to go to college or do something else to give purpose to her life and help her put the past behind her. Meanwhile, she just listened without responding. Maybe they were right. Maybe not. Making a decision required energy she didn't have.

As usual, the TV was on, some morning program showing on the screen. She liked to listen with half an ear to the banal chatter while she brushed her teeth, got dressed, forced herself to eat breakfast. The mundane subjects and simple pleasures they talked about lifted her spirits and helped her forget for a short moment. She could hear the TV from anywhere in her tiny apartment, half of a larger one that had been subdivided.

A famous model who had taken a year off to have a baby was

telling the two moderators how it felt to be back on the catwalk as a mother, how she'd ended a photo shoot early to nurse the baby, how easy it had been to get her figure back. Adi actually wanted to hear the last part, about the diet, but they ran out of time. The interview with the model who'd learned what really mattered in life after giving birth was cut short by the news.

Eight o'clock! She hadn't noticed the time. She had to leave now! She took a final sip of coffee and was taking her mug into the kitchen when she heard the newsreader reporting another brutal rape in north Tel Aviv. The mug fell from her hands, shattering in the sink.

She couldn't breathe. It felt as if all the air had been sucked out of the apartment. In a typical monotone, the man on the TV screen recited that the rape had taken place late the previous night on Stricker Street. The victim was a single woman in her twenties. The rapist had fled.

Stricker Street was right around the corner. Adi's knees buckled. She sat down on a kitchen chair. Even though the volume on the TV was turned down low, it seemed like the newsreader was yelling at her, screaming in her ear, as he related that a similar incident had occurred nearby two months ago. The perpetrator had been caught and had been allowed to plead to the lesser charge of aggravated assault due to a technicality. He'd been sentenced to two years' probation. Sources in the police force, he went on, claimed that because of the similarity between the two incidents, there was a very good chance the same man had committed the second rape as well.

With shaking hands, Adi picked up the remote and switched off the TV. The apartment fell silent. The words continued to echo in her ears—"another brutal rape in north Tel Aviv," "due to a technicality."

She was overcome by a wave of nausea, the granola and yogurt she'd eaten for breakfast rising in her throat. She ran to the bathroom and hurled—again and again. She couldn't make them stop, the nausea and uncontrollable weeping.

Finally, she got up from the floor. On her way to the living room she caught a glimpse of herself in the mirror. Her eyes were swollen, her face was blotched, her hair was disheveled. She'd taken hundreds of showers in the past two months, but suddenly she imagined she could smell his odor on her again, like another recurrence of an illness she thought she'd recovered from.

Tearing off her clothes, she ran to the shower. Just like she had that night, she stood under the scalding water, scrubbing and crying.

She recalled her last meeting with Inspector Nachum. Think how you'll feel if he does it again, he'd said to her, but she'd been so furious she didn't want to hear it. The prosecutor had also asked her to consider the possibility that he might do it again, but she'd ignored her too.

What had she done, what had she done? Her tears mingled with the stream of water pouring down on her.

She stepped out of the shower and lay down on her bed. Everyone had pleaded with her not to recant, but she wouldn't listen. A spoiled, self-centered brat, that's what she was. It was her fault he'd raped someone else. Just a few blocks away, another girl was lying on a bed somewhere, bleeding, sobbing, shaking. And all because of her.

Adi got up, opened the drawer of her desk, and pulled out Nachum's card. She'd ask him to forgive her, tell him she knew it was her fault, that she was ready to do anything, to help in any way she could, even testify in court if necessary. She'd do whatever they asked.

She picked up her cell phone and saw that her parents had called several times while she was in the shower. They must've heard the news too. With a shaking hand, she punched in the numbers on the card.

A woman answered.

"Can I speak with Eli Nachum, please?"

"Inspector Nachum is on leave," the woman replied drily.

"When will he be back?" Adi asked. She was surprised he wasn't there. He didn't seem the type to take a vacation.

The policewoman cleared her throat. "That information is not available at this time," she answered finally before hanging up.

Chapter 28

DETECTIVE Ohad Barel had been put in charge of the rape case, and he was nervous. He'd waited a long time for this opportunity, and now that it had finally arrived, he was plagued by self-doubt. Was he ready? Would he be able to prove himself worthy of the trust that had been placed in him?

A year ago, Superintendent Navon had called him into his office for a private chat. After he'd given a brief review of the cases he was working on, Navon told him the brass was very pleased with his work. He'd smiled to himself in anticipation of the announcement of a promotion that he was positive was coming next. But to his dismay, Navon had said that despite their appreciation, they could not offer him a promotion at this time due to the recent budget cuts. He'd waited in silence for Navon to make some promise for the future, give him an approximate timeline, but the superintendent had also remained silent as he stood up to shake his hand, indicating that the meeting was over. It was only at the last minute, when he was about to step out into the hall, disappointed and confused, that Navon had patted him on the shoulder and said: "We're expecting great things from you, Barel. My door is always open. If there's anything out of the ordinary, anything you want to tell me, anything that you think I ought to know, I'm here." Ohad got the message. Although Nachum's name had never been uttered, he understood that his promotion would only come at his boss's expense.

He didn't plan to do anything about it. He respected Nachum. Eli had taught him almost everything he knew about being a cop.

He had no intention of returning the favor by kicking him in the butt. His time would come. He considered himself a person of integrity, not the type to stab a good man in the back.

As time went by, however, it became clear to him from what other cops were saying, and what Nachum himself told him, that his boss's fate had already been decided. The higher-ups were just waiting for a chance to get rid of him. A detective from another unit even labeled him a "dead horse." Ohad did his best to convince himself that Nachum was not to blame for the fact that his own career was in limbo, but he found himself resenting him for standing in his way, for not making room for younger guys to move up the ranks. His opinion of Nachum began to change too. Suddenly he started to see what everyone else seemed to see: an old-timer who refused to change, a dinosaur who used outdated methods and wasn't open to new ideas.

When the Regev case landed on their desk, he knew that if Nachum botched it, he'd be out. Navon had thrown him a rope and Ohad had to grab it; he wouldn't get a second chance. Then he saw Nachum filing a false report for the court and went straight to Navon.

For days he'd been a nervous wreck, unable to look Nachum in the eye. The smile on Navon's face when he told him made it clear that it was only a matter of time until he put the information to good use. He'd even hinted he might leak it to that reporter, Giladi, who was making Nachum's life miserable. Eli would know immediately how Navon and the press got wind of it. Ohad was already preparing his defense for the imminent showdown with his boss. But he got lucky. Before Navon could decide what to do with what he'd learned, the prosecutor spilled the beans. Nachum was suspended without ever finding out that his second-in-command had betrayed him.

DANA Aronov lay on the bed in Ichilov Hospital with her eyes closed. The wounds on her face were covered in bandages, an oxygen mask was strapped to her head, and an IV tube was attached to her arm. This time the rape had been even more brutal than before. Dana was found lying unconscious in the yard of her apartment building by one of her neighbors. Just two days earlier, she'd returned from a trip to Eilat with a girlfriend.

Navon called at four in the morning to hand him the case. "This is your chance, Barel," he'd said. "Don't screw up and don't let me down." There was no need for him to add "like Nachum did." Ohad got the message loud and clear.

In less than thirty minutes he'd arrived at the hospital and asked to see the victim. After a glance at her mauled, swollen face, he'd felt compelled to look away.

"I can't tell you when she'll regain consciousness and you'll be able to talk to her. She may never wake up," the doctor had informed him at her bedside.

"Any DNA?" he asked. The doctor shook his head. "The tests haven't come back yet, but in my opinion we won't find anything. It doesn't look like he ejaculated. I guess the beating was enough for him."

Ohad looked at the doctor, his face registering his disappointment. He'd been praying for it to be an easy one. This was his first major case, and he wanted to show he could close it quickly. With the victim unable to ID her attacker and no DNA, it was going to be much harder than he'd hoped.

He'd have to use his brain. He couldn't screw up his first case. Nevo wasn't going to slip through their fingers this time.

His cell phone rang. As soon as Navon had hung up, he'd sent a squad car to Nevo's address. He knew he had to work fast. Every second counted.

There was no question in his mind that Nevo was their man. Navon was also operating on the assumption that they already knew the identity of the perp. All Ohad had to do was pick him up, lean on him until he got a confession, and then charge him with two counts of rape. There was no room for any doubt. The MO was the same in both incidents, the victims were similar, and the two rapes were committed in the same neighborhood. Nevo had already admitted to assaulting Adi Regev. He was only out because Nachum had fucked up. The fact that he'd gotten off so easy despite all the evidence they had against him must have given Nevo a sense of confidence. He probably felt untouchable, as if he could do whatever he wanted without paying the price.

"Nevo's place is empty," he heard from the cop he'd sent to arrest him.

"Did you try his ex?" He hadn't really expected him to be in his own apartment. He'd already ordered them to check out the ex as well. Even if he wasn't there, she might know where to find him. At least he hoped so. After all, they had a son together.

"Not there either."

"Does she know where he is? For all I care, you can bring her in too if you have to!"

"No can do. Nobody home."

Chapter 29

AMIT strode quickly through the hospital corridors. It was only five in the afternoon, but there weren't many people around. His footsteps echoed through the halls, adding to his sense of unease. The sharp odor of disinfectant reminded him of the last time he'd been here, when he'd come to visit his grandfather after a simple case of the flu had developed into pneumonia. The old man died three days later.

If he could, he'd turn and run. He didn't want to be here, but Dori had given him no choice in the matter. He'd managed to worm his way out of it last time, inventing an excuse not to interview Adi Regev in the hospital. Dori had let it go then but not this time.

He found out where they were from Ohad Barel, the detective who'd replaced Eli Nachum. He recognized them instantly. The victim's parents were huddled together in the waiting room outside the ICU.

Dori said it was part of the job description. "When a soldier dies, there's a picture of him in the papers the next day, right? Where do you think they get it? Who do you think knocks on the parents' door?"

Amit walked over to them. The father looked up for a second before returning his eyes to the floor, staring sightlessly at a random square of tile. He had to get it together and just do it.

"Excuse me," he said quietly.

The parents raised their eyes to him almost simultaneously. He'd planned his approach on the way over. He'd pretend to be visiting a relative and start a conversation that would yield a printable quote. But, standing in front of them now, he knew he couldn't lie to them.

"My name is Amit Giladi. I'm a reporter," he said.

They continued to gaze at him in silence. Maybe they don't speak Hebrew, he thought. Even without knowing their name was Aronov, he could see from their clothes that they weren't native Israelis.

He repeated the words, more slowly this time.

"Please go away," the father interrupted. He had a heavy Russian accent, but his Hebrew was fine.

Amit stayed where he was. More than once in his short career he'd been told to go away, get lost, fuck off. He was no more than a nuisance to most people. But it was his job to stand his ground and get the story.

"Do you know that the man who did this to your daughter was arrested, but they had to let him go because of a technicality?" He wanted to gain their trust. They might agree to talk to him if they felt they had a common enemy.

"I asked you to leave, Mr. Giladi," the father said, pointing to the exit. "We don't have the patience for this now."

"How's Dana doing?" he asked, trying a different approach.

Both parents looked at him in disgust, making it clear they had no intention of speaking to him.

"Has she said anything? Did she wake up? Did she tell you anything?" he asked, firing at them the questions Dori had dictated to him.

Silence.

"I'm not the enemy. On the contrary . . . ," he said meaninglessly.

The mother aimed a hostile expression at him. Other journalists would probably know what to say, what words to use to draw these people out. But Amit didn't have that skill, or maybe he didn't have enough experience to know how to get them to open up to him. He was going to leave here empty-handed.

"Do you have any comment about the rape? Is there something

you'd like me to put in the paper?" he said, making another attempt to elicit a response.

The mother stood up and came toward him. The father said something to her in Russian. It sounded like a reprimand.

"My husband told you to leave . . . Please respect our privacy," she said reprovingly.

"I'm going. Just tell me one thing . . ."

"Don't you understand? We don't want to talk to you. Leave us alone. We have nothing to say." She had raised her voice and he could see her lips trembling.

"I need something . . . something to tell the readers . . . to tell people . . . they care . . . they want to know how you feel, they want to know about Dana, about what she's going through . . ."

He wasn't prepared for it. It happened too fast. It was too unexpected. Without warning, the mother slapped him sharply across the face.

"Now you can tell them how *you* feel," she said, bursting into tears as he stood there staring at her, stunned. Her husband got up quickly and took her in his arms.

"I'm sorry," he muttered, his arms wound tightly around his weeping wife. "You have to understand, we're very upset. Dana's in critical condition."

Amit continued to stand there, his cheek burning, his eyes filling with stinging tears.

AS soon as he got to the paper, he saw Dori standing at the door to his office, going over the galleys. His figure towered over the partitions between the work stations. Amit was about to beat a quick retreat. He'd come back later. He didn't have the energy for a confrontation with Dori right now, but the editor caught sight of him and waved him over.

"Did you get it, kid?" he asked.

"They didn't want to talk to me," he answered, not meeting Dori's eyes.

"What do mean, they didn't want to talk to you?" From the tone of his voice, Amit knew his boss would start shrieking any minute.

Silently, he cursed Dori for saddling him with this assignment and cursed himself for working for this cheap rag. A couple of nights ago he'd run into Amir Hasner at The Cave. They'd gotten their degree in communications together. Not only did Amir tell him he was at *Haaretz* and not some ass-wipe local throwaway, but he also hinted he was working on a huge story that was about to explode into the headlines. "It has to do with the chief of police," he said with a wink. Naturally, Amit hadn't said anything, but he could feel his temples throbbing. That was supposed to be his story!

"Their daughter is in the ICU," he tried to explain.

"So what? I didn't think she was touring Europe," Dori snarled.

"I did my best to get something out of them, but they wouldn't talk. The mother slapped me in the face. She's got quite an arm on her."

"Poor baby," Dori said sarcastically. "The mother slapped you? I hope you went to the emergency room."

Amit didn't answer. What could he say?

"Come on, baby boy, why don't you turn the other cheek? Maybe it'll do you some good if I slap you on the other one."

Amit kept silent. That was the best way to handle Dori.

"I've always had my doubts about you, Giladi." Apparently, Dori wasn't going to let up on him. "I always knew that at the moment of truth you'd turn out to be a crybaby. You just haven't got what it takes. You're not cut out to be a journalist."

"Badgering parents who don't know if their daughter is going to live or die—that's what it takes to be a journalist?" Amit couldn't stop himself.

"That's exactly what it takes, asshole," Dori declared with a triumphant grin. "It's part of the job description. I already explained all that. Why can't you get it through your thick skull?"

"Forget the parents," Amit said, choosing to ignore the personal slur and try to divert the editor's attention. "That isn't the story. The story is why the police and the DA put a rapist back on the street so he could do it again. That's what I'm working on."

"You work on what I fucking tell you to work on," Dori screamed. From the corner of his eye he could see that everyone in the office was watching.

"Enough," he bellowed. "I've had it with the lot of you motherfuckers! I'll have to do it myself. I'll show you all what it means to be a fucking reporter. Maybe you'll finally learn something."

Amit stared at him in silence, shocked by the outburst that was even more violent than usual for his high-strung editor.

"Quit looking at me like an imbecile. What hospital is she in?"

AMIT sat outside Dori's office and waited to be called in. He'd been summoned to a meeting with the editor and had arrived promptly at the appointed time, which was fifteen minutes ago. Dori could see him sitting out there, but he was making him wait. He assumed he was about to be fired, and, as usual with Dori, it would undoubtedly be loud and messy.

"Here, read this," Dori ordered when he finally called him in after making him cool his heels for a good half hour.

Puzzled, Amit looked at the sheet of paper Dori shoved into his hand. The editor was in the habit of firing people verbally, not in writing.

"Read it," he said impatiently. "See how it's done. I had to do your work for you."

Amit didn't understand. When Dori asked him what hospital

Dana Aronov was in, he didn't expect him to act on the information. He thought it was just part of his public humiliation. He must have been wrong. A wave of relief swept over him. Ever since the scene in the office yesterday, he'd been miserable. Despite all his grumbling, his job had its advantages. Not only could he set his own schedule, but he still had hopes of a major scoop that would boost him into the national league. And on very rare occasions, it gave him the chance to make a real difference.

He scanned the article quickly, his eye picking up the words "mother weeping," "father chain-smoking," "police to blame," "Ziv Nevo," and "vacationing in Eilat with a girlfriend."

"This is your last chance, Giladi. You don't get another one," Dori warned.

"I understand, yes . . . ," Amit mumbled, still focused on the article.

"You're getting the byline even though you never got your act together, even though you played the virgin with me," Dori went on.

Amit nodded. Editors didn't generally get bylines, even when they wrote an item themselves. But he'd be happy to pass on the honor. From what he'd managed to read, Dori's piece was sentimental drivel of the worst kind. It was exactly the sort of article he'd expect to come from an attempt to talk to the victim's parents about their "feelings."

"We have to come up with a nickname for the rapist, something that packs a punch. I have the feeling he's going to be with us for a long time, especially when the cops keep proving how incompetent they are," Dori said, interrupting his thoughts.

"What about 'Northside Rapist'?" Amit suggested, tossing out the first idea that came to him.

Dori snorted, and justifiably so.

"Go talk to the cops and find out what they know about him.

Maybe the assholes will give you something to go on, something that sets him apart."

"You mean like he cries and begs the victim's forgiveness at the end, or threatens them with something unspeakable? Or he takes a lock of their hair or their panties?" Amit could see that Dori was pleased with him.

"Just don't go soft on me anymore, kid. I hope you've learned your lesson. You have to man up!" Dori called after him as he left the office.

"No going soft," he agreed quietly.

Chapter 30

ELI Nachum was sitting in his car waiting patiently for his former second-in-command to come out of the building. Ohad was now occupying his office. When Nachum read about the second rape, he hoped they'd cancel his suspension and reinstate him. But the call never came. No one even asked for his help on the sly. He'd been a cop for more than twenty years, and suddenly it was over, as if he'd never carried a badge.

He should have expected it. He had no doubt that everyone was blaming him, saying the second rape was on him, that he was responsible for allowing it to happen. If he hadn't bungled the investigation, if he hadn't created an impossible situation that forced the DA to let Nevo off with no more than probation, the creep wouldn't have been able to do it again. In the wake of the criticism in the press, with the headlines screaming that police incompetence had put a rapist back on the street, the police spokesman had been compelled to issue the standard statement: "The police force has looked into any errors that were made and drawn the necessary conclusions." That local guy, Amit Giladi, wasn't alone anymore. They were all out to get him. Nobody had to tell him what "the necessary conclusions" meant. It meant his dismissal. His career was over.

One of the few friends he had left in the precinct told him they were concentrating all their efforts on finding Ziv Nevo. There was no question in anyone's mind that his release had given him a sense of euphoria and complacency, provoking him to rape again. But so far they hadn't had any luck. He'd disappeared without a trace.

Nachum agreed with their basic assumption: the two rapes were committed by the same man. The MO, location, victims, and brutality were too similar. Of course, there might be a copycat, but it didn't seem likely. A single incident didn't usually generate that sort of response.

The second rape was horrible, but it was also his chance to get back on the job, to fix the mistakes he'd made. He'd work the case and bring them Nevo's head on a platter. He wasn't dead yet, and now he didn't have to answer to anyone. He wasn't required to follow orders or justify every move he made. In a way, he had resources at his disposal that he didn't have when he carried a badge, and he no longer needed his commander's authorization to work overtime.

At five minutes to nine, Ohad came through the door. He stopped by his car to shake hands with two people Nachum knew very well: Yair Bar, the crime reporter at *Ma'ariv*, and Amit Giladi.

Nachum looked at them with a sour face. He belonged to the generation of cops who didn't leak information to the press, who only talked to reporters when he thought it could further an investigation. But times had changed. Handling the media was part of the job now. If he'd internalized that a little sooner, he might not have found himself in this position with his future hanging by a thread.

Nachum waited until the three men had driven away before getting out of his car and heading toward the station house. Ohad was a good cop, but he didn't have enough experience. He needed a few more years to hone his instincts. Nachum figured the enormous pressure on him to find Nevo wasn't helping either. If he himself read the file, he might see something Ohad had missed.

The guard at the door looked at him in surprise. After twenty years on the job, he was incensed by the idea that he needed an excuse to be there.

"I forgot something in the office," he muttered apologetically as he hurried inside, hoping the guard was the last person he'd have to explain himself to.

He walked into his former office and turned on the light. Even before he took in the files thrown around haphazardly, the empty coffee cups staining the desk, and the papers covering every inch of space, he noticed that the odor was different. On the cabinet behind the desk, someone had placed a small bottle of air freshener that gave off an odd scent and turned the room he'd spent so many years in into an alien space with an unpleasant smell.

His heart seized up. He hadn't been in need of any more proof that his career was finished, but every additional bit of evidence still hurt. He was shocked by how quickly and cruelly things had changed. What was he going to do with himself? He wasn't a kid anymore. He'd been a cop his whole life. It was the only thing he knew.

As he'd expected, the file was on his desk, Ohad's desk, he reminded himself. Ohad had always been sloppy, so it wasn't surprising that he hadn't bothered to lock it away in a drawer. Nachum snatched it up and began reading, page by page, detail by detail. The similarity between the two cases was striking. Even the pricks under the chin appeared to have been made by the same hand. They were cut at the same angle and the same depth. There was no question that the second rape was also the work of Nevo.

There were, however, two differences. This time the attacker had beat his victim unconscious. Although Nevo had hit Adi Regev too, the blows hadn't been this violent. On the contrary, he wanted her to be awake, to cooperate, to beg for her life. The second difference was that this time they were certain Nevo hadn't ejaculated. In Adi's case, that question had remained unanswered. Too much time had elapsed before she got to the hospital for any traces of DNA to survive. The description she gave suggested that he had ejaculated, but they couldn't be sure, and Nevo refused to say. These two points needled him. They might be related. If he'd gotten what he wanted out of Adi and not Dana, and if he'd only beaten Dana unconscious, maybe it was because he wanted to keep her quiet because he was afraid of being seen. That meant he might have been interrupted by something or someone. Could there be another Mrs. Glazer out there?

He looked at the pictures of Dana Aronov. She was badly beaten. He didn't have to read the medical report to see that the perp had broken her nose. He started to examine the photographs more closely. Something was bothering him, but he couldn't put his finger on it. He pulled open the drawer of the desk. Good thing Ohad hasn't had time to empty it, he thought, taking out the magnifying glass he kept there. Bringing it up to his eye, he went over the pictures section by section. Police work was a painstaking job. The smallest, most insignificant detail might turn out to be critical. He put the photos back in the file and picked up the crime scene report, but he was finding it hard to concentrate. Something was still gnawing at him, some hidden asymmetry. Turning back to the pictures, he went over them again meticulously, but nothing jumped out at him. He didn't even know exactly what he was looking for. Suddenly he stopped. There. The right hand, the middle finger. He reached for the magnifying glass and looked again. He was correct. A ring was missing. The difference in skin color was clearly visible.

His eyes remain focused on the photograph. She could have taken it off before the attack. But there was also a chance it fell off in the struggle, if there was one. There was no way to tell.

By the time they got the report of the assault on Adi, it was already three days after the incident. She'd gone home, showered repeatedly, and thrown out the dress she'd been wearing. It was only because of pressure from her parents that she'd gone to the hospital and reported the rape. In vain, he tried to remember if he'd asked her if anything was missing afterward.

He looked through the office for the Regev file, but the case had been closed and apparently there was a limit even to Ohad's lack of order. It was probably already gathering dust in the archive room. If he were in charge of the Aronov case, one of the first things he'd do would be to pull the previous file and try to find more connections between the two cases.

Nachum sat down in the chair that used to be his and stared into space, thinking, as he had done so many times before in this very spot. The missing ring troubled him. There were all sorts of rapists. Was Nevo the type that collected trophies?

He'd questioned Nevo for hours on end. At no point in the interrogation had he seen any sign that the man was a psychopath, that rape was a ritual for him, or that he took pride in what he'd done. It was just the opposite.

He leaned forward and massaged his temples in an effort to relieve the pulsating pain that had come on suddenly. Now that he took the time to think about it again, he had to ask himself if Nevo was the type of obsessive sex offender who'd rape again even after getting caught. He seemed too apprehensive, too squeamish. It was highly unlikely that after facing the almost certain prospect of hard time, he'd risk that fate again such a short time later. He didn't seem the type to taunt the cops, to dare them to try to catch him. And he didn't seem the type to collect trophies either.

Nachum turned to the computer and typed in PCL-R, wanting to go over the checklist of antisocial characteristics to be sure he hadn't missed anything. His head was throbbing. He scanned the markers of a psychopath. Nevo didn't display any of them. Before his divorce, he'd maintained a steady long-term relationship with his wife, was devoted to his son, and held down a job that provided comfortably for himself and his family. The fact that he'd been an officer in a combat unit meant he was capable of respecting authority and worked well with others. His responses during the interrogation had been emotional rather than indifferent, and there was no record of juvenile delinquency.

Nachum looked up from the screen. He heard the elevator doors open at the far end of the hall, followed immediately by the voice of Superintendent Navon speaking loudly on his cell phone. Nachum stood up quickly. He couldn't let Navon find him here. If his independent investigation was to have any chance of success, no one could know about it. How could he explain his presence in what was now Ohad's office? The excuse he'd given the guard at the entrance wouldn't work with the superintendent.

He switched off the light and hurried out of the office. He only had a few short seconds before Navon turned the corner and was right in front of him.

HE looked at his face in the large mirror in the ladies' room. The place was spacious, clean, and smelled a lot better than the men's john at the other end of the hall. More to the point, it was much closer to his old office. He could still hear Navon screaming into the phone in the distance. How did he get himself into a situation where he had to hide in the ladies' room? How low had he come?

Until the car crash near Netanya, Nachum was sure he'd live out his days in logistics. Then one day he and a couple of other cops from the unit were on their way to the station house in Tel Mond when there was a horrific accident right in front of them: a truck collided with a sedan, and the car flipped over and caught fire. The gas tank could explode at any minute. He heard the screams of the woman trapped behind the wheel. Everyone else kept their distance, but not him. He was no different then. He'd always felt compelled to take action and not simply stay on the sidelines. He raced to the burning car, smashed the window, and pulled the driver out. The next day he was hailed as a hero in all the papers, but he didn't feel like a hero. When there was a job to be done, he did it. That's just who he was. He took advantage of the medal ceremony to tell the district commander about his ambition of becoming a detective. Two months later, his application was approved.

The missing ring was still eating at him. If the perp took it, it was much more than an insignificant detail. It told them something about his character.

Nachum pulled out his cell phone, went into a stall, and sat down on the toilet seat. He was stuck here until Navon left. Adi Regev's number was still in the phone. He had to talk to her, ask her if he'd taken anything. A ring, maybe?

She picked up on the third ring.

"Adi," he said softly, "it's Eli Nachum."

NACHUM leaned his head on the cold tiles and stared at the door of the stall. His eye was caught by a fading sticker with the number of a hotline for rape victims. You didn't find that sort of thing in the men's toilet. He was worried that Adi wouldn't agree to talk to him, that she was still mad at him, but his apprehension turned out to be unwarranted. She said she'd been trying to contact him ever since she heard about the second rape, but they told her he was on extended leave. She apologized over and over again for backing out on them. "I was confused, angry," she said, assuring him that now she was ready to ID Nevo as the rapist. He listened patiently, doing his best to calm her, insisting that he wasn't upset with her, that he understood.

THE hallway was quiet. Navon must have left.

The conversation with Adi convinced Nachum he'd made another mistake, probably his biggest one. One of her rings had been missing since the attack. She noticed it was gone as soon as she got inside her apartment and assumed it had fallen off when she was dragged on the ground. Since then, she'd been too scared to go back into the yard to look for it. She hadn't given it much thought. It wasn't expensive, and since the police hadn't found it when they searched the scene, she figured it was lost.

He might be able to blame Ohad for Sarah Glazer, but he couldn't blame him for this. He'd questioned Adi himself. Why hadn't he asked her if anything was missing?

Had he known then what he knew now, the whole investigation might have gone in a different direction. Ziv Nevo didn't fit the profile of a serial rapist who collected trophies and taunted the cops. Had he let himself be swayed by Yaron Regev's accusations, by his pain? Had he let fucking CompStat get to him, make him too eager to prove that he could close cases quickly, lead him to draw hasty conclusions and accept the easy answers, even if they were fundamentally flawed? He was so sure it was Nevo, so keen for him to be the attacker. He must have read what he wanted to into his words.

Nachum's head was about to explode. If Nevo didn't rape Adi, what was he doing on Louis Marshall Street in the middle of the night? Why did he look so guilty? That was one thing the detective was certain of. He knew his instincts didn't get that wrong. Nevo was guilty of something. But what? How could he have let himself conduct such a sloppy investigation?

Right now, it was imperative that he find Nevo and see if he had a tattoo. If he'd been correct the first time and Nevo was the perp, bringing him in would solve two cases and make up for his mistakes. Then maybe he'd get a second chance. But if he found him and he didn't have a tattoo, he'd have to catch the true rapist. He owed it to Nevo, to Adi, to Dana Aronov, and to the next victim or victims. He had a lot of debts to pay.

Chapter 31

"HE'S asleep," Merav said to her ex-husband, closing the door behind her. Ziv gave her a warm smile. She'd been dreading this moment all day. On her lawyer's instructions, she hadn't been alone with him even once since she kicked him out of her life a year and a half ago. But that wasn't the only reason she'd avoided any intimate contact with him. Her rage had made it unbearable for her to be anywhere near him, to look him in the eye.

And now here they were, all alone in this lovely house in the country in the middle of nowhere. They were hiding from the world because of something he'd done, and she didn't even know what it was.

When he'd shown up outside her office and told her that Gili was in danger and they had to go away, she was shocked and frightened. She would have called the cops if Ziv hadn't insisted they couldn't help, and it wouldn't get Gili out of harm's way. No matter how angry she was with him, she knew he'd never hurt Gili. She'd refrained from calling her parents and her brother in case it might put them at risk too. Besides, she was feeling so confused and vulnerable, she wasn't up to listening to their lectures and advice.

In the end, she'd decided to take Ziv's suggestion and call Orit. All their friends gathered in Orit's capacious backyard every year for a carnival-like Independence Day picnic, and Merav was hoping she'd be able to put them up for a few days. She caught her two hours before she had to leave for the airport. The family was going on a ski vacation in Europe. Without asking a single question, Orit invited her to use the house in their absence. She'd leave the key under the grill in the backyard.

As soon as she hung up and returned to the office, Merav felt all her strength deserting her. The thought of what awaited her—dealing with Gili, who made a fuss over any change in his routine, packing for the two of them, driving for four hours. It was too much for her to cope with on her own. Without giving herself time to change her mind, her fingers automatically tapped in the number she'd dialed so infrequently in recent months.

THEY barely exchanged a word the whole drive. Ziv seemed preoccupied, worried. When he got in the car, he told her to call her parents and Gili's preschool teacher and inform them that they were going away for a few days and would be out of reach. She didn't like the way he was ordering her around. Several times she almost told him to turn the car around and take her home. But in the end she held her peace. She was too scared, and anyway she didn't know enough about the danger they were in to be able make any rational decisions. But mainly she did it for Gili. He was thrilled to be with his father, had literally leaped into his arms the moment he saw him, and spent the whole ride singing silly songs and trying to make them laugh. His joy at this supposed family vacation tugged at her heartstrings. For a long time she'd been making a constant effort not to acknowledge how much he missed Ziv, not to admit to herself how much she missed him.

"I'm usually tearing my hair out by the time he falls asleep. I can't remember the last time he dropped off so quickly." Ziv followed her into the living room. She chose an armchair, just to be on the safe side.

"He was worn out. All that singing and jumping around," he said, and then fell silent.

They sat in tense silence. Both of them had focused on Gili all day, taking care to avoid each other's eyes, to exchange as few words as possible, functioning like two factory hands working side by side on an assembly line. Only once, when he complimented her on the salad she threw together from the vegetables they bought on the way, did she give him a tentative smile before looking away.

A feral wailing broke the silence, startling her.

"It's just a jackal," he said with a smile, telling her what she herself knew.

Should she return the smile? She had so many questions to ask him, but she was afraid that if they started talking she'd lose her temper and the temporary truce between them would come to an end. She was too drained to fight with him.

"I'm tired too," she said, rising and faking a wide yawn. She had to put a stop to the unexpected intimacy that had sprung up between them. It was making her strangely uneasy.

"I'll help you make the bed," he said, getting up.

She was about to tell him to stay where he was, that she could manage on her own, but instead she smiled. "Thank you," she said.

They went into the master bedroom and began pulling off the soiled sheets.

"Help me fold them up. I'll do a laundry tomorrow," she said from across the wide bed. They worked quickly in synchronized movements. After all, they'd done this an infinite number of times before.

Holding two corners of the blanket cover, he stepped toward her and then stood still, gazing into her eyes. His face was very close. She felt her heart racing as she breathed in his familiar scent. Her body's response took her by surprise, making her feel awkward. Quickly, she reached down for the bottom corners, folded the cover in half, and took it from him.

Without a word, she held out the clean bedding. When they were together, they used to change the sheets every other Saturday night when he got home from his basketball game. They had an ongoing rivalry to see who'd complete their side of the bed first. Now, even though they were working in silence and barely looking at each other, Merav followed his progress out of the corner of her eye and knew he was doing the same. She finished first and couldn't resist declaring her victory: "Done!"

"You gave me the tougher pillow," he said with a grin, and she laughed, reminded of his customary excuse. She wondered if he was thinking the same thing she was: this is the point when we fall onto the clean, fresh-smelling sheets and make love. Sex with Ziv was wonderful. No other man she'd ever been with had pleasured her so deeply, had been so attentive to her needs and knew how to satisfy them, had even cared about satisfying them.

She moved farther away from him. What was happening to her? How could she be so quick to forget what he'd done?

"Okay," she said, hoping he would take the hint. The desire he aroused in her was disconcerting. You haven't had sex in a long time, she reminded herself, trying to find an excuse for the sudden hunger for his touch. And maybe I'm just scared, she thought.

Ziv stayed where he was. "If you're not too tired, I'd like to talk to you," he said.

Without her asking, he told her in detail about the past few months. Not mentioning any names—"the less you know, the safer you'll be," he said—he related how he'd worked for the mob—"just a driver, nothing illegal"—and then found out they actually wanted him for the skills he'd acquired as a sapper in the army. Merav's initial reaction was shock, mainly because of his naïveté, but as the story unfolded she found herself taking pity on him, mainly because of his naïveté. She knew she should be angry at him for jeopardizing Gili's safety, and her own, but she couldn't help wondering if the divorce hadn't been more devastating for him than she thought. After all, she and Gili were the only family he had.

"What happens now?" she asked when he was done.

Ziv shrugged. "I'm hoping in a couple of days they'll see the cops don't come looking for them, and then they'll know I kept my mouth shut and they'll leave us alone."

She wrapped her arms around her chest, either because of the cold or her fear; she wasn't sure herself.

"I'm sorry," he said quietly.

Merav didn't respond. What happens if they don't leave us alone, she thought, standing up abruptly. "Do you want me to help you make up a bed in one of the other rooms?" she asked.

"Thanks. I'll manage," he said, rising.

They stood facing each other. She knew she should turn around, go into the bedroom, and close the door. She'd been through a lot in the past twenty-four hours. She couldn't afford to do anything she might regret later. But despite what her brain was telling her, she remained where she was.

She could deny it as much as she liked, but it would still be true—she wanted him. He had rekindled the flame of passion that had been extinguished by the divorce and a number of forgettable experiences with other men since then.

And she knew he wanted her too. She could see it in his eyes. After all, she knew him very well. But neither one of them moved, both too afraid or too embarrassed to do anything about it.

With a deep breath, Merav took a step forward, silently closing the gap between them. Her body quivered with excitement as he reached his arm around her waist and pulled her in for a kiss.

Chapter 32

SUPERINTENDENT Navon was in his office trying to ignore the headline in *Haaretz* on the desk in front of him. It screamed of senior officers close to the chief of police being rewarded for their loyalty with trips abroad to bogus training courses and staying at five-star hotels at the taxpayers' expense. The item below named names and cited specific cities, hotels, and figures. He couldn't say he was surprised, not even by the names of the officers involved, many of whom were attached to his district. It had been a long time since he himself had been sent overseas or enjoyed the luxuries afforded to those with friends in high places. It wasn't for lack of trying. He'd done his best to win favor with the brass, but something had always gotten in the way. There were too many fuckups under his command, too many mistakes that made their way into the press. And there were complaints from subordinates as well: old-timers who groused about the lack of authorized overtime, young upstarts who felt they weren't moving up the ladder fast enough.

Just recently he'd made an example of a highly respected detective in order to demonstrate his determination to make room in the higher ranks for younger cops and send the message that on his watch you paid for your mistakes no matter who you were. But meanwhile, the rapist had struck again, the investigation was going nowhere, and he had the press on his back.

Anonymous sources were quoted as demanding that the chief of police be asked to tender his resignation. But Navon didn't feel like gloating. He was familiar enough with politics in the force to know that when the chief of police was in a tight spot, the officers under him were going to feel the pinch.

Navon glanced at his watch. Nine thirty. Maybe the anxiety that had been building in him ever since he heard the news on the radio was unwarranted.

But the minute he headed out for yet another briefing, hoping the tidal wave had passed him by, his assistant informed him that the district commander wanted to speak to him urgently. Even before he picked up the phone, he knew his instincts had been spot on.

"We need an arrest," his superior barked, not wasting words.

Navon breathed a sigh of relief. It wasn't that bad. Normal procedure: you haul in some notorious bad guy, put on a show for the media, and then let him go. The crime syndicates knew the drill. They'd keep their heads down when he was released. If anyone said anything, you blamed the legal system for putting him back on the street and not letting the cops do their job. Yes, he was very familiar with office politics.

"Anyone in particular?" he asked, making an effort not to let any hint of sarcasm seep into his voice.

"We were thinking of Shimon Faro."

"No problem. I'll get it done today," Navon said. He almost added, "in time for the evening news," before thinking better of it. The chief of police needed a story that would push the corruption scandal to the end of the newscast or, even better, leave no time for it at all. He'd been tasked with the dirty work.

"One more thing," his superior said, clearing his throat. "We want a real arrest, not a catch and release."

Navon kept silent. His stomach was churning. His relief had been premature; he wasn't going to be let off so easy.

"You've got an informant in his organization, right?" the district commander said when he got no response. It was more a statement than a question.

Navon held the receiver to his chest and roundly cursed the district commander and the shit he was making him eat.

"He's not ready, Ilan. We'll lose him if we use him now. Faro's arrest will blow up in our face."

Navon's attempt at persuasion was met with silence. He knew his boss was just as unhappy about the situation as he was. Just like him, he was only following orders.

"The creep has been stringing you along for months. It's time to see if he can deliver," he said finally.

"He can deliver, and he will, but not yet. We need more time to convince him to switch loyalties. You know how these things work . . ."

The district commander cut him off. "Don't be such a pessimist, Moshe. He might surprise you and sing like a canary."

Navon didn't answer. He was enraged by the idea that months of careful planning would be going down the drain, that his cops would have to see all their hard work sacrificed for a mere photo op. Nothing would come of bringing Faro in now. Their informant wasn't ready. The arrest would spook him and he'd refuse to cooperate. They'd lose him for good.

"You still with me, Moshe?"

"I'm here." Navon decided there was no point in prolonging the conversation. The order had come down from above, and neither he nor the district commander could do anything about it. In view of the latest turn of events, it was in his best interest to appear to be a team player, not another thorn in their side.

Chapter 33

DAVID Meshulam was following Faro, making sure to keep two cars between them. That's how they always did it. Faro went first, and Meshulam had his back. He still felt miserable for not telling Faro how he'd gotten the idea to plant the bomb on Louis Marshall Street and recruited Nevo to do it. He never lied to Faro, never kept any secrets from him, never dreamed of betraying his trust. He owed the boss so much! But he didn't see any reason to upset him for no good reason. Maybe at first, when he thought Nevo had squealed. His suspicions were confirmed when the motherfucker ran.

The fact that the bitch's car had disappeared was another strike against him. He'd called Michael in the Department of Motor Vehicles. The guy owed Faro a big favor. But nothing showed up on the DMV computers. She hadn't gotten a ticket, driven through a toll booth—nothing. Gone. He couldn't get his head around it. He went back to her house again and again, but the car wasn't there. Then yesterday he'd seen her taking a cab to work. The bitch was still out there, free as a bird. It made his blood boil.

But days went by and nothing happened. No cops. Zilch. If he was right and Nevo had ratted them out, the whole fucking police force would have come down on them by now. His cell phone rang. Faro's driver told them they were stopping at Nisim's shawarma place up ahead. "No problem," he said. He could do with a good meal.

Maybe Nevo had done him a favor by disappearing. He'd been planning to take him to the warehouse and finish him off right then and there. Nevo wasn't a bad guy. The rape charge was a crock. He'd gotten off easy, but now he had a rap sheet. That meant the bastards had a free pass to harass him for the rest of his life. He heard on the news they were looking to pull him in for another rape. When those motherfuckers got their claws into you, they never let go.

Faro's car pulled up in front of the restaurant. He waited for Sammy to climb out and get their lunch. His too. He didn't have to ask. He didn't even have to tell him how he liked it. Sammy knew. Faro and his guys were family.

Meshulam stopped a safe distance from Faro. It was starting to rain. He switched on the windshield wipers and listened to Shlomi Saranga singing, "All the different words, just killing time, all the years of waiting, and what do I have." Maybe he was right. Like Faro said, maybe it was time to start thinking about settling down. He didn't have anyone special in his life. To be honest, there'd never been anyone special. The wounds of the past hadn't healed, even though it was a long time ago.

His musing was interrupted by the sound of sirens behind him. They came one after another, until the street was filled with a whole fleet of cop cars. He'd never seen so many in one place at one time. He straightened up in the seat. Something bad was going down. The squad cars surrounded Faro's ride from all sides. He was aching to get out and help the boss, but he stayed where he was, his knuckles going white on the steering wheel. Faro would be mad if he showed himself, and he'd be right to be mad.

A cop tapped on the door of the black Mercedes and the window was rolled down. Meshulam couldn't hear what they were saying, but he saw the cop gesturing for Faro to get out of the car. The lack of respect he was showing the boss, it made him see red. It felt like a slap in his own face.

Shit. They stopped here all the time. He told Faro it was too risky. But the boss liked Nisim's shawarma.

Faro stepped out of the car. The cop spun him around and cuffed him. Meshulam could feel his blood rising. He wanted to pop the motherfucker right between the eyes. Right here, right now. He didn't give a shit what it cost him.

He slammed his fist into the dashboard, silencing the music. A stampede of TV cameramen and press photographers was rushing at Faro like a herd of wild animals, like cannibals. Faro was used to being the focus of media attention, but this time Meshulam saw him turn away from the cameras that were clicking and flashing around him. It looked like everybody had gotten word that the arrest was going down. Everybody, that is, except them.

The cop led Faro to a squad car. Just before he got in, he looked straight at Meshulam. A knife went through his heart.

Meshulam sat there for a long time after the street had emptied out, compulsively punching the steering wheel and cursing under his breath. Faro'd been arrested before. The cops picked him up periodically just to flex their muscles, to show them who was in charge. But he'd never seen anything like this media circus before.

His thoughts turned to the expression on Faro's face. He'd looked flustered, as if he also sensed there was something different about this arrest, as if he could tell it wasn't just for show. An appalling idea suddenly formed in Meshulam's mind. Was it possible the whole thing with Nevo was part of a sting operation? He should have known something wasn't right when he couldn't find the bitch's car. The cops had been biding their time, waiting to pounce on them the moment they were confident Nevo hadn't squealed and they let their guard down.

Chapter 34

GILI climbed onto the bed, waking her up. Merav opened her eyes and watched him crawl between her and Ziv, cover himself with the heavy blanket, and lay his little head on the pillow beside her before closing his eyes.

It was all happening so fast. Too fast. If anyone had told her a week ago that she'd wake up like this one morning, she would've laughed it off as a preposterous fantasy. But here she was, lying in bed with her son and her ex-husband like the happy family they once were.

Gili flopped over and put his tiny hand on her shoulder, hugging her in his sleep. He didn't need time to adjust. As soon as he saw his parents together again, he settled blithely into the new-old reality. How would he react when they went back to real life, when they had to leave this paradise?

She got up carefully so as not to wake Gili and Ziv and slipped into the top and panties Ziv had pulled off her last night. She looked at the two of them sleeping, both lying in almost the exact same position, and tears welled up in her eyes. It seemed so right.

It was cold out, but inside the idyllic house was bathed in a pleasant warmth. Moving quietly, she went into the kitchen and switched on the electric kettle. She needed time to herself, time to think and process the events of the last few days.

The kitchen window looked out on the vast desert landscape. It's so peaceful here, so beautiful, so remote from everything we left behind, she thought as she gazed at the winter sun rising over the imposing rose-tinted mountains.

Last night was still fresh in her mind. She recalled how he'd stroked her belly, her breasts, her nipples, drawing tiny circles that gradually grew bigger, just the way he knew she liked it. Purring with pleasure, she'd passed her hand over him in the way she knew aroused him. It wasn't long before he was inside her, his body pressed against her, her body rising to meet his.

She was pouring the boiling water into two mugs when she heard Ziv getting out of bed. She'd been out with a few men since the divorce, but all they wanted was to get laid and be gone the next morning. A lonely, single mother was easy prey. One man turned out to be married, one hadn't gotten over the breakup from his wife, one wasn't looking for commitment—the excuses were endless and left her feeling hurt and bitter. Before falling asleep, she'd decided it would be best if they put last night behind them. It was only a temporary lapse, a momentary connection forged out of lust, fear, and solitude.

Ziv put his arms around her from behind, drawing her closer and kissing her neck. They held the embrace for a long moment, both gazing through the window at the glorious, endless desert spread out before them. How wonderful it felt to be cut off from the rest of the world.

"I could stay here forever," he said softly, giving her another kiss on the neck that made her body quiver. She raised her arms and twisted them around his head.

"Tomorrow I'm going back to Tel Aviv to talk to them," he said.

"You think you can get them to leave us alone?"

"The fact that the cops haven't come down on them should speak for itself, shouldn't it?"

"I don't know. I hope so," she said, making an effort to hide her anxiety.

"In the meantime, let's enjoy what we've got," he whispered in her ear. She nodded, pulling his head down for a kiss.

Chapter 35

SINCE Eli Nachum had no way of knowing where Nevo might be hiding, he decided to wait until after midnight, when he was sure everyone in the house was asleep, and then set out for the suspect's apartment in the hope of uncovering a clue to his whereabouts. He knew Ohad and his team had already turned the place upside down, but he also knew that Ohad could be sloppy. With his own orderly, methodical habits and greater experience, he might turn up something they'd missed.

He stood outside the building and looked it over. Despite the late hour, the lights were still on in several apartments, but, as he expected, the blinds were drawn over Nevo's windows. As far as he could tell, it was dark inside. He zipped up his jacket and strode quickly to the front door, making sure no one had eyes on him. What would he say if he ran into a cop, he wondered. But he very much doubted the place was under surveillance. Ohad didn't have the budget for it—police budgets were constantly being cut. When he saw the resources at the disposal of the police in American movies, he always felt jealous.

The stairwell was empty. To avoid attracting the attention of the neighbors, who'd probably been asked to report anything suspicious, he chose not to turn on the light, and climbed quickly and quietly up to Nevo's apartment in the dark. He was startled by loud barking behind one of the doors. "Quiet, Fritz," he heard a man's voice command. The dog went on barking, scratching at the door.

Nachum quickened his pace, taking the stairs nearly at a run. Finally, he stood outside Nevo's apartment, pausing to catch his breath. He reached for the door handle and was surprised to feel it give way. He'd assumed he'd have to jimmy the lock and was glad to find there was no need. The odor of stale air and mildew issued from the dark rooms. He felt on the wall for the light switch but came up empty. He could still hear the neighbor's dog barking. Then a door opened on a floor below. He slipped inside and closed the door behind him. He couldn't afford to be caught here.

The apartment was silent and almost pitch-black, with only a thin glimmer of pale light from a streetlamp below that seeped in through a broken slat in the blind. He moved rapidly along the wall until he finally found the light switch and flipped it on. Nothing happened. Another switch nearby produced the same result. He debated going into the hall and checking the fuse box but decided against it when he heard the neighbor step out of his apartment with the barking dog. He was reaching into his back pocket for the small flashlight he'd brought with him when he froze. Not far away from him, something, or someone, had moved. For a moment he thought he might be mistaken, that maybe the sound had come from outside, but his first instinct was confirmed when he heard it again, closer. Footsteps? Was someone moving toward him? He spun around, searching for the source of the noise.

"Who's there?" he called out in the darkness. Silence. Nachum's heart was pounding. He couldn't see anything, but he could sense a presence. Someone was standing there. He could smell the sweat on his body, hear the sound of his breathing. He should have realized something was wrong when he found the door unlocked. Maybe they were right and he was getting too old for this.

"Who's there?" he called again.

Everything happened very quickly. He felt a powerful kick to his left knee. He could actually hear the bone breaking. The pain was excruciating. He dropped to the floor like a sack of potatoes, fighting the scream that threatened to burst out of him. His blood froze at the realization that whoever had landed that kick knew exactly what he was doing, how to disable him.

Another kick to the left side of his face made his teeth rattle. He was shaking. His attacker wasn't finished. He aimed a third kick at Nachum's gut. The detective struggled to twist his body out of the way, but the stranger was too quick. He sat on him, immobilizing him, and pointed a harsh, blinding light at his eyes, which were already tearing up in pain. Nachum tried to look away, but the man seized his injured jaw, making it impossible for him to move his head.

"You his old man?" a raspy voice asked, disabusing him of the idea that the stranger might be Nevo himself.

Nachum felt his mouth filling with blood. His leg was screaming in pain, his ribs protesting loudly with every breath he took. Before leaving the house, he'd considered taking his gun but decided to leave it at home. He was still on suspension. Now he cursed himself for his high principles, his obsessive need to play by the rules.

The man applied more pressure to his ribs. It was too much for him. The sensation of being stabbed by a thousand blades at once forced a shriek of pain out of his throat.

"I asked you a question," his attacker said emotionlessly, almost indifferently. Nachum tried in vain to focus his eyes on the man's face, but he was blinded by the light.

"Who wants to know?" he heard himself ask. The words coming from his bruised, bleeding mouth were slurred.

The man put his hand on Nachum's throat and started to press down. "Cut the crap. I'll ask the questions."

Nachum couldn't breathe. He tried to fight the stranger who was pinning him down, but the slightest movement was agony.

"Where is he?" the man asked, loosening his grip on Nachum's throat.

Nachum coughed and fought for breath, flinching from the pain in his ribs. The man repositioned himself as if he were about to lean on his chest again. Nachum spread his arms to the side in a gesture of surrender. He was sure at least one of his ribs was broken. Any more pressure and it could puncture his lung. His outstretched hand touched something. Cautiously, he moved his fingers along the object and identified it immediately: a beer bottle.

"You got a death wish?" his attacker grunted. Nachum grabbed the bottle and swung it at his face.

Stunned by the unexpected blow, the man recoiled. Knowing he had to act fast if he wanted to take advantage of the element of surprise, Nachum aimed his fist at his assailant's face and landed a crisp punch smack on the nose. He heard him stifle a scream.

The man rolled off Nachum, holding his bleeding nose. The ball was now in the detective's court. Despite the pain, he managed to elbow his attacker straight in the groin. The man doubled over, shrieking in agony. With a supreme effort, Nachum slowly pulled himself to his feet, leaning his weight on the right leg, and looked down at the man on the floor. He didn't have a clue who he was or where he'd come from. His head was throbbing and the pain in his knee and face was torture. He had to use his momentary advantage to get out of there as quickly as possible. The man was younger and stronger than he was. It wouldn't be long before he recovered and came at him again. Nachum had a family that loved him and relied on him. He had responsibilities. He couldn't afford to tempt fate. If he left now, he would get out alive. But his curiosity and obsession with the case got the better of him. Police work was in his blood. It had always been. After the accident in Netanya, Leah had made him swear he'd never risk his life like that again. He'd promised, and he'd kept his promise, maybe because he'd never had the opportunity to break it. But here he was, years later, face-to-face with a thug who would rip him apart as soon as he got his breath back, and he wasn't able to turn and run.

The man struggled vainly to stand up. The blow he'd received had been too painful and precise. Nachum struggled to take a few deep breaths despite the pain in his ribs. He had to be calm, to slow down, moderate the flow of adrenaline in his blood. That was the only way he could control the situation. At times like this, a cool head was no less important than physical strength.

"Who are you? What do you want with my son?" he asked. The last thing he needed was for the guy to know he'd just hit a cop. His gut told him the best way to get anything out of him was to let him go on believing he was who he thought he was, Nevo's dad.

The man muttered something incomprehensible. Nachum leaned over him. The stranger rolled toward him and hit him in the injured knee. Losing his balance, Nachum tumbled to the floor. The man raised his head and butted it into his chest. Nachum curled up, knowing he had lost the upper hand. Not wasting any time, his attacker rose to his feet with a grunt and got a stranglehold around Nachum's neck.

Nachum could feel himself losing consciousness. He'd be dead in a minute. "Where is he?" The voice seemed to be coming from very far away.

"I don't know," he mumbled.

The man's eyes gleamed in the darkness, black and threatening. The rage the detective saw in them was terrifying.

Suddenly, the man released his grip. Nachum drew in air, again and again, until his ribs shrieked in protest. He would have been a goner in another second. His eyes cleared.

"Tell him he better not forget what Meir said in Abu Kabir."

"Who?" Nachum asked, puzzled. Who was Meir?

Ignoring the question, the man walked to the door. Nachum followed him with his eyes as he turned back one last time, raised his leg, and kicked him in the stomach.

Chapter 36

AS soon as he got on the Ayalon Highway, which crossed through Tel Aviv, Ziv felt a sense of repulsion. The time he'd spent with Merav and Gili in the south, just the three of them cut off from the world, had been the best days of his life. There'd been good days before his life fell apart, but that was a long time ago, when he'd taken it for granted that the family he'd built would always be there. Maybe the elation he was feeling now stemmed from the realization that their happiness was temporary. He and Merav knew only too well that it wouldn't last forever, that real life was knocking on the door and they couldn't go on ignoring it much longer.

"I want things to go back to the way they were, like this, together, a family," he'd whispered in her ear before getting in the car and driving away from their private paradise. "Me too," she'd said with a smile. He was overcome by emotion.

He had to eliminate the threat to his family from Faro and his organization. He'd made so many mistakes, and hurt so many people along the way, that he didn't deserve a second chance. But he'd been given one anyway. He didn't intend to waste it.

He considered the possibility of simply calling Meshulam or Faro and telling them he didn't inform on them, that he'd kept his mouth shut. He ran because he panicked. That was the only reason. He had nothing to hide. You can see for yourself, he'd say. I've been out almost a week and nothing's happened. If I ratted you out, the cops would have done something already, right?

But the more he thought about it, the more he understood that he had to meet with them face-to-face. They had to be able to look him in the eye and see he was telling the truth, that he wasn't hiding anything. That was the only way to win their trust.

HE parked Merav's car outside his apartment and glanced at the clock on the dashboard. Three a.m. What was he doing? He hadn't planned on coming back to this rat hole. Only bad things had ever happened to him here.

But during the drive, an urge had taken hold of him and he couldn't get rid of it. It was like he was possessed. He had to find his wedding band and put it on again. It had taken him a long time to bring himself to take it off. He'd kept it on even after the divorce was final. But in view of the events of the past few days, it was time for it to be back on his finger where it belonged.

What if someone was waiting for him upstairs? Was he risking everything just to get the ring? He pushed open the door and got out of the car. This was crazy. He'd never been one for romantic gestures. But he felt powerless to stop himself. He had to put it on. The ring would give him strength. And even more important, if he didn't come back alive, Merav would know that he was wearing it when they found his body, that in his eyes they were husband and wife again, a family.

The familiar stench in the stairwell made him sick to his stomach. He detested this place. It was a symbol of the loneliness of his recent life. The last time he'd been here was the day he was arrested.

He took the stairs rapidly. Fritz barked as he passed. "Hey, Fritz," he called to the dog through the door of the first-floor apartment, not slowing down. As he stuck his key in the door, he was surprised to find it unlocked. I should've known, he thought. Why should the cops take the trouble to lock the door after they finished searching the place?

The odor of mildew added to his nausea. All the windows must be closed, the blinds drawn. Was that how he left it? He couldn't remember.

The light switch wasn't working. He went out to the hallway and flipped the safety switch in the fuse box. The lights in the apartment came on.

Heading back inside, he pulled up short in the doorway, his heart missing a beat. A man was lying on the floor, a red pool still forming around his head and a bloodstained bottle at his feet. For a second he thought he must be imagining it, that he was delusional from exhaustion and all the anxiety and pressure he'd been under. But it wasn't a mirage. The man lying on the floor of his apartment was Eli Nachum.

NACHUM opened his eyes and gazed at him in silence. Ziv remembered those eyes all too well. He remembered how they'd stared at him piercingly in the interrogation room, filling him with fear. Now he saw fear in the detective's eyes.

Wary, Ziv moved closer, unable to comprehend the sight before him.

"What happened? What are you doing here?" he fired at Nachum.

The detective didn't answer, merely emitted a gurgling sound. Ziv noticed his unofficial attire. What was going on? Was it some kind of trap? But why? And who had done this to the formidable cop?

He bent over him to be certain it was Nachum. His face was bruised and swollen, blood was trickling from his mouth, and his hands were wrapped around his knee. He lay curled up on the cold floor like a frightened child.

"What happened?" he asked again. "Who did this to you?"

"Water," Nachum muttered with a look of pleading in his eyes.

Ziv didn't move. He just stood there staring in amazement. He hated this man. He'd begged him to listen to him, to believe him when he said he didn't rape the girl, but he didn't want to hear it.

Nachum coughed, his face registering pain. Whoever had beaten him had made a good job of it. He might be bleeding internally. If he left him here closed up in a deserted apartment, he could die.

Nachum raised his head slightly as if he wanted to say something, but it fell back to the floor before he could get any words out. A shiver went down Ziv's spine. Was he trying to tell him something? Was there someone else in the apartment?

Ziv straightened up quickly and looked around. He didn't hear anything. He went into the bedroom and turned on the light. The room was empty, and so was the small bathroom. They were alone. At least that.

Going back into the living room, he looked down at Nachum. He was still lying in the same position he'd left him in.

"Water," he repeated weakly. His eyes closed.

What was he supposed to do now?

Shit, Ziv said to himself, pulling himself together. What's wrong with you? What are you doing standing here like a statue? The guy might be the devil incarnate, but you don't have to repay him in kind. You've been given a second chance to prove you're a better person. You can't leave him like this.

He ran into the kitchen and filled a glass with water. Wetting his fingers, he cleaned the blood off Nachum's mouth and then held the glass to his lips.

"Sip it slowly," he said. "Not all at once."

Nachum opened his eyes and nodded his gratitude.

"Who did this to you?" he asked once more when he saw Nachum looked a little stronger, but the detective remained silent. His eyes closed again. Ziv wasn't sure he wanted to know the answer.

It was no random chance that Nachum had been beaten to a pulp in his apartment. Did Faro's men do this? Did they know Nachum was a cop? He suddenly realized he might never be able to untangle himself from the web he was caught in.

Nachum coughed again. "I'm taking you to a hospital," Ziv said firmly. With a practiced movement, he heaved Nachum over his shoulders the way he'd been trained in the army to carry the wounded.

As he was leaving the apartment, he stopped and swung around. With Nachum on his shoulders, he went to the chest near the door and pulled out the drawer. There it was. He reached in, fished it out, and slipped it on his finger.

NACHUM gave him an odd look as he laid him on the backseat.

"Take . . . off . . . your . . . shirt," he said haltingly.

Ziv stared at him in bewilderment. Their faces were close together, nearly touching. Nachum's breathing was labored.

"Take . . . off . . . your . . . shirt," the detective repeated.

"Why?" This was no time for cryptic requests. He hadn't said who'd attacked him, what he was doing in his apartment. Why the hell did he want him to strip?

"I have to check something," Nachum said. "Trust me, it's important."

Ziv scanned the area. The street was empty. Without knowing why he was doing it, he pulled off his shirt, baring his chest for Nachum.

"Turn around."

Exhaling impatiently, he did as he was told.

"Happy now?" He felt stupid standing there half-naked, and even more stupid for letting himself be manipulated by Nachum again.

"I'm sorry," the detective said softly.

"For what?" Ziv asked as he put his shirt back on.

"I was wrong. You didn't rape Adi Regev."

He didn't know whether to laugh or cry. "About time," he said finally as he got behind the wheel.

"DON'T take me inside. Leave me by the gate," Nachum said when Ziv turned into the street that led to the Ichilov Hospital complex. He glanced at Nachum in the rearview mirror. He looked terrible. His face was as white as a sheet.

"You sure?"

"There was another rape. They're looking for you."

"What?" Ziv couldn't believe it. "Why me?"

Nachum shrugged his shoulders.

"Who's 'they'?" he asked angrily.

"They are the ones who threw me off the force," the detective answered before being consumed by a fit of coughing that shook his entire body.

Ziv froze. He'd come to Tel Aviv to set Faro straight, and suddenly he was a suspect in another rape? What the fuck was going on?

"I'll help you, I promise," Nachum said, interrupting his thoughts.

"You? How? You said you're not a cop anymore, right?"

"I'll find the guy who did it. I swear." He just managed to get the words out before his head fell back onto the seat.

As instructed, Ziv stopped at the hospital gate, dragged Nachum out of the car, and settled him on a bench. He hesitated for a moment before sitting down next to him.

"Somebody will come by in a minute and call for help. You've done enough. Go," Nachum said when he saw that Nevo was reluctant to leave him there. "Disappear again for a few more days. The cops are looking for you."

"How long? How will I know when it's safe to come back?" Ziv asked, stunned by the detective's advice.

Nachum managed a smile. "You'll read about it in the papers."

Someone was coming.

"Go. I'll be all right here."

"Who did this to you? What were you doing in my apartment?" Ziv asked, ignoring the approaching figure.

"I don't know. He thought you were my son. He said to tell you not to forget what Meir said in Abu Kabir."

Ziv felt his heart start to race. It was one of Faro's thugs. He was never going to forget what Meir said.

"Who was he?" Nachum asked.

Ziv said nothing.

"What kind of trouble are you in? Maybe I can help."

Ziv stood up.

"It has something to do with what you were doing on Louis Marshall Street that night, right?"

Ziv continued to remain silent. How could he trust the cop who'd made his life a living hell?

"Take care of yourself," Ziv said as he turned to leave.

Chapter 37

DAVID Meshulam was ushered quickly through the border crossing at Shaar Ephraim, passing from Israel within the Green Line, where law and order reigned, to the West Bank, or what Faro liked to call the "Wild West." He should have left the minute Faro was picked up. He was familiar with the emergency plan: if anything goes wrong, hook up immediately with George's crew in Shufa.

But even though he knew he should get in the car and disappear, he couldn't leave everything behind and run like a rabbit. It was probably all his fault anyway. He wanted to get it off his chest, to admit to Faro what he'd done, but every time he tried, he couldn't get the words out. He couldn't stand the thought of seeing the disappointment on the face of the man he owed his life to. And now even if he wanted to come clean, who would he tell? The cops had Faro, and there was no one else he could trust.

He couldn't get his head around the arrest. Everything pointed to Nevo. Faro was hauled in after Nevo was released, Nevo ran, and, to top it off, the car with the bomb had vanished into thin air. Nevo's wife and kid were missing too.

But—and it was a very big but—if Nevo had talked, what was all the bullshit about another rape? He read the stories in the paper. Every fucking cop in the country was looking for him. Maybe it was just a smoke screen so Faro wouldn't know he ratted him out. Even the asshole cops weren't stupid enough to pin two rapes on a nerd like Nevo.

The whole thing was too confusing, too complicated, way above his pay grade. But what choice did he have? Faro wasn't there, so he had to rely on himself to make sense of all this shit. He decided his best move was to hide out in Nevo's apartment. Making his way over the rooftops, he slipped in without being seen. He figured sooner or later Nevo would have to come back for his stuff, or send someone else to get it. He'd left everything behind when he ran. The cops didn't scare him. It didn't seem very likely they'd put a watch on the place. Faro always told them to take advantage of the tight budget the police had to work with. Worse comes to worst, if he caught sight of a cop he'd take off.

He'd spent two nights there, and then yesterday, Nevo's old man showed up. At least he thought he was his old man. He couldn't even be sure of that anymore. He'd shown the old geezer no mercy, but he hadn't given up easy, and Meshulam had a bloody jaw and a broken nose to prove it. And despite the hammering he'd taken, he hadn't volunteered any information about Nevo.

He'd keep looking, but for now his busted face would attract too much attention. He had to get out of there for a couple of days until things quieted down. Then he'd go after him again. In the meantime, he'd be safe with George. The cops couldn't touch him there.

He sped down the winding road. He wasn't ready to give up yet. It was just a minor delay. It'd work out in the end. He'd find Nevo and get him to spill his guts. After that, who knows what might happen.

Chapter 38

ZIV was terrified. All of a sudden he was the target of a double man-hunt. Both the cops and the mob were looking for him.

Despair almost got the better of him. He didn't have the street smarts to deal with this shit. He ran through possible scenarios in his mind but was paralyzed to make a decision. Every scheme led to a dead end. How was he supposed to decide between different shades of disaster?

His first thought was to take Nachum's advice and disappear for a few more days. He'd go back to Gili and Merav and go on pretending nothing was wrong, just ignore the world and everything that was happening around them. But as soon as he got on the road heading south, doubt began gnawing at him. He filled the tank and then parked at the edge of the gas station. Was he making a mistake? Running away again would make the bad guys more convinced than ever that he'd informed on them. And eventually he'd have to come back and face reality.

He felt unbearably lonely and powerless, like a tiny pawn in a game between two titans. Why the hell were Faro's guys still after him? He'd been out long enough for them to see he hadn't betrayed them. If he'd told the cops what he was doing that night, they would have picked up Faro and Meshulam by now, and they certainly wouldn't be accusing him of another rape. Why was the mob still looking for him when he was wanted in connection with the second rape?

Given the circumstances, he was less anxious about the cops. He was shocked to hear they suspected him of another rape, but he could deal with that. Merav would testify that he was hundreds of miles from Tel Aviv when it happened. Even if they didn't believe her—and there were no other corroborating witnesses—the worst they could do was throw him in jail. At this point, that seemed the safest option.

Faro's organization was still his biggest problem. There were no lines they wouldn't cross. They wouldn't hesitate to hurt him or Gili. Nachum's attacker said to tell him not to forget what Meir said in Abu Kabir. The words sent a shiver down his spine.

Feeling stifled, he cracked the window to let in the cold air. He debated going to the police and telling them what he knew about Faro in return for protection for his family and him. But how could they protect them? He'd have to keep looking over his shoulder for the rest of his life. Faro wouldn't give up. You never got free of guys like him. What kind of life would they have? He'd be condemning Gili and Merav to living on the run.

A huge semi behind him honked, startling him. He turned the key in the ignition and got back on the road.

He had to talk to Faro. If he sat down with him face-to-face and told him he hadn't given him up, he'd see in his eyes that he was telling the truth. He had to. Meshulam was no more than a thug, but not Faro. He was a clever guy. Ziv was sure he could convince him. That's why he'd gone back to the city in the first place.

But what if it didn't go the way he hoped? The image of Nachum's bloody face and battered body floated up before his eyes. That's what he'd look like, assuming Faro decided to let him live. If he hadn't shown up in time, Nachum would be dead. Who would save *him* if his plan didn't work?

Before leaving for Tel Aviv, Ziv had written a letter detailing everything, had put it in a sealed envelope, and had given it to Merav for safekeeping. He wasn't sure he was doing the right thing. After all, the less she knew, the better. The letter could put her at risk, make her a target too. But it was also his insurance policy if his plan didn't work. "Don't open it unless I don't come back and you and Gili are in danger. Only if you have no other choice," he said as he handed it to her. She'd promised. If he told Faro about the letter, it might give him some leverage. Of course he'd never tell him where it was, just that it existed and that the cops would get it if anything happened to him.

For the second time that day, he saw the skyline of Tel Aviv in the distance.

Once, at one of their fancy picnics at Orit's house before his world collapsed, he'd said he'd give his life for Gili. They weren't just words. He really meant it. But still, it was the sort of thing parents say. It's easy to mean it when there's no danger in sight, when you can't imagine you'll ever actually have to do it.

"ZIV?" Noam sounded very surprised to hear his voice.

He'd thought long and hard about the best way to make contact with Faro. He considered calling him directly, but he'd never called him before for any reason whatsoever. He was afraid it would be regarded as presumptuous, as if he weren't showing Faro the proper respect, and he certainly didn't want to piss him off any more than he already was. He was scared to call Meshulam. In the end, he decided to go through Noam. Despite everything that had happened, he might still have some credit with Noam in view of their history. He'd been his commander way back when, and Noam had gotten him the job with Faro. And he wasn't actually part of the organization, just Faro's nephew. He'd dialed the number a dozen times that day, but Noam's phone was switched off. It was eleven at night by the time he reached him.

"Where are you?" Noam asked.

"Listen, I need a favor," Ziv said, getting the words out quickly before he changed his mind. "I have to talk to your uncle . . . as soon as possible."

"You kidding, Nevo, or what? Are you nuts?" There was an unfamiliar harshness in Noam's voice.

"I swear by everything I hold dear, I didn't do anything, Noam. They've got no reason to come after me. I didn't do anything. I've got to talk to your uncle."

No response.

"Five minutes, that's all I need. Just to explain. I don't know what to do. I need your help."

"Where are you?" Noam asked again.

"Here, in Tel Aviv. Tell me where to go and I'll be there. Five minutes, that's all I'm asking for."

"Let me check with a few people and I'll get back to you," Noam said, hanging up.

Ziv got out of the car and paced back and forth, his cell phone in his hand. Had he made the right decision? Maybe Faro wouldn't want to hear what he had to say. Maybe he'd just give the order to kill him.

His phone rang.

"I talked to them," Noam said. "Wait at the top of the Ayalon North ramp at the Halacha exit. Someone will be by shortly to pick you up."

Chapter 39

NACHUM moved slowly, flinching with pain at every step. The doctor had told him to stay in bed and not put any weight on the leg. He'd nodded and promised Leah to do as he was told. But the second she left the room he was out of bed, leaning on crutches and keeping out of sight of the ward nurses. The thought that she was lying in a bed only two floors above him gave him no peace.

He couldn't remember how many times they'd told him how lucky he was, that, considering the beating he'd taken, his injuries weren't too severe. Still, his whole body hurt, especially the left knee and the ribs. At the slightest incautious movement, he could almost feel his broken bones rubbing up against each other.

As he tottered, panting, along the empty corridors, stopping from time to time to rest, he kept hoping they'd be there, that this trek, which would take a healthy person five minutes and was taking him half an hour, was not in vain. He breathed a sigh of relief, insofar as his broken ribs allowed, when he saw him sitting in the waiting room, staring sightlessly at the TV screen on the wall. He was afraid he might not recognize him, but he identified Michael Aronov immediately. The resemblance between Dana and her father was striking.

NACHUM had had a flood of visitors all day. Everybody wanted to know what happened to him, but he told no one. Even when he was alone with his wife, he refused to answer her endless questions. He'd decided to keep it to himself for the time being. He even declined to cooperate with the local cops who came to question him after they were notified by the hospital of a possible crime.

Had he made the right choice? If he shared the information he'd gotten from Sarah Glazer about the tattoo on the man's arm, and the fact that Nevo didn't have one, Nevo wouldn't be their prime suspect anymore. They could stop concentrating all their efforts on looking for the wrong man and start focusing on finding the true rapist.

There'd been a few times during the day when he'd almost dialed Ohad's number, but he'd never made the call. He'd been part of the system long enough to know it wouldn't make any difference. They'd convinced themselves that Nevo was the perp, and they were trapped in that mind-set. It all fit: the similarity between the two attacks, the fact that Nevo had already been convicted and had only gotten off because of a technicality. At this point, admitting that he didn't do the crimes meant admitting they'd been wrong from the outset, that they'd helped convict an innocent man.

He couldn't really blame them. He'd just now arrived at that conclusion himself, while he was on suspension. It didn't mean he wouldn't have gotten there if he was still carrying a badge. But when you're on the force, the considerations are different, the thinking is different. It's easy to join in the consensus, to go with the flow. Much easier than taking an unpopular stance and expressing doubts. One guy says something, another seconds it, and then two more add their voices to the choir and they all make perfect harmony. Even if the fifth guy down the line thinks differently and decides to say so, who's going to listen?

If he gave them the information, chances are they wouldn't give it the proper weight. They'd probably focus on the facts of secondary importance: How come he was conducting a private investigation? Where did he meet with Nevo? Why did he let him get away?

NACHUM lowered himself onto a chair in the waiting room. The sharp pain in his side forced a groan out of him. Michael Aronov took his eyes from the TV screen and looked at him suspiciously. There were only five other people in the room, leaving plenty of empty seats farther away that he could've chosen. He imagined his battered face wasn't a pretty sight either.

He watched Michael Aronov in silence. Part of a detective's job description is knowing how to cope with the tragedies he encounters on a daily basis, how to steel himself to the pain and focus on the investigation. He'd sat opposite parents like the Aronovs too many times to count. But this time he felt ill at ease because he wasn't officially a policeman. He was conducting an independent investigation. But he couldn't stop himself, couldn't ignore the connections between the Adi Regev case and the rape of Dana Aronov. Like the ring, for instance. The more he found out, the closer he'd come to the rapist.

He saw Aronov's leg twitching and the pack of cigarettes in his shirt pocket. The only way he'd have any chance of drawing him out and getting him to tell him what happened to his daughter would be to take him somewhere private. And he couldn't reveal his identity. After all, if it weren't for his own mistakes, they might have caught the real perp in time and prevented the attack on Dana.

He glanced again at the cigarettes making a bulge in Aronov's pocket. He hadn't smoked in twenty years.

"Can I buy a cigarette? The pain is killing me," he said, nodding to the small balcony outside.

Aronov held out the pack without looking at him.

"Would you mind helping me get the door open?"

Aronov stood up.

NACHUM watched him walk back inside. In a minute, he'd get up and start the trek back to the ward.

It hadn't been easy, but in the end he'd managed to get Dana's father to open up. He wasn't sure what triggered it. It could be that he mentioned his own daughter, or that he groaned about his pain and the man took pity on him, or that, having grown up in the USSR, Aronov felt more comfortable talking to a stranger than to anyone in uniform. Maybe it was simply boredom, a way to pass the time or ease the hurt a little. And it could have been all those things together.

He didn't have much to say. He and his wife lived and worked in Beersheba, remote from their daughter's life in Tel Aviv. The police called to inform him of what happened to Dana. He was at work, in the bank, when they got the horrendous news. She was unconscious when they found her, and she'd been that way ever since. The doctors couldn't say when she'd wake up, or if she ever would. His wife had gone to Dana's apartment to get a few hours' sleep. She'd be back soon and then it would be his turn to get some rest.

Dana was a receptionist in the Weizmann Fitness Center, right near the hospital. She didn't tell him a lot about her life in the city. As far as he knew, she didn't have a boyfriend. She was closer to her mother, but she didn't know about anyone in particular her daughter was seeing either. They had no idea who could have done it. That's what they told the police, and the two reporters who came to pester them too.

Nevertheless, Nachum's excruciating journey from the ward might not have been wasted. Aronov told him that before she got the job at the gym, Dana had worked as a waitress at the Zodiac Café, a popular local coffee shop. As a rule, he wouldn't give much weight to her previous place of employment, but he'd heard that name before. Yaron Regev told him that Adi spent a lot of time there. Nachum had even questioned the servers about anyone matching the description Adi had given of her attacker, but nothing came of it. "A lot of people who come here match that description," he was told.

This might be the connection he was looking for. Dana was in a coma and couldn't provide any further details about the rapist, but now that he had a clearer picture of his personality, the questions put to the servers could be more focused.

He stood up, biting down on his lip to stifle the yelp of pain. He'd call Ohad tomorrow and tell him what he'd found out. If he could, he'd continue the investigation on his own. But for the time being, that was impossible, considering the shape he was in. Anyway, the cops had more resources.

He made his way tortuously through the empty corridors smelling of illness and pain. Yes, he'd call Ohad tomorrow and tell him everything. Or would he?

Chapter 40

ZIV was about to give up hope. He'd been waiting at the top of the highway ramp for half an hour, and no one had showed up. A few cars slowed down, but none of them stopped. Why didn't they come? Whoever "they" were.

The cold of the early December night reached down to his bones. He shifted his weight from foot to foot in an effort to keep warm. Then a squad car came by and he turned his back to the road. The last thing he needed now was to be picked up again for a rape he didn't commit and miss his meeting with Faro.

When he saw the silver Land Rover slowing down around the curve, he figured it was another false alarm. But he was wrong. The car pulled up beside him, the front door was thrown open, and a man he didn't recognize ordered him to get in. He spoke with an Arabic accent.

This time, the man in the back wasn't Meshulam. Ziv's relief was nipped in the bud when he heard the click of the doors locking. There was no chance he'd be able to get away again. There was no trick he could pull that would get him out of here.

A shiver went through him when he saw they were on the road to Shaar Ephraim. Why the hell were they taking him to the West Bank?

He hoped the soldier at the border crossing would order them to stop, or at least ask where they were going, but he just gave them a bored look and waved them through. He didn't seem to care why an Israeli car was heading to a place no more than spitting distance from Tulkarem at one thirty in the morning. He looked at the winding road up ahead. At this time of night, it was totally deserted. This wasn't the first time he'd been here. He'd passed through the same border crossing dozens of times as a soldier. But then he'd been traveling in an armored military jeep and carrying a weapon, not riding unarmed and unprotected in a civilian car, being transported to an unknown destination. Back then he thought he was invincible, that the difference between wishing for something and making it happen was only a matter of believing in yourself. What a naive fool he'd been.

A car was coming toward them at high speed, its headlights blinding him. He knew that what he was doing was crazy, but what choice did he have? What other course of action could he take? If he didn't do what they wanted, they'd hurt Gili. The only way to get them off his back was to convince them he hadn't informed on them to the cops, that the fact they were looking to charge him with another rape was proof enough he hadn't said anything.

A car appeared behind them, sitting on their tail. The driver leaned on the horn. Was he going to end up getting killed in a car crash? He turned to look at the man beside him, but he kept his eyes focused indifferently straight ahead, apparently unconcerned by the car no more than a couple of yards back.

All of a sudden, the second car sped up and passed them, disappearing around the next bend in the road. Ziv peered out the window. All he saw was darkness. What would he do if they ordered him out of the car here in the middle of nowhere? Or worse, they could order him to get out and then shoot him, leaving his dead body by the side of the road. Maybe that's what Faro wanted, to stage his death to look like the work of terrorists.

They passed a sign showing the distance to Shufa, Safarin, and Beit Lid. Not far beyond was the settlement Einav. Where were they taking him? The sound of a ringtone made him jump. The driver answered, speaking rapidly in Arabic. After disconnecting the call, he said a few words to the man in the back, and Ziv saw him nod in response through the rearview mirror.

Another car appeared close behind them, blinking its lights. The driver slowed and stopped on the side of the road. The second car passed them and pulled up in front. It was a Subaru van. Clearly, the operation had been mapped out very carefully. Nothing was being left to chance.

"Get out," the driver commanded. Ziv heard the sound of the doors unlocking.

He stepped outside, his body trembling from fear and cold. This was his last opportunity to change his mind. He wouldn't get another one. He might still be able to make a run for it and try to lose them in the darkness. Why was he doing this? Why the fuck was he sticking his head in the lion's mouth?

He knew why. He had no choice. He'd been over it a million times in his head and each time he reached the same conclusion.

Taking a deep breath, he strode quickly toward the van. The back door was open, a sign for him to get in.

Chapter 41

MESHULAM figured he must be hearing things when he thought he recognized Nevo's name in a phone conversation one of George's guys was conducting in Arabic. Impossible. What did they know about Nevo?

He hadn't been here long, but he was already climbing the walls. He was forced to sit like a prisoner in a tiny room in a godforsaken village in the middle of the West Bank, surrounded by Arabs. In an endless cycle, he paced back and forth, sat down on the bed, got up, and paced again. He didn't have a moment of peace. The idea that he was responsible for Faro being under arrest was driving him crazy. The worst part was that there was nothing he could do about it.

The man was still talking on the phone. Meshulam lay down on the bed. It was late. Maybe he could get some sleep. At least it would be a way to pass the time. Tomorrow or the next day he'd go back and resume the search for Nevo. He was closing his eyes when he heard Nevo's name again. What was wrong with him? When did he start hearing voices? Was the hunt for Nevo fucking with his brain?

He got up and opened the door. Samir, at least he thought that was his name, stopped in midsentence and stared at him, the phone still pressed to his ear. The two organizations had an efficient working relationship, what Faro liked to call "synergy." George brought the drugs in from Lebanon to the West Bank, and Faro sold them in Israel.

Meshulam motioned for him to ignore him. He wanted to be sure he'd heard right, that he hadn't imagined it. But Samir was obviously surprised to see him there, probably thinking he was asleep. He ended his conversation with an abrupt "yalla."

"Who were you talking about?" Meshulam asked.

Samir didn't answer. To be honest, he hadn't expected an answer. He knew very well that wasn't the sort of question he was allowed to ask.

"Did I hear you mention Ziv Nevo?" He had to know.

Samir turned his back and walked away in silence.

Meshulam knew he shouldn't be doing this, that he was taking a big risk, but he couldn't stop himself. He called the attorney, Shuki Borochov, to try to find out why George's people were talking about Nevo. If anyone knew the answer, it would be Borochov.

"You won't believe it," Borochov said when Meshulam made the call from a public phone half an hour later. The tense wait for an opportunity to slip away almost drove him out of his mind. "All the cops in the country are looking for the stupid motherfucker, and out of the blue he contacts Noam and says he wants to talk to Faro."

"Faro? What about?" Meshulam asked, stunned. Why would Nevo want to talk to Faro? Did he know the bomb was his idea?

"The asshole didn't even know that Faro was arrested." Borochov laughed maliciously.

"What did he want to talk to him about?" Meshulam asked, cutting off the lawyer's hearty laughter.

"Noam says the guy's clueless. Nevo told him he's innocent, he didn't rape anyone, he needs help."

"What kind of help?" Meshulam was still having a hard time making sense of it all.

"Maybe he needs money, an attorney, you know, help. What difference does it make what he wants? Noam's got a brain in his head. He called me right away, and I did the math," the lawyer said, sounding very pleased with himself.

"What do you mean?" Meshulam couldn't stand the way Borochov was always patting himself on the back.

"We can use the idiot to negotiate with the cops. He gives us leverage. They're dying to get their hands on him."

"So he's coming here?" Meshulam was beginning to understand.

"You got it. It's a good thing you're there. A real stroke of luck. You keep an eye on him. Faro needs him. He could be his ticket out."

Chapter 42

NACHUM was lying on his side on the lumpy hospital bed, gazing out the window at the city below. Despite the splendid view of the low-rise buildings crowded together in the foreground and the blue sea beyond, he was anxious and restless. For the twenty years he'd been a cop, no one had ever questioned his loyalty. He'd always seen himself as a company man. Although he himself was critical of certain procedures, he'd steadfastly defended the force whenever it was attacked, emphasizing the good work they did that never made it into the papers and proudly wearing the shield. And now he of all people was about to do something that could only be defined as the exact opposite of loyalty.

He stared in frustration at his bandaged knee. If only he could, he'd go it alone. But that wasn't possible. He needed help. All morning he'd debated whether or not to make the call. He still wasn't sure he was doing the right thing.

Yes, he could call Ohad and tell him what he'd found out. But the simple truth was, he didn't want to. This was his investigation, and he intended to see it through. He'd show Ohad and Navon and all the other backstabbers in the precinct that he wasn't dead yet. He could still do his job. They didn't deserve to have the fruits of his labor fall into their lap so easily. His ribs were aching, impelling him to change position. Besides, it was his mistake and his responsibility to fix it. Being on suspension made it that much harder for him. He didn't have any authority or the resources of the system to rely on. But it also helped him see things from a fresh perspective, without any vested interest. He wouldn't get in the cops' way, but he wouldn't give them a leg up either. We'll see who gets to the finish line first, he thought.

There was a soft rapping on the door. He turned his head quickly, flinching from the pain.

Before he could say, "Come in," Amit Giladi walked through the door and stood by the bed, shocked at the sight of his battered face.

"What happened to you?" he asked incredulously.

THE last time they'd met had been in his office, when he'd tried to convince Giladi that the Regev case was still a high priority and they were making every effort to find the rapist. The reporter had been skeptical. His questions were pointed and snide, and he'd refused to accept his explanations. There was something disconcerting about Giladi. A pale, skinny guy, he looked harmless and insubstantial, but when Nachum tried to brush him off with vague answers, he proved to be very determined.

Other reporters tried to ingratiate themselves with him in the hope of gaining his cooperation, but Giladi never made an effort to be likable. He asked probing questions with dogged persistence. Nachum despised him as much as he despised every other journalist he'd ever come into contact with, but he had to admire this quality in him. In a way, he reminded him of himself.

"I've got a proposition for you," Nachum said, gesturing to the bright orange plastic chair by his bed.

Amit didn't take him up on the invitation to sit. He just stood where he was, staring at Nachum, waiting for the answer to his question. The detective had no intention of satisfying his curiosity.

"I want you to help me catch the north Tel Aviv rapist," he said quietly.

Giladi looked at him in surprise. "You mean Ziv Nevo?" he asked.

"No," Eli said, shaking his head. A wave a pain shot through his jaw. "The real sonofabitch."

The reporter listened in silence as Nachum expounded on his theory of the rapist's personality. He debated whether to tell him about Mrs. Glazer and the tattoo she'd seen or about the rings taken from the two victims but decided to keep the information to himself for the time being. He'd share those facts with Giladi if he showed himself to be reliable. And it was a good idea to hold on to a few things he could use later as incentives to keep the reporter going if their independent investigation got bogged down, as investigations often did.

"Why are you telling me this? What do you want from me?" Amit asked when Nachum was done.

The plan had taken shape in his mind last night after he talked with Michael Aronov. Since he was incapacitated, he needed someone else to be his eyes, legs, and mouth. Amit Giladi was the most viable option on the meager list of candidates for the job. Besides, even if he didn't like to admit it, there was a certain similarity between the work of the cops and the press, particularly when it came to investigative reporters.

"I'll tell you what to do. Together, we can solve this case. It needs a fresh pair of eyes. And with your energy and hunger for a scoop, the role fits you like a glove."

Unexpectedly, Giladi didn't jump at the opportunity. He seemed reluctant to take him up on his offer. When Nachum had envisioned how this conversation would go, he'd anticipated questions and objections, but also excitement and eagerness to collaborate with him. He was giving Giladi the chance to get in on a major case, to do something that would culminate in an unprecedented scoop, as well as another occasion to embarrass the police and show up their incompetence.

"What's the problem?" he asked, leaning toward the reporter to create a greater sense of intimacy between them, even though the slightest movement was agony.

Giladi passed his finger lightly over his upper lip and remained silent.

"I understand it's an unusual proposition," Nachum said, looking him in the eye, "and I can imagine what you're thinking—'I'm a reporter, not a cop. I don't have the time or resources to spend months investigating a rape.' But listen, Giladi, I'll be guiding you the whole way. And there are some concrete actions we can take. If they pan out, we'll catch the creep much sooner than you think."

"Like what?" Nachum was happy to see he was finally showing interest.

"Like the Zodiac Café," he said, telling him about the lead he'd gotten from Aronov.

"So you're suggesting I plant myself there for hours, maybe days or weeks, waiting for Mr. Rapist to show up? And then what? How am I supposed to know it's him, and what am I supposed to do about it?" Nachum couldn't tell if it was mockery or disappointment he detected in his voice.

"I'm suggesting we work out a plan. There are things I can teach you that'll make it easier." He couldn't give up now. Some people couldn't see the positive until you cleared away all the negative.

"What about the cops?" Giladi cut in.

"The cops need time to rethink their initial concept. They'll get there eventually, but it'll take a while, and that's time we can't waste."

"Do you know where Nevo is?" Giladi asked abruptly.

"No," Nachum answered firmly. "I have no idea."

The reporter gave him a skeptical look.

"Honestly, I don't know," he repeated, keeping his voice calm and steady. "But it doesn't matter. He didn't do it."

"What happened to you?" Giladi asked again, gesturing toward Nachum's battered body.

"That doesn't matter either. It has nothing to do with the case," he said, earning another skeptical look from the reporter. He was annoyed that Giladi was focusing on side issues and not the big picture.

"I'm offering you the chance of a lifetime," he went on, not letting up. "If it works, you'll get the credit, the recognition. The Sokolov Prize, that's what they give outstanding journalists, right?"

"I'll make a deal with you, Nachum," Giladi said after a short pause. "I'll quit asking you about the beating you got if you give me another tip about the case. Something no one else knows."

"I think I've already given you quite a lot." Giladi's cockiness was getting on his nerves.

"That's the deal. Take it or leave it."

Nachum looked at him in frustration, wondering what he was thinking when he chose Giladi to be the partner who would help him crack the case. He didn't really know anything about him. But then again, he didn't have many options, did he? He could barely move.

Beggars can't be choosers, he thought to himself. If he wanted Giladi's cooperation, he'd have to let him in on what he knew, he'd have to trust him.

"The rapist takes a ring," he said finally, telling him about the connection between the Regev and Aronov cases.

Giladi remained silent. Nachum had decided that was all he was going to get. If that wasn't enough to persuade him, he'd give up.

Giladi rose.

"I'm in, Nachum. I have to get my editor's approval, but I'm in," he said, reaching out to shake the detective's hand.

NACHUM lay in bed replaying the conversation in his head. Something was needling him, something in Giladi's smile, in the fact that he was so anxious to leave. Something seemed off, despite the reporter's promise to return as soon as he got approval from his editor.

Chapter 43

GILADI was sitting in a coffee shop near the hospital gazing at the egg sandwich in front of him. He felt hungry when he ordered it, but he couldn't eat. His conversation with Nachum had thrown him for a loop.

He'd never dreamed that was why Nachum wanted to talk to him. He'd almost ignored his call. The old cop couldn't have anything worthwhile to tell him after he'd been so unceremoniously kicked off the case. He thanked his lucky stars that he'd finally decided to go see him.

He stuck his hand in his pocket to confirm that the recorder was still there. He'd been afraid Nachum would check to be sure he wasn't being taped, but he hadn't even asked. In his eagerness to share what he'd found out, to rope someone else into his investigation, to find a partner who'd agree to work with him, he hadn't taken the most basic precautions.

Nachum's proposition was tempting. Under other circumstances, Amit would grab it with both hands. But he'd learned his lesson from "Deep Throat." If he'd run with the story right away and hadn't insisted on proof, it would've been his byline on the scoop, not Amir Hasner's.

He had no intention of playing cops and robbers with Nachum. He didn't have the time to play detective. He had to strike while the iron was hot. Nachum had given him enough for a big story: former detective accuses police of ignoring leads, framing an innocent man, proceeding on mistaken assumptions while the true rapist was still at large, endangering the public. It was a shame he couldn't get him to reveal who worked him over.

In a way, he felt sorry for Nachum. There was no doubt in Giladi's mind that he genuinely wanted to catch the criminal, and believed he could do it too. He wasn't entirely comfortable with what he was about to do. But like Dori said, that's life and that's the job. And he'd promised himself he'd keep his feelings out of it from now on.

Having made his decision, his appetite returned. He wolfed down the sandwich and leaned back in his chair. There was a pile of newspapers on the table in front of him. The headlines were filled with the prime minister's official visit to the United States, the drought, Shimon Faro's arrest. The north Tel Aviv rapist was old news.

Never mind, he thought. He'd be back in the headlines very soon. On Thursday the national press would carry an ad about his scoop, and on Friday it would be on the front page of his paper.

He pulled out his cell phone and punched in the number.

Dori would be over the moon. He might even start treating him better, appreciating him more. And maybe that didn't matter, because after the story appeared, the national papers would be calling him and he could say good-bye to the local rag.

"What's up, Giladi?" Dori barked as usual.

And then it came to him. He didn't just have a story, he had a name too: The Ring Rapist.

Chapter 44

SUPERINTENDENT Navon thought he was about to have a heart attack. He'd just gotten off the phone with the district spokesperson. He'd been asked to comment on Eli Nachum's accusations regarding the investigation of the rapes in north Tel Aviv. The story would be in the paper tomorrow.

He leaned forward and buried his face in his hands. The bombshell had landed on him just after he got back from a very pleasant lunch. Now he could feel it stuck in his gullet like an elephant. Tomorrow he would be the laughingstock of the entire country and, even worse, the entire police force.

Navon got up and paced his office restlessly. He remembered what his late father always used to say: "Those who ravaged and ruined you shall leave you." He once heard someone explain that the biblical phrase was originally meant to be comforting and had been turned on its head in popular usage, but what difference did that make?

How could Nachum do this to him?

He considered ordering his arrest. Nothing was stopping him. By talking to the reporter, Nachum had given him legal grounds to charge him with obstruction of justice. But despite his rage, he backed down from the idea. The conflagration that would erupt tomorrow would be hot enough without adding fuel to the fire and turning Nachum into a martyr. He could already see the headlines: "Police Arrest Honest Cop Who Blew the Whistle on Their Incompetence." Even if his arrest was thoroughly justified, it would be the stupidest thing he could do at this stage.

Never mind. Nachum would get what he deserved. The interview he gave spelled the end of his career on the force. With the rape investigation going nowhere, Navon had been weighing the possibility of bringing him back in to take over the case again. There was no way that was going to happen now. After what he'd done, Nachum would pay in blood for every drop of sweat that fell from Navon's brow. He could kiss the job good-bye. They wouldn't even take him back in logistics, the hole he'd crawled out of, not even if he saved a whole planeload of passengers.

Navon went back to his desk and sat down. He picked up the phone and told his assistant to get him Ohad Barel, ASAP.

Why didn't he see it coming? He knew Nachum resented his suspension. He should have expected him to try to get revenge. And it wasn't unusual for losers who got canned to air their dirty laundry in the press. When Navon was new on the job, he accepted the fact that he was nothing more than a peon. But the higher he climbed on the ladder, the more he realized that nothing had changed. Here he was, a superintendent, and he was still just a pawn in the game the chief was playing by arresting Faro. He was a pawn in Nachum's game too.

The phone rang. "Ohad's on the line," his assistant said.

The only way to extinguish the blaze that would burst out tomorrow when the paper hit the stands was to catch Ziv Nevo. The fact that his prime suspect had fled and they hadn't managed to track him down was an embarrassment.

Besides, when it came down to it, he didn't understand what Nachum was going on about in the interview. The claim that Nevo didn't fit the psychological profile of a rapist sounded like bullshit to him. The guy confessed to the first rape, and two days after he was released he did it again. The two attacks were almost identical. Add to that the fact that he'd run. There was no doubt the creep had something to hide. As soon as they caught him, Navon would roll up his sleeves and show the numbskulls how to conduct an interrogation. He gave Nevo two hours at most before he confessed to the second rape too. Then he'd shove it up Nachum's ass.

"You wanted to talk to me?" Ohad asked.

"You've got twenty-four hours to bring Nevo in," Navon said, not wasting words. "I don't care how you do it, I want to see him here!"

Chapter 45

AMIT was in no hurry to get out of bed. He tossed from side to side staring idly at the ceiling. He had no reason to get up. He'd called Dori excitedly and given him the details of the amazing scoop he'd gotten from Nachum, but the editor had thrown cold water on his plans. Unbelievably, he preferred Nachum's suggestion, that he collaborate in his private investigation.

"You wanted to be an investigative reporter, didn't you?" he said mockingly.

Amit did his best to convince him they had to run the story now, that it couldn't wait, but Dori was adamant. He claimed it was better to hold on to what they already knew and use it to get an even bigger story: revealing the identity of the true rapist and showing up the cops.

"Think big, Giladi, and you'll be big," he'd pronounced condescendingly.

Amit had crawled back to the hospital with his tail between his legs to get detective lessons from Nachum. The instructions he was given just blackened his mood even more. He had to question the employees of the coffee shop about a tall, thin man who frequented the place, usually alone, but sometimes with a girl, a different one each time. "It's hard to imagine it's one of the servers or kitchen workers, but you have to check them out too," Nachum said.

"Why should they tell me anything?" Amit asked.

"Why do people talk to you when you're covering a story?" Nachum threw the question back at him, making it clear he had no intention of going easy on him, especially not now when he had his editor's blessing for their partnership. Great. Now he had two bosses, one worse than the other.

He'd spent yesterday in the busy coffee shop, examining every man who came in, ingratiating himself with the servers so when the time came and he asked them about a "tall, thin man," they wouldn't give him a strange look and walk away. After several useless hours, he'd decided to go home. He'd had enough. There was just so far you could push him. Tomorrow he'd try to draw out Tamar. She'd been especially friendly, and he'd left her a tip that was almost double the check.

For a minute he thought Nachum had him under surveillance. As soon as he got on his bike, the detective called for a report. "Zilch, nada, that's what I got," he said, irritated. Nachum ignored his tone and gave him more instructions. Talk to people at the neighborhood convenience stores, hair salons, gyms, parks. The cops knew about Adi Regev and Dana Aronov, but there might be more victims. Lots of rapes were never reported. The women were too scared or ashamed, or they didn't want to go through the painful process that followed on an official complaint. But sometimes they told their girlfriends or their family, or called a rape crisis center. Moreover, the guy they were looking for was violent and used a knife. Amit might be able to identify other victims by the scars or bruises on their body. They could tell the story, even if the women themselves had kept it secret.

"Why didn't you do all that when you were still on the case?" Amit asked petulantly.

"I made a lot of mistakes. Now I have to fix them."

Amit debated calling Dori to complain that Nachum was running him ragged, but he thought better of it. Dori would only insult him again and call him a spoiled brat. He'd follow Nachum's directions for a few days, until the editor saw for himself that they weren't getting anywhere and he was neglecting other stories, and then Dori would draw his own conclusions.

"Nothing. Wasted day. Coffee shop receipts for 127 shekels. Will try again tomorrow," he texted Dori.

"Nachum can pay for your fucking coffee, asshole," Dori texted back an instant later.

Finally, when he was sick of lying in bed, he got up and left the house for another day of "work," courtesy of Dori and Nachum. The moment he entered the coffee shop, he sensed that something was wrong. It had been crowded yesterday, but today it was nearly empty. What's more, the few customers who were there were all male. Even the waitresses were gone. He looked around for Tamar. She'd said she'd be here this morning, but he didn't see her.

He took a stool at the counter and ordered a cappuccino.

"What's going on?" he asked the barista who'd been racing to keep up with the orders yesterday and was now bent over a newspaper.

The man looked at him as if he were an alien from outer space.

"Terror attack?" Amit asked, tentatively.

"Something like that." The barista pushed the paper under his nose and pointed to a headline reading "Zodiac Rapist at Large." The name in the byline was none other than Dori Engel.

He picked up on the first ring. No surprise there. The man had no scruples.

He wanted to go to the office and confront Dori in person, but he was too upset to drive. And he couldn't wait. He had to talk to him right here and now, to scream, yell, curse, and let it all out, everything he'd wanted to say to him ever since he started working at this fucking paper.

"I expected to hear from you sooner. I guess you've been on vacation," Dori said calmly.

"Don't you have an ounce of integrity? How could you do this to me? It's my story!" He was shouting so loud that passersby were stopping to look.

"Calm down. I did it for you," Dori said in the same mild voice that was making him even more furious.

"For me? What do you mean for me? You stole my story! My name should be on it, not yours."

Dori laughed. Amit imagined he could see his thin lips stretching into a satisfied smile.

"What's so funny?" He was so mad he could hardly talk. "I want you to know I'm not going to keep quiet about this. I'll go to the ethics committee, I'll sue you, I'll go to the cops—whatever it takes."

"Pardon me," Dori broke in, "but isn't it your name on the interview with the Aronovs? Who wrote that one, Giladi? You or me?"

"You're kidding me, right? That was your call! I didn't want anything to do with that sentimental garbage."

"Okay, Giladi, calm down. Come in and I'll explain why I did it. Then you'll . . ."

"No way. I quit. And I don't plan to look the other way." The words spilled out of his mouth before he even had time to think about what he was saying.

"Just give me five minutes. Then you can go tell whoever you want. It's not like anyone'll believe you anyway."

"Five minutes," Amit spat. He was so enraged he just wanted to go on shrieking at him, but Dori's words had made an impact. Who would believe that Dori had stolen his story? His editor was an old-timer with a solid reputation. And who was *he*? A nobody.

"You listening, baby boy?" Dori said, interrupting his thoughts. "Good," he went on when he got no answer. "I gotta admit, it took me a while to decide what to do with the story. Like I said—and I meant it—I want you to work with Nachum and get the real scoop.

There's nothing I want more than to have our paper reveal the rapist's identity. But the interview deserved to be printed. The two things just didn't go together. One of them had to go. I was gonna call you and tell you I was running the story, and then I figured out a way we could have our cake and eat it too. If your name was on the story, Nachum wouldn't want anything to do with you. He wouldn't even piss in your direction. But with my name on it, you can go and cry to him that your editor fucked you over, stabbed you in the back, whatever you want. You can say you want to go on working with him. You can milk it even more and tell him you quit. Get it, Giladi? Two birds with one stone. We run the story and you go on looking for the pervert."

Amit was struck dumb by Dori's explanation. He'd never have the gall to concoct such a scheme.

"Think about it," Dori went on. "What choice did I have? You know very well I'm not the type of motherfucker to steal a story from one of my reporters. Just the opposite. But I have responsibilities as the editor. I have to see the big picture. I want you here, Amit." It was the first time Giladi had ever heard him call him by his first name. "And I want you on this story. You work with Nachum and you'll find the guy. I'd bet my bottom dollar on it. This is a big one, and it's gonna be all yours."

"How do I know you're not going to screw me over again?" Amit asked, but he could feel his resistance wavering.

"Come into the office and I'll put it in writing. You know what? I'll even sign a statement saying you did the interview with Nachum, not me. How's that?"

Amit didn't answer. He hated to admit it, but there was a certain logic in what Dori was saying.

"Why didn't you tell me? Why did I have to read it in the paper?" His temper was rising again.

"I'm trying to educate you, kid. You gotta learn how the world works."

Amit kept silent. That was Dori's stock excuse for all the grief he gave his employees.

"Now stop crying like a fucking baby and get to work." The old Dori was back. "And remember, this is the last time you take a morning off," he said, disconnecting.

Chapter 46

AFTER thirty-five years as a prosecutor, Tel Aviv district attorney Rachel Zuriel thought she'd probably seen everything. Nevertheless, time and again she discovered there was no end to the surprises her job could conjure up.

She rose to greet Joshua Borochov. "Good to see you, Shuki. How've you been?" she forced herself to say amicably.

"How are Ariel, the kids, the grandkids?" he asked, shaking her outstretched hand warmly. Not for the first time, she wondered if the loathing she felt for this man was reciprocated.

In the course of her long career, she'd faced off against countless defense attorneys. Some she respected more, others less. But Shuki Borochov belonged to a separate category: those who crossed over to the other side. They didn't just represent the crime syndicates, they actually functioned as full-fledged members of the organization. It was a well-known fact. Nonetheless, Borochov was still entitled to put "Esq." after his name and even served on several Bar Association committees. He showed up at every event or convention to rub shoulders with noted judges and lawyers, amusing them with his jokes and regaling them with stories about the fine restaurants he dined at in London, New York, or Paris. When she was a candidate for DA five years ago, he was on the Bar Association's National Council and had played a large role in deterring several leading attorneys who were opposed to her appointment from launching a smear campaign against her. Although they never spoke of it, she had a strong feeling it was not by chance that she'd learned of his efforts on her behalf.

Yesterday morning, she'd called a meeting to discuss Faro. The atmosphere was tense. The cops were treading water and the investigation was going nowhere. Superintendent Navon didn't say it in so many words, but she got the impression he thought Faro's arrest was a mistake from beginning to end, that it was forced on him by his superiors.

Inspector Nachum's interview in the local paper didn't improve the mood either. "There's something rotten in the district of Tel Aviv," she heard a commentator declare dramatically on the radio on her way to work. Despite Navon's efforts to assure her that it was all bullshit, that Nevo was their guy, they both knew what the repercussions would be if it came out that they'd not only charged the wrong man but had been complicit in ensuring his wrongful conviction.

When the meeting broke up, Navon asked to speak with her in private. He told her their informant in Faro's organization had gotten cold feet and gone missing since the arrest. The higher-ups were leaning on him to make Faro believe they had a trustworthy informant who was cooperating with them. But the bottom line was that all they'd gotten from him was that Faro used some guy named George to smuggle drugs into Israel from Lebanon near Ghajar, the village that straddled the border. That's all they had, two names: George and Ghajar. They didn't know who George was, the extent of his activities, how he moved the drugs, or what part Ghajar played in the operation. If they had had more time to work the informant, to massage him until he was ready, they'd probably know more. "But that's a lost cause now," Navon said with a sigh.

The superintendent looked troubled and exhausted. What they had might not even be enough to make Faro break a sweat. And there was also the chance that the names would lead him directly to the informant, which meant that if they used them in the interrogation, they'd be handing the guy a death sentence. Two words—that's all they had. "You may be able to build a case on them, but the whole structure is just as likely to collapse," Navon concluded.

AS she looked at Borochov sitting across from her, Zuriel wondered if those two words were the real reason for this meeting. He'd called last night, saying Faro's remand hearing was two days away and they should talk. It was a perfectly normal request. He was simply asking to meet with her before the court hearing.

As soon as she hung up, she rang Navon and told him about the call. They were both experienced enough not to give it too much weight. Faro hadn't so much as twitched a muscle when they dropped the words "George" and "Ghajar," he reported. He'd sat opposite his interrogators for hours, saying nothing, aside from periodically intoning, "On the advice of counsel, I invoke my right to remain silent." "Maybe the names made an impression on him, and maybe they didn't," Navon said, reiterating the same assessment of the situation he'd offered yesterday.

"I assume you realize Faro's arrest has exhausted its usefulness," Borochov said, crossing his fleshy arms on his enormous paunch. To anyone who didn't know him, he looked like a benevolent uncle, a fat jolly man with a round, bald head and a kindly smile.

"We happen to see it differently," Zuriel answered calmly.

Borochov laughed.

"You want to tell me what you have on him?" he said when he saw she wasn't similarly amused.

"I assure you, you'll find out when we issue the indictment."

"Come on, sweetheart," he said with what he apparently thought was a disarming smile. It only intensified her repulsion. "We've both been at this long enough. If you had anything solid, you'd tell me. Why play games?"

"We know about George and Ghajar," she announced. "Actually, we know quite a lot about your client." She watched him closely, trying to read the effect of her words from his expression.

Borochov leaned back and straightened his expensive tie. "Yeah, yeah, George and Ghajar. My client told me they were grilling him about some guy named George. He has no idea who they're talking about," he said, not losing his composure for a second.

Zuriel continued to watch him. Her instincts told her he was lying, that they knew very well who George was and that was the reason the lawyer was here. Faro was feeling the pressure. There's an element of luck in any investigation. Sometimes two little words can do what mountains of evidence, surveillance tapes, and wiretaps can't.

"So why did you ask for this meeting?" She decided it was time to cut to the chase.

"I told you. Faro's arrest has exhausted its usefulness. I can guarantee that if you release him now, if you save us the hassle of judges and hearings, he won't talk to the press. Total media silence from our side. In a day or two, no one will remember that the cops bungled his arrest."

"I want to thank you and your client for your concern for the good name of law enforcement," she said with a smile. He responded with a grimace.

Despite his silence, Zuriel felt there was something else the attorney wanted to say. He was just waiting for the right moment.

"If all you've got to offer is media silence, you wasted your time coming here," she said, breaking the silence in the hope of forcing him to show his hand. "But you know I'm always happy to see you," she added with a fake smile.

"You got an offer for me?" he asked.

She hadn't expected him to start the haggling so soon. She had no idea what kind of charges they'd be able to file against Faro. Tossing out a number off the top of her head would be irresponsible.

"Seven years," she fired at him. This was too good an opportunity to pass up. And years of bargaining had made her very good at the game.

Borochov rose. "I guess you're right. We're both wasting our time here," he said, straightening his bright red tie again. But it seemed to her the number didn't really faze him.

She rose as he held out his hand. "Tell Ariel I said hi. Remind him he owes me a tennis match at the next convention in Eilat," he said with a smile.

Had she just missed her chance to put Faro behind bars? As things stood, even a twelve-month sentence would be an achievement. It was in the public interest to get a man like him off the streets.

Borochov started toward the door. She debated calling him back and telling him she was willing to try to work something out, that she was ready to listen. But she held back. She was the DA, not someone hawking her wares in the market. Besides, if she gave in too quickly, he'd realize how weak her hand was. Borochov was a smart man. He was testing her.

He opened the door and she inhaled deeply. They wouldn't have closed a deal now anyway, she reassured herself. On the other hand, if George wasn't worth seven years, she'd missed her opportunity. Borochov would go back and tell Faro that under the present circumstances, their best option was to fight it out in court. And she didn't have any weapons at her disposal.

She was on her way back to her chair when he turned around.

"I almost forgot," he said.

She repressed a smile. She'd done the right thing by resisting the temptation to call him back. Plea bargaining was no different from haggling over the price of a carpet in a Turkish bazaar.

"One of my clients may have information about the Tel Aviv rapist," he said, coming to stand across the desk from her.

"What kind of information?" she asked, struggling to understand what was going on and how the topic of Ziv Nevo had suddenly come up.

"Where he is, for instance. You interested?" His smile grew wider.

"Which client?" she asked, although she had the feeling she knew the answer. He ignored the question.

They stood opposite each other in silence. Catching Nevo would enable the cops to save face, to say nothing of removing the threat to the women in the area.

"What does your client want in exchange for the information?" she asked, knowing nothing came free in their world.

"My client only asks that you not be greedy."

She waited.

"Seven years is too much. You know that as well as I do, sweetheart," he declared before turning to leave for the second time.

ZURIEL looked out the window at the traffic on King Saul Street. She'd consult with a few people in the office, get the necessary approval, but in the end she'd reject Borochov's proposal. It wasn't worth losing out on a chance to strike a deal in the Faro case for a lead to the whereabouts of a rape suspect, no matter how dangerous he might be.

If she agreed to listen to what Faro had to tell her, she'd have to offer him a reduced sentence in exchange. And every day a man like that was locked up was a day with less criminal activity, and that was clearly in the public interest. When she was new to the DA's Office, decisions like this kept her up at night. She was playing with people's lives. A rapist versus a crime lord. One type of victim versus another.

She still didn't take such things lightly. But over the years she'd grown accustomed to making tough decisions. You had to weigh the cost against the benefit, victim against victim, crime against crime. Being responsible for putting Faro behind bars would be the crowning glory of her career as district attorney. Everyone would know that, on her watch, one of the most dangerous crime syndicates in the country had taken a fatal blow.

Chapter 47

IT took a supreme effort for Meshulam to resist the urge to give Nevo one last kick as he lay at his feet on the floor. When Borochov said he was on his way, he'd promised himself he'd keep his cool until he got the lousy motherfucker to spill everything he knew. But as soon as he laid eyes on him, he lost it. That was always his problem, his short fuse. His rage took over and he didn't stop to think.

When Nevo got out of the van, Meshulam told George's crew he needed a minute alone with him. "He's all yours," they said, turning the prisoner over to him. Nevo was obviously shocked to see him there.

"Whaddya want Faro for?" His body still ached from his encounter with the geezer in Nevo's apartment, but that didn't prevent him from giving Nevo a punch in the gut that made him double up in agony. "What you gotta say to him you can't say to me?"

"I didn't do anything. I kept my mouth shut," Nevo mumbled.

"I asked you what you need Faro for, you motherfucking loser."

"I'm sorry," Nevo said, struggling to straighten up. "You're right. I should've come to you. I get it."

"Where's the car?" he asked, grabbing Nevo by the shirt and yelling in his face.

"What car? I don't know what you're talking about." The terror showed on Nevo's face.

"Don't play dumb with me," Meshulam whispered ominously. "You know exactly what I'm talking about—the car with the bomb, the car from Louis Marshall. Where is it? You tell the cops why you were there, shithead?"

"I don't know. Honestly. I don't know what you want me to say. If I knew, I'd . . . But I don't . . ."

Nevo's servility just enraged Meshulam more. He despised weaklings, men who had no self-respect, who whined like little girls. He even despised weepy broads. He head-butted Nevo and heard the bone break in his nose.

"Where'd you hide your family, huh? Don't lie to me!"

Without answering, Nevo brought his hands up to his bleeding nose.

"I'm warning you. I want the truth."

Silence.

"Who was in your apartment?" he shouted.

"The cop investigating the Tel Aviv rapes. I've got nothing to do with him." Nevo himself could barely understand the muffled words coming from his mouth.

"What was he doing there?" Nevo's answer had taken Meshulam completely by surprise.

"I don't know . . . looking for me, I guess . . . they think I did it . . ." His speech was becoming increasingly slurred.

Meshulam landed another punch in the gut, bringing Nevo to his knees. He didn't believe the motherfucker for a second. He and that cop had something going. They were working together. Fact: Nevo knew the cop was there. He talked to him. Fact: The car was missing. Fact: His family was in hiding. Fact.

"Where're your wife and kid?" he asked again.

Nevo still didn't answer.

He kicked him in the head.

He could tell the bastard was too far gone to withstand another blow. That's the way it always was: he used his fists first and his head later. Nevo's eyes were closed. Was he dead? Borochov had told him to keep an eye on him, that he might be Faro's ace in the hole. He held two fingers to Nevo's neck and felt for a pulse. Not dead, just unconscious. Meshulam breathed a sigh of relief.

Chapter 48

THE quiet of their desert hideaway that had been so enchanting when they got here had turned menacing. Ziv had been gone for three days, and Merav hadn't heard a word from him. When he said it would take time, she thought he meant a day, two at most. But it had been three days, and the silence was deafening.

Gili was also getting impatient. He kept asking when Daddy was coming come back. "Everything's fine, sweetie," she promised over and over again, the fear in the pit of her stomach growing sharper each time she said it. She had a feeling something bad was coming.

Orit's spacious home had begun to seem claustrophobic. Merav felt caged in as she tried to keep herself busy cleaning and cooking. But the fear wouldn't let go, the terrifying scenarios she envisioned never stopped filling her head. The vast landscape she'd found so beautiful at first only intensified her loneliness.

Ziv had given her explicit instructions not to try to get in touch with him and not to contact her parents under any circumstances. A few hours ago she'd broken down and called his cell phone, only to discover it was switched off. Then she called her parents. Her mother sounded panicky, on the verge of hysterics. "Where are you? I'm going crazy," she said again and again, but Merav merely answered, "I'm fine, Mom. Don't worry about me," before quickly disconnecting like they do on TV so a call can't be traced.

She didn't sleep a wink last night, just lay in bed with her eyes open, every nighttime noise making her jump. Gili often pleaded to be allowed to sleep in her bed, especially after the divorce, but in the past she'd always refused. Now she invited him in. She lay down beside him, watching him sleep, listening in dread to the jackals howling in the wilderness, waiting anxiously for the sound of her car pulling up at the house, and then she'd hear the front door open and close and Ziv would walk in and say the nightmare was over.

She went into the room of Orit's eldest son and turned on his computer. Up to now, she'd refrained from using it because she didn't want to encroach on the family's privacy any more than necessary, but she couldn't go on living in the isolation she'd imposed on herself. Ziv could be in trouble.

The headline on the news site she went into told of a man in the north who murdered his wife. She scrolled down slowly, looking for any item that might give her a clue to what happened to Ziv. She didn't find anything. The night he opened up to her, he said he'd gotten himself mixed up with the mob, but for her own protection he refused to mention names. She could easily read something that had a bearing on his fate and not even know it, she thought.

She heard Gili playing with his stuffed animals in the other room, chatting to himself. How long could she keep him locked up here? Orit and her family would be back from their vacation in three days, and then she'd have no choice. She'd have to leave.

She went into Google and typed "rape north Tel Aviv." As she'd expected, she got a lot of hits. The attack had been covered by all the media. She'd read about it herself at the time.

She concentrated on the items from the last seven days. Incredibly, she discovered there'd been another rape, and the police were again looking for Ziv. It occurred to her that he might've been lying to her the whole time, that he was guilty, and he'd been out raping another girl while she was waiting anxiously for him to return. But she dismissed the idea as soon as she saw the date of the attack. He'd been here with her when it happened.

Tears welled up in her eyes. What had they done to deserve this? How come Ziv was the prime suspect in two rapes?

Merav sat in front of the computer weeping uncontrollably. She felt lost, helpless. If Ziv hadn't been so adamant about keeping the cops out of it, she'd call them right now and tell them that he'd been with her, lying beside her in bed when they claimed he was raping a woman in Tel Aviv. But Ziv had made her promise she wouldn't involve the police.

She was about to switch off the computer when her eye caught the headline of an interview with Inspector Eli Nachum. Ziv had told her about the detective with the vicious piercing eyes who tricked him into confessing to a crime he didn't commit. Skimming through the interview, she saw that Nachum was now saying that Ziv was innocent and he'd been wrong all along.

The flicker of optimism she felt when she first found the article died out very quickly when she read it more carefully. She learned not only that Nachum had been kicked off the force but that they rejected his opinion out of hand. In the official eyes of the police, Ziv was the rapist. A tremor ran through her body when she read they were now mounting a nationwide search for him.

Merav turned off the computer and started pacing the floor. All she wanted was for Ziv to come back so they could go to the police together and she could tell them he was with her the night of the rape.

Her intuition was right. Something very bad had happened. She knew that now.

She wanted desperately to help him, but she didn't know how. What could she do? Then she remembered the letter he'd placed in her hand before he left. Should she open it?

WITH trembling hands, she dialed the first number on the list she got from Information. It turned out there was more than one Eli Nachum in the Tel Aviv area. She prayed she wasn't making a terrible mistake and putting Ziv in even greater danger.

But she couldn't just sit here and do nothing. She was placing all her faith in the detective. After all, he'd made it very clear that he didn't believe Ziv was guilty. And it wasn't like she was calling the police. The papers said he'd been booted out.

"Stop calling me, Giladi. I have no intention of talking to you, and you can quote me on that in your fucking rag." The voice at the other end was furious.

"Is this Eli Nachum?" she asked.

"Yes. Sorry about that. I thought you were someone else."

"Inspector Eli Nachum?"

The longer she spoke with him, the more she began to trust him, despite her initial apprehensions. He sounded deeply sorry for what he'd done to Ziv and she heard, or imagined she heard, a desire to help that was entirely genuine.

"You have any idea where I can find him?" he asked.

She looked at the letter she'd just read. She was still reeling from what it said. The mob had forced Ziv to plant a bomb under a woman's car, he didn't know who. "Don't open this letter unless you and Gili are in danger," he'd warned her before he left.

"Merav? Are you still there?" Was she doing the right thing? For the moment, at least, she and Gili were safe. Nothing had happened to make her feel they were in any imminent danger. And he'd made her promise she'd only use the letter as a last resort.

"He left me a note with the name of the man he went to see," she said finally, her heart pounding. It didn't seem wise to tell him everything. If the letter fell into the wrong hands, it could have serious consequences for Ziv. She didn't know Eli Nachum and couldn't be sure what he'd do with it. She had to use her head. To play it safe, she wouldn't tell him about Faro.

"Who is it?"

"David Meshulam," she said, her voice shaking as she uttered the name of the man mentioned several times in Ziv's letter as the one who gave him his instructions.

Chapter 49

SERGEANT Ohad Barel was very pleased with himself. At last, all the pieces were falling into place in the investigation he was leading. He'd had to go through what Nachum called "legal shit" to get the warrant, but he finally had what he wanted: a record of the calls Nevo's ex-wife made from her office on the day he disappeared. A few minutes before leaving work, she'd called the cell phone of a friend by the name of Orit Berger. The call had lasted four minutes and fifteen seconds. Berger lived in the south, but he found out from Border Control that she and her family were currently overseas. There was no doubt in Barel's mind why Merav had called her.

Now he was on his way south to bring Merav in for questioning. With any luck, he would find Nevo there too.

He drove at high speed, enjoying the fine weather and the company of Shiri, the policewoman on his squad whom he'd brought along for the ride. He'd had his eye on her for a while, and he had the impression it might be mutual. A day that started out so well was bound to end well too.

Just three minutes after he turned onto the southern highway, his cell phone rang. It was Dr. Dan Mizrachi from Ichilov. "Dana Aronov has regained consciousness. You can talk to her," he said blandly, as if he were speaking about the weather.

"What? When?" he asked excitedly.

"Yesterday," the doctor answered drily.

"Why didn't you say so before?"

Dr. Mizrachi apologized. "Sorry. My fault. We're very busy here.

I'd advise you to get here as soon as possible," he added before hanging up.

What was he supposed to do now? Navon told him to do whatever it took to bring Nevo in, and his gut was telling him Merav knew where to find her ex-husband. On the other hand, Dr. Mizrachi told him to get to the hospital quickly. Aronov's testimony was critical to the case. He couldn't risk missing out on it.

"We don't have any choice. We have to go back to Tel Aviv," Shiri said, smiling at him. After cursing the doctor one last time, he turned the car around. If everything worked out as he hoped, Aronov would ID Nevo as her attacker, and he'd head south again that night to finish what he'd started.

BAREL was excited. This was his time to shine. Just as he'd expected, the description Dana Aronov gave matched Adi Regev's description of her attacker. More to the point, it fit Ziv Nevo to a tee.

Like everyone else, he'd read the bizarre interview Nachum had given to Dori Engel. He didn't see eye to eye with him one bit. And he couldn't figure out why Nachum had decided to go to the press with his crazy ideas. Nothing good would come out of it, not for the case, and definitely not for Nachum himself.

He remembered what his former boss had said about a lineup: that it was like baking a cake, you had to follow the recipe. And since this was the first cake he'd ever baked by himself, he'd decided to go by the book and conduct an unimpeachable photo lineup. First he'd gone to the DA and gotten a green light: if they didn't have Nevo, there was no legal impediment to presenting the victim with a photo array. For the record, he'd left a brief message on the cell phone of Assaf Rosen, Nevo's attorney, informing him they were planning to conduct another lineup and asking him to contact him. He just didn't bother to leave a number. So far, Rosen hadn't called back.

He looked over the pictures numbered one through eight that were pinned to the corkboard. All the faces were similar to Nevo's. He wondered if he hadn't gone too far in his determination to follow the recipe impeccably. The faces might resemble each other too closely. But he put that thought aside. In his interview with Aronov, he'd asked her several times to describe her assailant, and each time she'd given him the answers he was looking for. He was convinced she'd do the same at the moment of truth and point to Nevo. He was so positive that he'd even resisted the temptation to "accidentally" leave a picture of Nevo in her room.

The technician taping the proceedings signaled that he was ready. Barel entered the room. He thought he saw tears forming in Dana's eyes, their clear blue intensified by the bruises and swelling on her face. "Practically a medical miracle," Dr. Mizrachi called it when he described how she'd woken up from the coma. Now he was standing by her bed in case the experience of identifying her rapist had an adverse effect on his patient's condition.

Barel stood next to Aronov and explained, for the record, what was going to happen. When he was done, he spun the corkboard faceup, more like a TV entertainer than a police officer, and held it where she could easily see it. He kept his eyes trained on her as she scanned one picture after the other, concentrating so hard that he was actually following her eye movements. Number one, number two. His heart nearly stopped when she quickly passed over number five, Nevo, and went on to the next one.

Finally, she raised her eyes to him. He could see by her expression that she was unable to ID the rapist. His stomach hurt. The last thing he needed was for the lineup to fail to produce a result. Navon was breathing down his neck. If he didn't bring him Nevo's head on a platter, he'd take the blame for the screwup. He'd tried too hard, the pictures were too much alike, they'd say.

Aronov continued to look at him in silence. "Take your time. There's no reason to hurry, no pressure. I know this is hard for you," he said, making an effort to keep his voice calm.

"I don't know . . . I don't recognize any of them."

Barel's heart fell. He was beginning to think he was suffering from bad karma, that all the problems he was encountering were punishment for what he'd done to Nachum.

"Take another look," he coaxed, shifting slightly so that his back was to the camera.

As she brought her eyes back down to the board, he passed his finger inconspicuously over the photos, pausing for a fraction of a second at number five before moving on. She looked up at him and he gazed back at her meaningfully. That's the one, point to that one, he screamed silently. Please, please, just do it. My career is on the line, his eyes said.

"I'm sorry," she whispered, turning her head aside.

Barel drew in a sharp breath. He could hear Nachum's voice in his head: never take anything for granted, always have a Plan B in case something goes wrong. He cursed himself for the overconfidence that had bitten him in the ass.

"Please take another look at number five. Is that the man who raped you?" Barel found it hard to keep his voice steady. He knew the risk he was taking. An ID based on a single photo carried much less weight than the result of a photo array, but it was better than nothing. In the present circumstances, he'd grasp at any straw not to leave here empty-handed.

Dana focused on the photo of Nevo.

"I'm sorry. That's not him," she said finally.

"How can you be sure?" he said, regretting the question the moment the words were out of his mouth.

"His face was pitted. He had a broader noise, thinner lips."

Chapter 50

RACHEL Zuriel swallowed the pill without water. The Tel Aviv district attorney had read about the danger of pain pills, especially the Optalgin she took regularly. She'd tried to cut down, but the headache that started after her meeting with Galit Lavie left her no choice.

She'd summoned Lavie to her office to tell her about her meeting with Shuki Borochov and the information he claimed to have about Ziv Nevo. Lavie was in charge of the Nevo case, and even beyond that, Zuriel respected the young ADA's opinion. She was astonished to learn from her that the second victim had woken up and they'd conducted a photo lineup in the hospital, but she hadn't fingered Nevo. In fact, when they'd pointed him out to her, she'd said she was certain he wasn't the man who raped her.

It looked like Eli Nachum was right. Nevo didn't rape Dana Aronov and there was a good chance he didn't rape Adi Regev either. They'd been chasing the wrong man, and in their misplaced zeal, they'd gotten him convicted of a felony he didn't commit.

"Rachel, I'm asking you to include Nevo in the deal with Faro," Galit said after hearing Borochov's offer.

"Why would I do that?" she asked in surprise, wondering if she should tell Galit she'd had no intention of taking the deal even when she thought Nevo was guilty. Now that they knew he was innocent, what interest did it serve to bring him in?

"We owe it to him, Rachel," Lavie went on when she got no reply. "We've done him an injustice. And it's very likely that Faro's people are more involved than just knowing where he is. They're probably holding him. There's no telling what they'll do if you inform Borochov that we know Nevo's innocent and the cops have no further interest in him. They might very well decide that killing him is the best way to keep him quiet."

"I think you're exaggerating, Galit," she said, although she knew the ADA could be right. No one knew more about Faro's organization than Lavie. Just a few months ago she'd gotten a murder conviction against one of his soldiers, Yariv Cohen. They'd leaned on him hard and tried to seduce him with all sorts of perks, but he refused to give up his boss. He got a life sentence. Lavie had received death threats during the trial, but she hadn't backed down. She was a brave woman.

"We owe it to him, Rachel," she repeated. "He's got a little boy. If it weren't for us and our mistakes, none of this would be happening to him."

"I understand what you're saying," Zuriel said sympathetically, looking the young attorney in the eye. "But the chances of something happening to Nevo are very slim. It's just speculation. What we have to consider . . ."

"No, Rachel. When it comes to people like them, it's not just speculation. And even if it is, he's the one who'll pay the price if I'm right, and he doesn't deserve that."

Zuriel closed her eyes. Her head was still throbbing painfully. Beyond her closed door she could hear the noise of the office, people chatting, telephones ringing. She'd promised Galit she'd think about what she said.

She'd never admit it, in fact, the very thought made her cringe in shame, but deep down she hoped Faro's organization would make the problem called Ziv Nevo go away. Both the police and the prosecution had come under heavy attack in recent years. The public was out for blood. They didn't understand that the barrage was instigated by criminal elements. Even her best friends believed the DA's Office fabricated evidence, hounded politicians for no good reason, and in general had too much power and regularly abused it. The Ziv Nevo fiasco would be another blow to their reputation. He'd talk to the press, give in-depth interviews to the media about how he was coerced into confessing to a rape he didn't commit, how he was incarcerated and tortured, how his life was ruined. And they'd have to hang their heads in shame once again, to come up with some lame excuse, to admit they were wrong, but of course it was all done in good faith.

She dialed Borochov's number.

"It turns out Nevo didn't do the rapes," she said, telling him about the photo lineup arranged for Dana Aronov in order to remove any suspicion he might have that she was trying to outfox him: attempting to get her hands on Nevo without giving Faro anything in return.

Borochov said nothing.

"The offer of seven years still stands," she said. It was her job to look out for the public interest. Even Lavie would come to see that in time. She was a smart girl.

Borochov continued to remain silent. She didn't like that. Had there been further developments since he left her office?

"In view of what your client is accused of, I think . . . ," she began, but he cut her off. "Seven years isn't something we'd even consider."

Now it was Zuriel's turn to be silent. She'd handled countless plea bargains. He'd throw out a number, she'd counter with a higher one, and in the end they'd meet in the middle.

"I spoke with Faro. We'll take our chances in court," Borochov announced.

She waited, ready to pounce the moment he gave her an opening to continue their horse trading, but he said nothing.

"So I guess I'll see you in court," she said finally. "I have to admit I'm a bit surprised you're choosing to waste everyone's time and risk a much harsher sentence, but it's your decision. Not a very wise one in my opinion, but that's your prerogative." She was doing her best to sound confident.

"Don't waste your breath, Rachel. We're no longer interested. Go issue an indictment on the basis of what you've got. We'll cope."

Zuriel chewed on her lip. Up until a few minutes ago, she was sure the only question was how much time Faro would spend behind bars. Now she had nothing. She couldn't go to court with no more than two words.

"So I assume we're done here," Borochov said, and started talking about the upcoming legal convention in Eilat.

She didn't take in a word of what he said. She was furious with the cops for this stupid arrest that had put her in the hot seat and with herself for giving in to the temptation to play along with it. The whole house of cards had come down around her. They'd have to release Faro, and they'd thrown Nevo to the wolves to boot.

"There's just one request I'd like to make," she said, interrupting Borochov's monologue. "Tell your client to let Nevo go."

"Oh, about that. I forgot to tell you. It was a matter of mistaken identity, someone who looked like Nevo. My client has no idea where Nevo is."

Zuriel fell back in her chair. No pill in the world would make her headache go away now.

Chapter 51

MESHULAM was standing on the corner watching the paramedics wheel a stretcher carrying the body of Yossi Golan out of the apartment on Jeremiah Street in Tel Aviv. He still ached all over from the brush with the man in Nevo's apartment, and his face was swollen, especially his nose. It was probably broken. When he looked at himself in the mirror this morning, his face seemed even more menacing than usual.

He knew Golan well, was actually fond of the bastard. But he wasn't sorry he was dead. The traitor had dug his own grave. There was only one punishment for loose lips in their organization. Golan knew that. So did Meshulam.

He tried to get the image out of his head, but he couldn't help seeing the day thirteen years ago when he watched the paramedics wheel his mother's body out of the house. He was the one who found her. She died of an overdose, just like Golan. He remembered every detail of that day, including the sour smell of death in the apartment. He was only sixteen. Miriam Meshulam hadn't been much of a mother, but her death still hurt. It meant he was all alone now.

The memory of that awful time engulfed him. He was irritated with himself. The past was the past. He had work to do. And work was all he had left. Without it, who was he?

Shuki Borochov called last night and told him their cop informant had come through at the last minute. It turned out Navon's squad didn't have anything solid on Faro. In fact, they didn't have squat. Golan had let slip a few inconsequential words to his brother-in-law about their drug operation, and the brother-in-law had told his best friend, who just happened to be a cop. How stupid can you get?

The cops and the DA had been keeping their cards very close to their chest, but they were bluffing the whole time. Shuki said that when the DA called, he more or less told her where she could stick it.

The paramedics opened the back of the ambulance and rolled in the stretcher with the body bag. Golan knew the rules. He shouldn't have talked to his brother-in-law. There was no place in their organization for weaklings, for people who didn't know how to keep their mouth shut, who showed no respect or loyalty.

The order to take out Golan had come directly from Faro in Abu Kabir. Borochov conveyed the message. "Be discreet," Meshulam was told, and he understood perfectly: no bullets, no fireworks, do it quietly. As soon as he got the call, he set out from Shufa, leaving Nevo, still licking his wounds, in the hands of George's crew.

He arranged for Golan to get some crystal meth cut with a little something extra that would do the job. The cops might suspect it was a hit, but they'd never be able to link it back to Faro. The dope had passed through too many hands along the way, and they all had good reason to keep their lips sealed. Nobody would risk going up against Faro because of a loser like Golan.

The ambulance passed him as it sped away. He could see the two paramedics laughing in the front. What did they care? When they came for his mother, they didn't even try to resuscitate her. She was just a lousy junkie. She didn't matter.

Meshulam turned and headed to his car. It was cold. He zipped up his jacket. He had to go back and deal with Nevo. Borochov had relayed Faro's instructions to let the asshole go. The clowns on the force had finally figured out that he didn't rape anyone.

There was no reason not to cut him loose. It was clear to them now that he'd been telling the truth, that he didn't squeal. And it's what Faro wanted. But from Meshulam's point of view, Nevo knew too much. So far, he'd managed to keep his little side venture on Louis Marshall from Faro, but that could change. Nevo might blab. Maybe not to the cops, but to the boss, or to his buddy Noam. The last thing he needed was for Faro to take pity on Nevo and give him his old job back, and then one day while he was driving him somewhere they'd start talking and it would come out.

He didn't want to have to live with that fear. The fact that Nevo had kept his mouth shut up to now didn't guarantee anything. One day you're strong and the next day you break, and then the shit hits the fan.

Faro wanted him to bring Nevo back from the West Bank, but a lot can happen on the way. Faro might be sorry about it, but he wouldn't grieve for him. With Nevo out of the way, Meshulam could put the whole thing behind him, there'd be no evidence of the one time he fucked up in all these years. And if there was one thing he'd learned from Golan, it was that you pay for your mistakes. It could just as easily be him in a body bag if Faro found out what he'd done. He didn't have a choice. He had to look out for himself. He couldn't rely on anyone else.

Chapter 52

ELI Nachum parked on a side street not far from the palatial house. After the call from Nevo's ex-wife, it didn't take him long to put all the pieces together. In the eyes of most cops, he was public enemy number one ever since the interview appeared, but he still had a few old pals on the job. He found out from them that Meshulam was one of Shimon Faro's soldiers. They faxed him some pictures, and he recognized the bad guy immediately as the thug who'd attacked him in Nevo's apartment.

He'd hardly left the house since he was discharged from the hospital. He sat at home like a frail old man, useless, sluggish, in pain. When he saw the interview in the paper, he kicked himself. How could he have been so dumb? Why didn't he realize they were playing him for a fool?

Navon called and reamed him out over the phone. Everyone else kept their distance. That was no less hurtful than Navon accusing him of being a Judas. He knew their silence meant they agreed with the superintendent. He debated calling and trying to explain, but the lame excuse that he'd been outsmarted by a twentysomething reporter made him sound even more pitiful than letting them believe he'd given the interview of his own free will.

Giladi kept trying to reach him, calling him incessantly on his cell phone and his home line. He'd even come and stood outside the house a few days ago. He claimed he was screwed over by his boss and said he'd quit his job because of it. Nachum didn't want to hear it. He didn't have the energy anymore. The world could go on without him. He hardly slept at night and was barely able to get out of bed in the morning. He couldn't turn off his brain, couldn't get rid of the constant thoughts about unsolved cases, about cases he'd solved but now wasn't so sure, about what his future would look like if he couldn't be a cop.

The call from Merav yanked him out of his funk in an instant, waking him up abruptly like an alarm clock. It reminded him that he wasn't yet entitled to sink into the abyss that had begun to swallow him up, that there were still things he had to set right. Nevo had saved his life, and now he was in deep trouble. And the rapist was still at large and could claim another victim, all because of the mistakes he himself had made.

As he'd promised Merav, he didn't tell his pals on the force why he was looking for information about Meshulam. He didn't mention Nevo's name either. He wasn't surprised to learn that Nevo was mixed up with Faro's organization. As soon as he realized he wasn't the rapist, he knew he was hiding a bigger secret by refusing to say what he was doing on Louis Marshall Street that night.

Nachum pulled himself gingerly out of the car. Any incautious movement sent him a sharp reminder of his nighttime encounter with Meshulam. He looked at the wall around the house across from him with the security cameras that were plainly following his every move. He'd had a diverse career as a detective, but he'd never dealt with organized crime. There was a first time for everything.

The heavy door opened and a tall crew-cut gorilla dressed all in black came out.

"Tell your boss Inspector Eli Nachum would like to talk to him," he said in a loud voice in case the cameras were equipped for sound.

"You're on private property, sir. You have to leave," the man said, gesturing to Nachum's car.

"Tell your boss that if he doesn't want to see the inside of Abu Kabir again today, it's in his best interest to let me in," Nachum said, even louder.

The man's eyes glazed over, and Nachum realized he was getting instructions through an earbud. He went back inside and closed the metal door behind him, leaving the detective standing in the street.

He was back a few minutes later. "Follow me," he said impassively.

"What can I do for you, Inspector Nachum?" Faro asked in a deep voice when Nachum was standing in front of him. He was sitting in a solitary lounge chair beside a pool with an elaborate waterfall in the middle of a huge lawn, taking the sun in a short-sleeved shirt and sweatpants.

"You can leave Ziv Nevo alone. I don't know what connection he has to you and I have no intention of asking, but I want you to release him, let him go back to his family." He'd decided not to beat around the bush. With people like Faro, the less talk the better. Especially when you know so little.

"Ziv Nevo has no connection to me whatsoever, Inspector Nachum. I can assure you I don't have him. He drove me around a few times. Nice guy. I understand you were looking for him in relation to a rape case and that he's no longer a suspect. I have no idea where he is. My attorney has already explained this to Ms. Zuriel. I suggest you check with her," Faro said coolly, turning his head to watch a gardener working in a flower bed on the other side of the lawn.

The crime lord's remarks threw Nachum for a loop. Why had Rachel Zuriel been speaking to Faro's lawyer about Nevo?

"Anything else I can help you with, Inspector Nachum?" Faro asked derisively.

"One of your men, David Meshulam, was in Nevo's apartment looking for him. He sent regards from Meir and referred to certain threats made in Abu Kabir." Faro could be lying about Zuriel, trying to mess with his head. But it didn't matter one way or the other. Nachum had come here for a reason.

Not a single muscle twitched in Faro's face, but Nachum had spent enough hours in the interrogation room to see that he'd just told the man something he didn't know.

"I know that because I ran into him there," he went on, gesturing to his bruises and pressing home his advantage by catching Faro off balance again.

Faro continued to say nothing.

"You've got twenty-four hours," Nachum said, pausing before he added, "It would be a shame for you to go to prison for complicity in an assault on a police officer."

Chapter 53

FARO heard the door slam behind the old cop with the battered face. He was just released from Abu Kabir this morning, and now there was a new threat hanging over his head.

He wasn't pleased by what Nachum had told him. Shuki Borochov said Nevo had called Noam to ask for help, and Noam had contacted him. Shuki got the idea to use Nevo as a bargaining chip to procure Faro's freedom. Now he discovered that Meshulam had been looking for Nevo, that he'd waited for him in his apartment and assaulted a cop.

What was Meshulam hiding from him? What was he doing at Nevo's place? Why the hell did he beat up a cop?

Faro got out of his chair. He never got a moment's rest. It was stupid things like this you had to avoid like the plague. He spent his time running large-scale operations, and in the end he'd be brought down by something picayune. Bigger men than he, men who built empires, wound up behind bars convicted of petty crimes because they were too busy to pay attention to the little things.

He waved Yaki Klein over. He smelled a rat. Someone was lying to him.

Chapter 54

AMIT looked at the name on the screen of his cell phone and decided not to pick up for Dori this time either. The man was a deceitful snake in the grass, and he was sick and tired of his games and abuse. There was no point in talking to him anyway. He knew what Dori wanted from the dozen text messages he'd already sent. He'd seen on the Internet that today was the day the judge rendered his sentence in the case of the teenage gang convicted of robbing convenience stores in south Tel Aviv, and he wanted his crime and education reporter to get to the courthouse and cover the story. But that wasn't all. Naturally, Dori had more up his sleeve.

The prosecutor on the case was Galit Lavie. As usual, Dori was looking to kill two birds with one stone: a small item on the gang-bangers and an interview with the ADA who signed off on the indictment against Ziv Nevo for a crime he didn't commit. "Ask her how it feels to be responsible for convicting an innocent man, what they're doing to catch the real rapist," he'd texted.

Under normal circumstances, Amit would do as he was told. The chances of getting Lavie to answer his questions were slim, but he ought to give it a go. He couldn't deny that it was part of his job. He'd tried to get something out of her after Nevo's conviction, but she'd brushed him off.

But he'd had enough. He'd been marking time ever since the interview with Nachum. The detective refused to talk to him. He'd called dozens of times, even waited outside his house. But it didn't get him anywhere. Tamar, the server at the Zodiac Café he'd been hoping to talk to, had quit. In fact, the busy coffee shop had been nearly empty since the story came out. He'd tried several times to talk to the employees, but all he got were suspicious looks, as if they thought he was the rapist.

This morning he'd decided to try one last time. He stopped playing games and went straight to the owner. "My name is Amit Giladi. I'm a reporter, and I'm here to help you figure out which one of your customers is the rapist," he said. "If we can do that, your business is sure to pick up again." He didn't expect a warm welcome, but he wasn't prepared for the response he got. It turned out the owner had known Dori for a long time, and not just as a regular customer.

The man didn't only refuse to talk to him, he kicked him out, screaming that Dori was "a motherfucking jackass." Dori had fucked with him again. Would it have been so hard to warn him? He could already hear him say for the umpteenth time, "Man up, kid." The idea of having to listen to his jeering remarks about how he was scared by loud voices infuriated him so much that he was simply ignoring the editor's calls.

His phone beeped again when he was getting on his bike. "Go now. Get an interview with her!!! No one else to send!!!" Dori texted.

Asshole. What did he do to deserve this? When he was new at the paper, everyone told him Dori was a hard man to work for. A talented journalist but a very difficult boss. He hadn't listened. So maybe he did deserve what he was getting.

"Working on another assignment. Go yourself," he texted back belligerently. He started the bike, not waiting for an answer.

He had to persuade Nachum to give him another chance. He couldn't work with Dori anymore. The only way he could stay in the profession was to get a humongous scoop, and to do that he had to find the rapist. That would be his ticket back in.

He sped toward Nachum's house. He'd been wrong to underestimate the veteran detective. Everything he'd told him in the hospital turned out to be true. He'd realized before anyone else that Nevo was innocent, that the real creep was still on the loose.

It was Amit's turn to atone for his mistakes. Nachum was also trying to make amends for the blindness that had gotten Nevo convicted in the first place. Together they'd make a good team, he'd tell him. He'd give it his all, not leave any stone unturned. Eventually, just like Dori believed (and he had to give him credit for his journalistic instincts), they'd find the perp.

Then he'd show that snake in the grass who was king of the jungle. He'd take the story and give it to another paper. He'd crush Dori like the reptile he was. If it gave him a chance to make that dream come true, it was worth it to him to get down on his knees and beg Nachum to forgive him.

Chapter 55

MESHULAM decided to wait until dark before starting out from Shufa. The more he thought about it, the more determined he became. He couldn't allow Nevo to leave the West Bank alive. He had to repair the damage he'd done, even if it meant disobeying Faro's instructions again. He swore to himself it would be the last time. He'd learned his lesson. Starting tomorrow, he'd go back to being the disciplined soldier he'd always been, that he was meant to be. The way he'd fucked up that night, everything he'd been keeping from Faro, it would all be buried along with Nevo.

His first thought was to leave him on the road near some isolated village and let the Palestinians do the job for him. But what if he survived? If he made it back alive, he'd still be a threat. No, it'd be best to stop on a dirt road somewhere, order him out of the car, and put a bullet in his head. He'd have to dig a deep hole for the body. He didn't need some stinking goatherd to find him and notify the authorities. He'd tell Faro he'd dropped him off in Tel Aviv and he had no idea where he went from there.

Meshulam got up and went into the room where they were holding Nevo. He was lying on the bed, his face black-and-blue from the beating he'd taken from him yesterday. That was another reason he couldn't bring him back to the city. On second thought, he saw he wouldn't have to risk using a gun. In the shape Nevo was in, he could finish him off with his fists.

He went back into his room, lay down on the bed, and closed his eyes. The stomach cramps that had started yesterday were still tormenting him. He had to get some rest. It would be dark in an hour and a half and then he'd get going. It would all be over soon and he could put it behind him.

YAKI Klein was standing over him when he opened his eyes.

"Get up, Meshulam. We're leaving."

He looked around. It was dark out. How long had he slept? Had he missed his chance? He leaped out of bed and stood facing Klein.

"Everything okay? What's going on?" he asked, trying to hide his surprise.

"Faro wants you back in Raanana now," Klein said.

"What're you doing here?" Meshulam didn't understand.

"I told you, Faro wants you back in Raanana," Klein repeated.

Meshulam moved aside and looked at the closed door to Nevo's room. Klein was the last person he wanted to see now. If Faro wanted him in Raanana, why didn't he call? Why did he send Klein?

"Fine," he said after a short pause. "I'll go take care of the package and I'm coming." He nodded toward the closed door.

"He wants you to bring Nevo with you," Klein said.

"What? Why?" This was bad, very bad.

Klein shrugged.

What was going on? Why was Klein here? What did Faro want with Nevo? Did he know? No, that wasn't possible. Nevo had been here the whole time. He hadn't talked to anyone.

"Go back and tell Faro I'm on my way," he said in a last-ditch effort. Having Klein around jeopardized his plan. But maybe he still had a chance. After Klein left, he'd get Nevo and make sure to lose him on the way back.

"No can do. Faro told me to bring you with me. He wants you both in his office in an hour."

Chapter 56

ZIV sensed that something was coming, but he didn't know what. Meshulam dragged him by the shirt from the tiny room where they'd been holding him captive and put him in a car waiting outside. A man he'd never seen before was behind the wheel.

They drove at high speed, hitting every pothole in the bumpy road. Each time the car bounced, Ziv felt a sharp pain in his ribs. They'd thrown him onto the passenger seat with Meshulam in the back, just like the time they snatched him after he was released from jail. No one said a word. Outside, the countryside was dark and deserted. They could kill me here and nobody would ever know, he thought.

Locked up in that room, he'd debated endlessly whether to play his last card: the letter he'd placed in Merav's hands. He'd never tell them he'd left it with her. He'd say he sent it to some lawyer and refuse to give his name. But the more he thought about it, the more he decided against it. He regretted giving it to Merav in the first place. What if it put her in even greater danger? What if they figured out she had it?

"Pull over for a second. I need to take a leak," he heard Meshulam say from the rear.

Ziv took a deep breath. They were going to do it now. They'd pull him out of the car and kill him right here in the West Bank, in the middle of nowhere. He wondered if he should say something, but what could he say that would do any good? The order to take him out probably came directly from Faro. There was nothing he could do to change their minds.

The car came to a stop and the rear door opened. His time had come. He'd prayed with all his heart that they'd leave him be, let him go back to Merav and Gili and start a new chapter in his life. But he knew when he called Noam and placed himself in their hands that things might not go the way he hoped.

He heard Meshulam get out of the car. His heart was pounding. He had to keep it together.

Meshulam rapped loudly on the window. A tremor passed through Ziv's body. He kept his eyes fixed straight ahead, not wanting to turn his head and see the finger gesturing for him to get out. And maybe the gun that was going to go off very soon too.

"You wanna piss?" Meshulam asked.

He gazed at him in surprise. What was going on? Since when did Meshulam care what he wanted?

Without thinking, he shook his head slowly.

Meshulam stood there motionless, staring at him.

"Get a move on, Meshulam, we haven't got all night. Do what you gotta do and get back in," the driver said. Meshulam moved away from the car.

Chapter 57

RATTLED, Galit Lavie left the courthouse and walked rapidly toward her office. What was wrong with her? How could she blow up like that? It wasn't the first time she'd been hounded by reporters when she stepped out of a courtroom. She'd grown accustomed to it over the years, even when they sometimes crossed the line. But despite her distaste, she'd learned to keep her cool. It was part of the job description, both hers and theirs.

But this time she'd snapped when Dori Engel approached her after the judge rendered his sentence in the case of the convenience store gang. Maybe it was because once again they'd gotten off lightly and she was mad at all the judges who were afraid to take a stand. Or maybe it was because his questions about Ziv Nevo touched a nerve. Or it could simply have been the way he did it, blocking her path, announcing imperially that he was the editor of the local paper himself, invading her space, acting as if he was entitled, as if it was her duty to stand at attention and answer his questions.

ONCE, a long time ago in one of her first murder trials, she'd given in and spoken to a reporter about the case. The next day she found herself misquoted in the paper and, even worse, the defense attorney had used what she'd supposedly said to complain to the court that the prosecutor was trying his client in the press. Ever since, she'd promised herself never to talk to reporters. She knew some of her colleagues took advantage of the media to get their message out, to influence public opinion and counter the slanderous comments of the defense and the accused, or even—no, make that mainly—to make a name for themselves. But she'd resisted the temptation since that incident early on. It takes a certain talent to manipulate the press, and she didn't have it. Besides, like her father used to say when she was little, "If you burn your fingers, you watch your toes."

"You'll have to address your questions to the Justice Ministry's press liaison," she'd said to Engel, using the standard formula, but her words had no effect. He continued to follow her down the hall, calling out that she ought to be ashamed of herself, that because of her an innocent man had been convicted, that in any other civilized country she would've been kicked out on her ass by now.

She kept walking rapidly, ignoring his provocations, but it didn't do any good. He ran after her, accusing and embarrassing her, not letting up. When she felt she couldn't take any more, she turned around and yelled at him to fuck off and leave her alone.

Everybody in the courthouse corridor turned to look at them with concern. Even Engel seemed taken aback by her outburst and shut his mouth.

As usual, as soon as it happened, she was sorry she'd lost it. She wasn't a drama queen by nature. But before she had a chance to apologize, he came up to her and hissed warningly, "You're gonna regret you did that. When the story comes out on Friday, you'll be sorry you weren't nicer to me, Madame Prosecutor."

Chapter 58

MESHULAM had to fight hard to hold back the tears. The man who never wept, who had nothing but contempt for crybabies, felt his eyes welling up.

On the way here he'd tried to persuade himself that things would work out in the end, that fate would smile on him. But the moment he saw the expression on Faro's face or, more precisely, the lack of expression the boss adopted when he was deliberately ignoring someone, he knew it was all over for him. He'd willed Faro to look at him, maybe even forgive him. He'd be satisfied with any reaction, a word or two. But nothing. Faro said only, "I guess this is the day of the walking wounded." Meshulam didn't understand.

He asked for five minutes of his time. He needed to apologize, to explain why he did it, to convince him that his intentions had been good despite what it looked like, that he did it for him because he thought it was what he wanted. But Faro ignored him completely, as if he were invisible.

It was Nevo who was now getting the warm reception, the hand on the shoulder, the avuncular "How're you doing?" He'd made a last desperate attempt to get rid of Nevo on the road. If he'd just gotten out of the car, he could've shot him and claimed he was trying to make a run for it. But that didn't go his way either. The motherfucker had more luck than sense. Meshulam sat in the backseat and saw Nevo's fear slowly evaporate. When he first dragged him out of the house in Shufa and threw him into the car, he was scared and nervous, probably expecting to be dead soon. But the idiot eventually got the picture when he saw they weren't taking him deeper into the West Bank but back across the Green Line, and they weren't driving on back roads either but on the main highway. When they pulled into Faro's driveway, he could see something close to a smile on Nevo's face. He finally realized he was safe, that if anything was going to happen to him, it would've happened by now.

"Why did you call Noam?" Faro asked Nevo when the three of them were in his study.

The whole story came spilling out of Nevo's mouth. He told Faro about the bomb, about the police interrogation, about Meir's threat—everything.

Meshulam sat in silence, his face going pale. Every word out of Nevo's mouth was another nail in his coffin. He tried several times to catch Faro's eye, but it was useless. The boss sat there in silence, listening closely to Nevo's story.

Whatever Faro decided, he'd take it like a man. Even if he ordered him killed. When it came down to it, that might be for the best. His life would be worth nothing without Faro. What else did he have in this fucking world? There was a time he thought he could turn his life around, that even though his mother was a junkie and a whore, he'd make something of himself. Faro would save him. But you can't screw with fate. He was destined to be a loser. He was his mother's son. The man who had pulled him out of the garbage was about to throw him back in.

Faro rose and held out his hand to Nevo. Pulling himself out of the chair with effort, Nevo extended a trembling hand.

"I wish you a happy life. Give your wife and kid my regards," Faro said with the hint of a smile.

Nevo remained standing there like a statue, uncertain what to do. He'd spent the past weeks fleeing, eluding his pursuers, hiding from Faro and the cops, and now all of a sudden he could stop running.

Faro gestured for Yaki, who'd been standing in the back of the room the whole time, to take him away.

"Look out for yourself," he said as he sat down again. Yaki escorted Nevo out.

WHEN the door closed behind them, Faro turned his eyes to Meshulam for the first time.

"David, David, David. What am I going to do with you?" He sighed.

Chapter 59

NACHUM listened in a mixture of boredom and anger as Amit Giladi apologized, again blaming his editor for everything. His mind
wandered back to what he'd done earlier that day. Although Faro
didn't promise him anything—he hadn't expected him to—he'd
left feeling more confident. If Faro had Nevo, he believed there
was a good chance he'd let him go. If not, he'd carry out his threat.
He didn't care how many doors he'd have to bang on or how many
people tried to get in his way, in the end he'd force the cops to take
action.

He'd driven around for a while instead of going straight home.
He considered heading to north Tel Aviv and questioning the resi-
dents, the job he'd assigned to Giladi, but changed his mind. He
didn't have a badge or the authority to question anyone. If he wanted
people to talk to him, he had to gain their trust and make himself
likable, but the limp and the bruises on his face were more apt to
scare them off.

In the end, he found himself sitting on a bench facing the ocean,
watching the waves lapping at the shore. Like every day lately, he
was putting off the time he'd have to go home and look in the faces
of the people he'd let down, the people who'd relied on him and no
longer could.

When he finally went home, he found Giladi waiting for him.
The reporter came up to him as he was parking the car. His immedi-
ate instinct was to brush him off, like the last time. But he held back.
Not so fast, he thought. He'd wait at least until he'd heard what the
kid had to say. After the meeting with Faro, he felt he had the wind

at his back, that he still had the power to make things happen. Besides, the main reason he'd approached Giladi in the first place still held: he needed someone to be his legman, to do what he couldn't do himself.

Giladi didn't stop talking. He didn't want to cover the rape, especially not that way. It was all his editor. Dori Engel was a snake in the grass. He'd pushed, manipulated, made all the calls. It was Dori's fault Amit had waited outside for Adi Regev to come out of her house and been yelled at for harassing her, his fault he'd gone to the hospital to talk to Dana Aronov's parents and been slapped in the face by her mother, and his fault he'd said all those malicious things about Nachum in the paper.

Nachum watched him, not saying anything, listening with only half an ear to his excuses and pleas for forgiveness. The truth was, he almost felt sorry for the kid. He wanted desperately to be a man and didn't know how.

The only question was whether he could still be of use to him. He was no genius. And as it turned out, he was also irresponsible. Despite how mad Nachum had been when he read the interview in the paper, he'd at least taken comfort in the fact that Giladi hadn't revealed the information he'd given him about the rings. But he now learned that the omission wasn't the result of the reporter's urge to further the investigation, of his understanding that certain details had to be kept secret from the public. It was simply because his editor didn't fancy the label "Ring Rapist" that he suggested.

He couldn't send him back to the Zodiac Café. Giladi told him about his altercation with the owner, how he'd thrown him out when he learned which paper he worked for and who his editor was.

Nachum leaned his head back and drummed his fingers on his knee. What should he do? What *could* he do now that so many avenues for his investigation were closed to him because of this stupid kid?

Most perps got caught because they made mistakes. Real life wasn't like the movies where the crooks were super-clever and solving a crime took a brilliant mind and a spark of genius. Nachum knew the value of persistent, painstaking work, but he also knew that a little luck never hurt. He remembered his old commander, Amnon Mizrachi, who liked to paraphrase Napoleon. "Get me lucky detectives," he'd always say.

If he were a betting man, he'd say the rapist had already made a mistake. It was his job to find out what it was and examine it under the light. And as always, as soon as he found it he'd wonder why he hadn't seen it before.

Ziv Nevo's name had come up too many times in relation to the rapes. He didn't do it, Nachum was positive. But maybe it was someone connected to him, someone he knew or had dealings with.

Chapter 60

AMIT forced himself to remain quiet. Nachum's eyes were closed. He hoped his invitation to come upstairs meant the detective was willing to give him a second chance, but meanwhile he seemed to have other things on his mind. Amit wasn't even sure he'd been listening to him outside. And he'd been very aware of the look of contempt that came over him when he told about his recent unpleasant encounters. "You've taken a lot of abuse," Nachum had said sarcastically.

He shouldn't have whined so much about Dori. Nachum must think he was a little kid who couldn't cope.

"Is there anything I can do?" he asked to be sure Nachum hadn't dozed off.

Nachum promptly opened his eyes, gazed at Giladi, and pulled himself up straight in his chair.

"You have any pictures of other people on the paper, other reporters?" he asked.

"What?" The question took Amit by surprise.

"Facebook, e-mail. I want to see pictures of the people you work with. I've got an idea," Nachum repeated, not taking his eyes off the reporter.

"What do you want them for?"

"Do you or don't you?" Nachum admonished him impatiently.

"I don't know. Why would I?" He knew very well where he could get the pictures, but he was hoping that by pretending ignorance he could get Nachum to tell him what he was looking for.

The detective stood up abruptly.

"I don't have time for games, Giladi," he said menacingly, closing the distance between them.

"I can get you Facebook pictures from an employee outing to a water park. Will that do?" he said, recoiling. Under ordinary circumstances, he'd demand to know exactly what Nachum wanted them for, but in view of his past behavior, he didn't dare. He had to cooperate if he didn't want Nachum to throw him out and slam the door behind him. Besides, the old guy was a little intimidating.

Nachum smiled, and Amit realized he'd never seen him smile before.

"Come with me," he ordered.

Nachum led the reporter into a small study crammed with books. A computer sat on the desk in the middle of the room.

"Sit down and log on to Facebook," he commanded sharply.

"Can you tell me what I'm doing this for?" Amit couldn't resist asking.

"Soon. First let's see if you've got anything to show me."

Amit clicked on his Facebook account and opened the file with the photos from the water park. "Here you go . . . pictures . . . Now can you tell me?" He looked up at Nachum, but the detective ignored the question, gesturing for him to get up so he could sit down at the computer.

He looked over Nachum's shoulder as he quickly scanned the photos on the screen.

"That's your editor?" he asked, pointing to a picture of him with Dori and Tzila on the way to a water slide.

"Yes," he said, nodding, remembering how Dori had announced the day before that they'd each have to pay for their own ticket, and when Stav said the employer usually pays, he'd shrieked at her that if she didn't like it she could find herself another job. No way he was going back to the paper, whatever happened, he thought as he watched Nachum. What the hell was he looking for?

Suddenly Nachum stood up and turned around to face him. "I want to talk to your boss," he said.

Now it was Amit's turn to offer no response. He was tired of Nachum's games, of the orders he kept firing at him. If he wanted to be someone's whipping boy, he'd stay at the paper.

"Well? What're you waiting for?"

"I want to know why first," Amit said firmly.

Nachum walked out of the room without answering. Amit followed him reluctantly. When they reached the living room, Nachum handed him the cell phone he'd left on the coffee table. He got it: he was being thrown out. Nachum was onto something and he wasn't going to tell him what it was.

"Call him and see if he's home," the detective ordered.

"Why?" Amit insisted. The last thing he wanted to do was talk to Dori after ignoring his calls all day.

"Just make the call. I'll explain soon enough," Nachum said impatiently.

"I'm not really comfortable . . . ," Amit stammered, starting to tell him how Dori had told him to go to the courthouse and interview Galit Lavie.

"What's Galit Lavie got to do with it?" Nachum interrupted.

Chapter 61

GALIT kicked herself. Why was she such an idiot? "Let me off by the supermarket. I have to pick up a few things," she'd just heard herself say. Assaf threw her a puzzled look, baffled. She could read the question in his eyes: Shopping? Now?

If she could, she'd tell him the truth, but she couldn't. Not yet. She had to keep her mask on, play the game. If it weren't for all the rules, she'd confess she was nervous about the inevitable awkward silence at the end of a first date. She routinely cross-examined murderers and rapists on the stand, but in those final moments she never knew what to say to a man and just went dumb.

It didn't matter when it was someone she wasn't attracted to, but this time was different. She liked him. She'd been a basket case for the past ten minutes, nodding and smiling from time to time so he wouldn't realize she wasn't listening to what he was saying. Her brain was actually occupied trying to frame memorable good-night phrases. Those two minutes at the end of the date were crucial. That's what stuck in a man's mind.

HE'D phoned her two days ago. She was sure the call was prompted by the rumors that had spread like wildfire throughout the local legal system: his former client, Ziv Nevo, was innocent. The cops and the DA had got it wrong from the start.

But she was mistaken. Like her, he was an eloquent speaker in a courtroom or plea-bargaining session, but now he sounded hesitant. He'd wanted to ask her out for a long time, he explained, but he'd held back because of their professional relationship. He'd finally decided to put his reservations aside. He found himself very attract-ed to her, he stammered at the end, bringing a smile to her face.

She didn't really know what to expect. He picked her up at nine and broke the initial uncomfortable silence by asking if she was still walking to work.

"You remember?" she said, pleased that he'd paid such attention. "For the time being. My brother's leaving in two or three weeks and I'll finally get my car back, I hope. He was supposed to be here for ten days, but he keeps putting off the flight back to Germany. My mother's thrilled, but I'm going crazy without the car." She heard herself babbling like a schoolgirl and shut up.

"If you miss your car so much, we can go karting," he suggested.

She was ashamed to have to admit she had no idea what that was.

"Go-kart racing," he explained.

"You watch or drive?"

"You drive," he answered with a smile, searching her face for her reaction to his suggestion.

"Sounds like fun," she said, returning the smile.

She was pretty sure she wouldn't put karting at the top of her list of favorite activities. Actually, she was certain she wouldn't. She hated to drive fast, preferring to crawl down the road under the speed limit. And she didn't think helmets were her thing. But when all was said and done, she had a good time. She liked the fact that he'd given it thought, had come up with a cute, original idea. Maybe he took all his dates here. He probably did (she thought she saw the guy in the ticket booth wink at him when he showed up with her, but she might have imagined it). So what? In the dating world, with all its strict rules, she was impressed by anything out of the ordinary.

BUT then she had to go and ruin everything. Instead of the eve-ning ending on a positive note like it should have, she had to blurt out, "Let me off by the supermarket. I have to pick up a few things."

He stopped the car in front of the supermarket, looking just as disappointed with her as she was with herself. A car honked for them to get out of the way. Eleven thirty at night and the traffic was almost as heavy as midafternoon. "You'd better get out," he said quietly, nodding toward the car behind them.

She was out of time. She had to say or do something to salvage the situation. If she were in his place, she'd think she was blowing him off.

"I had a good time tonight," she said with a smile.

Assaf remained silent. Taking a deep breath, she leaned over and kissed him.

AS usual, the walkway to her building was dark, Brenner, her upstairs neighbor, insisting on turning the light off. She'd asked him time and again to leave it on, explaining that it made her uneasy to walk down the path in the dark, especially after the incidents in the neighborhood. But he stood his ground. Eighty years old and a skinflint to boot. He didn't give a damn about young women and their phobias.

But tonight it didn't matter. She was in too good a mood. She'd just gotten a text from Assaf saying he'd had a good time too. In dating-speak, that meant he wanted to see her again.

She strolled toward the entrance carrying the bag of groceries. This might be the start of something good, she thought to herself.

Suddenly she froze. Someone was standing by the front door. Despite the darkness, his presence was unmistakable. What should she do? Turn on her heels and run? She stuck her hand in her purse and clutched the canister of pepper spray.

"Hello." She was sure she'd heard that voice somewhere today.

Galit breathed a sigh of relief when he stepped into the light and she saw his face.

"What're you doing here? You startled me," she said angrily.

"I've been waiting for you," he replied, coming closer.

"What for?"

He didn't answer.

Her relief was short-lived. Something didn't feel right. Why was he waiting for her in the dark?

"You weren't very nice to me today," he said. She could feel his breath on her cheek.

She took a step back, but he was faster. He grabbed her arm. She struggled to free herself.

"You were mean to me. I treated you with respect and you humiliated me," he said, tightening his grip on her. The reek of his sweat was making her sick to her stomach. Again she fought to get free, but he pulled her closer.

"What're you doing?" she asked, her voice unsteady.

Now she could see a large knife in his other hand.

"I always give them a chance. But you're special, aren't you? So you'll get special treatment, just for you."

Galit stared at him in terror. Her pulse was racing. Both Adi and Dana said the rapist had threatened to kill them if they didn't play along. He wanted them to beg for their life. Is that what he meant when he said he gave them a chance?

She realized her best move would be to apologize for offending him, beg for his forgiveness, promise to do whatever he wanted, but she couldn't get the words out. The only sound she made was the scream that escaped from her throat when he grabbed her by the hair and threw her on the ground.

Chapter 62

DORI wasn't answering his phone. Amit kept trying, but all he got was a recorded message saying the number was unavailable. "That's odd," he said after the fifth failed attempt to reach him. "Dori never switches off his phone."

Nachum was still weighing everything Giladi had told him, examining the image that took shape in his mind as the reporter was talking. He hadn't paid much attention when Giladi started spouting excuses, but as the words sank in, he gradually found himself focusing on the picture he was painting of a man who enjoyed demeaning his employees, who had an obsessive interest in the rapes, who kept pushing Giladi to find out more about the investigation, who took great delight in putting the cops to shame. He wasn't sure he agreed that the editor had left the rings out of the story in the paper merely because he didn't like the name Giladi suggested. Add to that the fact that he was a regular customer at the Zodiac Café.

Although the facts seemed to be leading him in one direction, Nachum was reluctant to draw hasty conclusions. He was too seasoned a detective for that. It was all circumstantial, easily explained. Besides, the last time he'd jumped to conclusions he'd found himself chasing the wrong man, and he'd ruined the poor guy's life and gotten himself kicked off the force in the process.

That's why he needed to see a picture of Engel. He'd asked Giladi to show him photos of all the people he worked with because he didn't want him to know where he was going with this, but the only person he was really interested in was Dori Engel.

Giladi called him a snake in the grass. Nachum's heart missed a beat when he saw the photo of him standing by the pool in bathing trunks. The man he was looking at matched Adi's description, and even bore a certain resemblance to Nevo in terms of height, build, and complexion. Most damningly, tattooed snakes slithered up both his arms.

It all fit: his physique, face, tattoos, and character profile, as well as the attempt to keep tabs on the rape investigation and the way he taunted the victims, their families, and the cops. It all fit.

What should he do with it? The right thing would be to take it to Ohad. But what if he was wrong? He didn't have a single piece of solid evidence, just a hunch. They wouldn't be in a hurry to arrest a respected journalist, and surely not solely on the word of a disgraced ex-detective.

"Try again," he instructed Giladi. He needed to come face-to-face with Engel before he went to Ohad. He wanted to get the feel of the man, to draw him out, get him talking, learn more about him.

While Giladi was trying to reach Engel, he dialed Galit Lavie again, but she still didn't pick up. Her phone also seemed to be switched off. He was troubled by Giladi's assumption that Engel had gone to the courthouse to interview her himself. He knew her well enough to know there was little chance she'd agree to the interview, and her refusal might enrage Engel, and then . . . He nipped that thought in the bud. He didn't want to get ahead of himself.

It was eleven o'clock at night.

"Are you finally ready to tell me what the hell is going on?" Giladi said, interrupting his thoughts.

Nachum gazed at him for a long time without saying anything, trying to come to a decision. He couldn't just sit here twiddling his thumbs. He had to get out there. He had to do something.

"Come on, we're leaving," he said.

HE drove rapidly, swerving through the traffic. Galit had once told him she lived down the block from Adi. Same street. He tried her number again. No answer.

He had a very bad feeling in the pit of his stomach. What if his theory was right from start to finish? What if Engel was going after Galit tonight? What then? His instincts had let him down badly the last time, but until then he'd always been able to trust his gut. He had to trust it now too, not hesitate simply because he might be wrong again.

He tried to reach Galit one more time. Still no answer. Engel wasn't picking up either.

He had no choice. He had to risk it. If he was wrong, he'd have to learn to live with it. But if he wasn't, he'd never be able to forgive himself.

Ohad sounded drowsy when he answered the phone. Nachum could hear the television in the background. He spoke quickly, outlining his theory, explaining where it led, or at least where he thought it led. Ohad listened in silence. Out of the corner of his eye, the detective could see Giladi's mouth gaping wider and wider.

"What do you want me to do?" Ohad asked when he was done. His tone was now crisp and purposeful.

"Send a couple of squad cars to the area around Louis Marshall, and make sure one goes straight to her house," Nachum answered, leaning harder on the gas pedal.

"This's blowing my mind. I'm in shock," Giladi said when Nachum hung up.

"Relax, it's just a theory. I'm not sure I'm right. I just don't want to take any risks," Nachum said in an effort to calm the reporter. He knew Giladi would be the first to plunge a knife into him if he was wrong.

"It makes sense, it all fits. I always knew he was a psychopath.

Now I get why the maniac kept pressuring me to stay on the story. He must have been very pleased with himself when you arrested the wrong man. I bet he was licking his lips when he sent me to bug Adi Regev and when he harassed Dana Aronov's poor parents in the hospital."

Nachum kept his thoughts to himself.

"I can already see tomorrow's headline," Giladi muttered to himself. " 'Engel Is the Devil.' "

Chapter 63

SARAH Glazer was dreaming she was a little girl riding a bicycle through the streets of Tel Aviv when she was startled awake by the noise of sirens. She looked at the alarm clock by her bed. A quarter to twelve. She had a doctor's appointment tomorrow morning and she wanted to get there early so she didn't have to wait. She'd asked to be Dr. Shaham's first patient of the day, but she didn't trust him to keep to the schedule.

She closed her eyes, hoping to sink back into her cozy dream, but she had trouble getting back to sleep. It was hard enough for her to fall asleep these days, even without all the noise outside.

Sarah dragged herself out of bed and turned on the light. The wailing of the sirens was now joined by the sound of a helicopter overhead.

She walked through the house, switching on the lights as she went. Knowing she was all alone in the apartment made her feel anxious, especially in the dark. Ever since Sefi died, there was no one there to grumble, "What's all the racket. Do they think it's Independence Day?" or "How do you expect me to pay the electric bill?" She got her binoculars and opened the blinds. She was immediately blinded by a flashing blue light.

"This is the police. Stay inside and keep your doors closed," she heard a metallic voice call through a megaphone.

She focused the binoculars on the street below and saw that nice police officer who'd visited with her last month. He was running down the street, limping badly. She didn't recall a limp when he was in her house. She'd read he was fired, but that must be a mistake. He was so professional, so courteous.

She continued to follow him through the binoculars. When he got to the corner, he stopped by a police car. Several people were milling around him. She adjusted the focus and saw that he had his arms around someone, a young woman with long hair.

Sarah's heart started racing. She wondered what new catastrophe had struck her street. She had to find out, but she remembered Dr. Shaham's orders to take a pill immediately when she had palpitations like this.

She stuck a pill under her tongue and went into the bathroom to wash her face. The binoculars were still hanging from her neck, so she decided she might as well see how the cats were coping with all the commotion. In contrast to the noise and excitement in the front of the house, it was dark and quiet in the back. She couldn't distinguish anything in the blackness until she pressed the night-vision button. She froze. A man was lying there on the ground, curled up like a baby, hiding.

Her heart was still pounding despite the pill. Images from that horrible night floated up before her eyes. She left the bathroom and hurried into the living room. With shaking hands she opened the drawer in the credenza and took out the police officer's card. Inspector Nachum, she read.

He answered on the second ring. She took a deep breath. This time she was going to do something.

"Inspector Nachum? This is Mrs. Glazer, Sarah Glazer. One of the neighbors. The man you're looking for is hiding in the backyard of my building."

Chapter 64

ZIV fiddled nervously with his cell phone while Merav was buying Gili a lollipop. From time to time she glanced up at him and their eyes met. He hadn't made the call yet. He'd promised her he'd wait till the last minute.

IT was three months since Faro had given him his life back. He still didn't understand exactly how it happened, why they let him go so casually after they'd been so determined to get their hands on him.

He'd allowed himself a glimmer of hope when the car passed through the border crossing. After all, it would have been easy to kill him before they left the West Bank. It was the middle of the night and they were traveling on a dark, secluded road. But he was still afraid to believe he'd get out alive. So many things had gone wrong in his life. Even at the end, when Faro said, "Look out for yourself," and his body responded with a shudder of relief, his brain still refused to take it in.

In less than a minute, he was standing in the street outside Faro's imposing house. A heavy door slammed shut behind him and he was free. He walked away quickly, lengthening his strides the farther he went, until he was running as fast as he could in his condition. His body shrieked in pain, but he had to get as far away as possible.

Gasping for breath, he kept on running. He stopped only when he was about to collapse. Leaning against a utility pole, he looked back to be sure no one was following him, that it wasn't just another trick. The street was empty. He was all alone.

"EL Al Flight 325 to Paris is now boarding at Gate Two. Passengers are requested to proceed to the boarding gate." He looked over at Merav again. She was just leaving the candy shop with Gili in her arms. She smiled at him and nodded. It was time. He could make the call.

SOME nights he woke up covered in sweat, his heart pounding, petrified by the thought that he'd imagined it all, that he was still living the nightmare, that it wasn't over yet. It was only when he felt the stroke of her soft hand and heard her say everything was all right that he could breathe normally again. Sometimes in the middle of the day he felt compelled to go by Gili's preschool to see for himself that he was safe. If he could, he'd never let them leave the house.

He didn't know how it happened, but all of a sudden all the bad had vanished from his life. The police were finally convinced that he didn't rape anyone, the true criminal was caught (it turned out to be the editor of the local paper, the headlines screaming "Engel Is the Devil" on the day his name was released to the press), Faro was out of the picture, and what mattered most: he had his family back. It was like someone had waved a magic wand and banished the darkness, bathing him in a bright, warm light.

HE made his way to an empty gate, his mind echoing Merav's apprehensions. Taking a deep breath, he pulled out his cell phone. His heart was racing. Was she right? Was he making a mistake? "Stop it," he admonished himself. "You've made your decision. Quit agonizing over it." He knew he might live to regret it, but it was the right thing to do.

TWO weeks ago, he and Merav had decided to accept her uncle's offer of a job in his flowerpot factory in Strasbourg. Ziv had always laughed off the suggestion that he go all the way to France just to sell flowerpots. He didn't know a word of French.

But after everything they'd been through, it didn't seem like such a bad idea anymore. After all, they say that when one door closes, another one opens. Besides, Faro was liable to change his mind, and as for Meshulam, the hatred he'd seen in his eyes during the meeting with his boss had sent a shiver down Ziv's spine.

He kept reminding himself that even though he was on top of the world at the moment and surviving the ordeal made him feel reborn, the euphoria was bound to wear off and then he'd go back to life as usual. He'd have to leave the security of his home and go out looking for a job, which meant he'd have to deal with the same questions about his former position and why he had been laid off. No one wanted to hire him before, and he could be certain they wouldn't now that there was a cloud of suspicion hanging over his head, no matter that his conviction had been overturned. Where there's smoke there's fire, people said. In France, nobody knew who he was, nobody knew about his past, and his name didn't immediately arouse associations with manhunts and rapists. He'd be able to start over with a clean slate.

"HELLO?" He heard Nachum's voice through the phone.

"It's . . . Ziv . . . Ziv Nevo," he said, clearing his throat.

He agreed with Merav that it was very likely he owed his release to Nachum. Something the detective said or did must have induced Faro to back off. But even though he'd saved Nachum's life, and Nachum had probably saved his, he still couldn't forget that night in the interrogation room, the man's terrifying eyes, his refusal to listen, his callousness.

AS soon as the decision was made, they started getting ready to leave. Merav quit her job and they took Gili out of preschool. Ziv was about to say good-bye to his old life, but he couldn't stop thinking about what he'd done, about the bomb that was under a car somewhere waiting to go off.

Merav tried to persuade him to forget it. There was nothing he could do about it now, even if he wanted to, she said. And the price was too high. Ziv had to agree. Meir's words in Abu Kabir still echoed in his head, and even Faro's parting "Look out for yourself" contained a thinly veiled threat.

The smart thing to do was to keep going and not look back, but he couldn't do it. The more he thought about it, the clearer it became to him: if he wanted to open a new door in his life, he had to close the old one first. And he couldn't do that without fixing what he'd broken.

For a week he'd walked the streets around Louis Marshall Street looking for the car. Having learned his lesson from the last time, he conducted his search during the day with Merav by his side. But the car was gone. He went back time and again, but he couldn't find it. After a while he gave up. If he hadn't found the car by now, he never would. He consoled himself with the thought that the bomb might have gone off without causing any harm, or Faro might have had it dismantled in time.

Then last night as they lay in bed looking around at their empty apartment, its contents already on the way to France, he brought it up again. "I have to wrap this up before we leave," he said to Merav, telling her he wanted to talk to Nachum. "That's insane," she protested. "He's not your friend, he's a cop. What happens if he decides to have you arrested? You committed a felony! You want me and Gili to go to the airport while you go to jail? I don't want to lose you again," she said, bursting into tears.

He gathered her in his arms and kissed her hair. He didn't want to lose her again either. There had to be another way.

"HOW'S Merav? Gili?" Nachum asked.

"They're fine, thanks," he mumbled. In the distance he could see the passengers lining up at the gate to board the flight to Paris. Merav and Gili were already there. He didn't have much time.

Naturally, he wasn't going to mention Faro's name. Or Meshulam's either, for that matter. He'd just give him the license plate number. That was enough. The cops could take it from there. He wasn't going to let himself worry about what conclusions the detective drew or what he did with the information. If he wanted to, he could order his arrest and the government could request his extradition from France. He didn't kid himself. He knew he was taking a risk.

"What's that noise? Where are you?" Nachum asked when the last call for the flight to Paris was announced.

Chapter 65

GALIT was enjoying the feel of the warm sun on her skin. She didn't have to be in court today, so she'd decided to take advantage of the opportunity to bring her car in for its annual safety inspection. She'd only gotten it back yesterday after her parents had intervened when they heard her arguing with her brother about it.

"Go for it," Assaf had joked, kissing her before he left for work. They'd been together for a month, and so far it was going great.

She stretched and felt a stabbing pain in her back, a reminder of that night. If Eli Nachum hadn't acted on his hunch so quickly, she would've been Dori Engel's latest rape victim. Maybe even his first murder victim.

The line of cars was inching forward slowly. She should've listened to Assaf and let the garage take the car in for its inspection. She could've used the time to get some rest.

Her cell phone rang. Nachum. Any other day she would have answered immediately, but now she decided to ignore the call and switched the phone to MUTE. She'd promised herself a day off, and she didn't want to think about work today.

IN a few months, she'd have to testify against Engel in court. For the first time in her life, she'd be on the witness stand, not at the prosecutor's desk. Engel's conviction was a slam dunk even without her testimony. He had a tattoo on the back of his left arm (a snake, not a dragon as Sarah Glazer thought), and the rings he took from Adi and Dana were found in his apartment, along with two others from unknown victims, despite Nachum's prediction that he'd probably gotten rid of them.

"Right turn signal, ma'am. Left turn signal," the inspector shouted at her, interrupting her thoughts.

They'd gotten a confession out of Engel, but Sivan, the ADA on the case, told her he'd recanted. It seemed his attorney was planning to argue diminished responsibility. It was all because of his difficult childhood: his father had abandoned him, the schools and welfare agencies had turned a blind eye, and he'd been sexually molested by a friend of his mother's. She'd heard those sob stories before. Scum like Dori always had a list of people to blame and tales to tell. He'd probably say the women asked for it, that they teased him, that it was their fault—all that chauvinistic crap. She never bought their excuses. People had free will. They didn't have to be the product of their upbringing. Assaf thought her attitude was too simplistic and inflexible. Maybe that's why he was a defense attorney and she was a prosecutor.

They never talked about what happened that day in her office, how they put together a plea bargain that led to the conviction of an innocent man. He knew why she'd done it. After all, it was in all the papers. But she'd probably never know why he agreed to it. He'd never break lawyer-client confidentiality. Whatever Ziv Nevo told him, the reason he didn't want to fight to prove his innocence would forever remain a secret.

But she did talk about it with her colleagues in the DA's Office, including Rachel Zuriel. It shouldn't have happened, we have to be more careful, but the bottom line is that these things happen. That's what everyone said, and it's what she told herself.

"We don't have all day, ma'am. Put it in reverse, please. Brakes," the inspector shouted, and she did as she was told.

Her cell phone flashed. Nachum again. She'd call him back when she was done here. He was more than just "work." She owed him her life.

She'd seen him in the courthouse last week when he came to testify in one of her cases. They took advantage of the opportunity to sit down together in the cafeteria. Over coffee, he'd hinted there was a reason Faro's henchmen had been holding Nevo. Apparently, he'd gotten mixed up with them even before that. She didn't ask for details and he didn't offer any. If it was true, Nevo hadn't said a word about it when he was questioned. Faro was a dangerous man who didn't forget and didn't forgive. She'd gotten a taste of the brutality of the crime lord and his organization in Yariv Cohen's trial.

"The lights are okay. Move forward, ma'am," the inspector shouted. She drove on to the next station, stopping over the pit for inspection of the undercarriage.

Nachum called a third time. She'd be through in a minute and get back to him. He hadn't been reinstated yet. Everyone knew he belonged on the force, but no commander wanted him on his team. In the cafeteria he'd said he might relocate to Haifa.

Galit was so wrapped up in her thoughts that she didn't notice the commotion outside.

"Get out of the car, ma'am," someone shouted at her over his shoulder. He seemed to be running away.

She looked around and saw that everybody had moved as far away from her as possible.

"What's going on?" she said, sticking her head out the window.

"There's a bomb under the car!" one of the inspectors yelled.

"What?"

"Two hand grenades stuck under your car. Get out! Now!"

Chapter 66

ZIV was sitting at the kitchen table looking out at the rain. It hadn't let up for two days. The weather here was depressing. It was too cold, too wet. He missed the sunshine back home. At this time of year the days were warm and bright.

Merav and Gili were still asleep. The house was quiet, the silence broken only by the sound of the Israeli newscast coming from his computer. The newsreader was reporting breathlessly about rumors that the defense minister was preparing to announce his resignation within the hour.

Getting up from his chair, Ziv yawned and stretched. It was Sunday, the start of a new week in Israel. It was still the weekend here. That was another thing it was hard for him to adjust to. Even though they'd been in France for several months now, he kept having to remind himself that the weekend started on Saturday, not Friday. His biological clock was still set for Israeli time.

A parade of commentators followed one another on the computer screen, each analyzing the effect of the minister's resignation on the stability of the government, the peace process, tensions with Israel's Arab neighbors. As usual, Israelis were convinced that whatever happened in the country had global impact.

He wasn't happy here. He didn't belong. He didn't have any friends. Merav's uncle had given him a job in the warehouse in his factory. He spent his days arranging flowerpots on shelves. Her uncle promised him something better as soon as his French improved, but unlike Gili, who could already chatter away like a native, Ziv was still struggling to make sense of the language.

There were plenty of times when he felt he couldn't do it any-more, especially when he started thinking about what his future here was going to look like. But he didn't let those moments get the better of him. It took no more than a glance at Merav and Gili to remind him of what he had, of what he'd nearly lost for good. The experi-ences he'd been through had made him a better husband, a better father. At least, that's what he wanted to believe. He and Merav were trying to get pregnant. No luck yet, but never mind. In the mean-time, they were having fun trying.

Knowing he'd done the right thing helped too. He'd saved the life of that ADA, Galit Lavie. A few days after they arrived here, he read on the Internet that they'd found live grenades under her car and defused them in time. She was unharmed. He couldn't be-lieve the target was the prosecutor in his own case. He had no idea why Meshulam wanted him to rig a bomb to her car. He'd probably never know.

He turned on the radio. They were playing a familiar song, and he hummed along. He still knew all the words. It had been popular during his army days. They used to sing it in the car on the way to some disco in Tel Aviv when they were both on leave. When Merav got up he'd ask her if she remembered it.

The song tugged at his heart. It was always the little things that got to him: the hummus he found in a supermarket near their new home, a man walking down the street with a yarmulke on his head, pictures of the first snow in Jerusalem. "Look how beautiful it is!" he'd exclaimed, calling Gili to come see the pictures on the com-puter. Dressed in white, Jerusalem looked so serene and majestic. It seemed peaceful, not the scene of conflict and contention. His son gave him a puzzled look. It snowed almost every day in Strasbourg in winter. "Remember when we went to Jerusalem to see the snow?" Ziv asked, still trying to infect Gili with his excitement.

"I remember," Merav chimed in. "We were stuck in traffic for hours at the entrance to the city."

Two months from now, Merav and Gili would fly to Israel for her nephew's bar mitzvah. As much as he wanted to, he wouldn't be going with them. There was a warrant out for his arrest. He'd never be able to go back. He'd consulted with a French attorney and learned that he was safe as long as he stayed in France. Even if Israel requested his extradition, the French government wouldn't agree, he was told. Meanwhile, no such request had been filed. Sometimes he wondered if his current situation wasn't the result of a deliberate decision, a unique form of punishment tailor-made for him. He wasn't behind bars, maybe because Lavie wasn't hurt. Instead, he was condemned to serve out a life sentence remote from Israel.

Ziv sat down again and began surfing the news site. The defense minister's resignation still occupied the headline. But it turned out the reports were unfounded. His office issued a firm denial. The rumor mill had been working overtime. A small item farther down caught Ziv's eye. The police had identified the body that had washed up several days ago on the beach north of Caesarea. Ziv had been following the story. It was the badly decomposed body of a man in his late twenties. The police had no clue as to his identity. No one answering his description had been reported missing.

He heard Merav moving around in the bedroom. He got up and put the kettle on to make her coffee. The three of them would have breakfast together when Gili woke up. All things considered, he was a lucky man.

He went back to the computer. There was a new headline: Shimon Faro had been arrested for murder. Ziv's heart raced as he quickly scanned the article. The body on the beach was one of Faro's soldiers. With a shaking hand, he clicked on the link to the picture.

His jaw fell when he saw the face of the man whose identity they now knew. It was David Meshulam.

The night he'd gone to Faro's house was still fresh in his mind. He remembered the fury that had flashed in the crime lord's eyes when he told him what Meshulam had ordered him to do. Although Faro remained silent, Ziv was certain it was the first he'd heard of it.

He devoured every word in the news item. It didn't provide much information because the judge had issued a gag order. The report concluded with a quote from Inspector Eli Nachum, head of the special team in the Haifa district that was investigating the incident. He said the police had ironclad evidence against Shimon Faro; the murder was related to another case that had been under investigation several months ago. How come Nachum was back on the force?

Merav came into the kitchen. Ziv jumped up from his chair.

"What's wrong?" she asked, looking at him questioningly.

"Nothing, nothing at all," he mumbled. He needed time to think, to process what he'd read. And there was no reason to upset her with this the minute she got out of bed. She didn't like it that he wasn't able to cut his ties with their former life. She wanted to bury the past, to focus on the future.

"Really?" she asked, stroking his face.

"Really. Everything's fine," he said with a smile.

What did this murder mean for them? Deep down, he'd always been afraid he'd hear from Meshulam again, that he was still looking to get back at him. He couldn't forget that the man had tried to get rid of him there in the West Bank.

It was a few seconds before Ziv realized that Merav was waving something in front of his face with a big grin. Then it dawned on him.

"That's right, you got it," she said with a laugh, holding out the plastic stick. "We're pregnant!"

Acknowledgments

THE name of the editor appears in small letters (too small) on one of the front pages of every book. For this book, I had the honor of working with two. I met regularly, week after week, first with Amnon Jackont over a beer in the evening (after the kids were in bed), and then with Noa Menhaim over coffee early in the morning (before they got up). Not only did I relish every minute and learn a great deal from these editors, but a large part of the final product is the result of their ideas, insights, and suggestions.

I am very grateful to applied criminologist Dana Kiser, who taught me about the profile of rapists, and to my sister, Einav Shoham, for her input on legal issues.

To Assaf Nachum for reading the first draft, and to his father, Eli Nachum, who didn't object to the coincidental use of his name for one of my characters.

Thanks are also due to Nurit Waisman for agreeing to read the book before it was published and for the valuable opinions she offered, and to Tamar Bialik for always rooting for me, for her wise comments, and, no less important, for the title of the book.

To Yehiel Shamir and Nir Farber for allowing me to talk things through with them along the journey, and for their positive reinforcement.

To the staff at Kinneret Zmora-Bitan for their encouragement and support, especially when times were hard and pressure was high (times like this, for instance), and to Dov Alfon and Sefi Bar who, despite the fact that they are no longer with the publishing house, are happy to offer their advice whenever I ask.

To Ziv Lewis of Kinneret Zmora-Bitan, who began the journey into foreign lands with me and was a smart, enthusiastic, and patient partner (I had a lot of questions); to Jonny Geller, Kate Cooper, and the entire team at Curtis Brown, whose tireless and professional efforts have made it possible for you to read this page in English; to Sara Kitai, my talented translator. When reading the English translation, I sometimes forget the book was originally written in Hebrew. To Claire Wachtel from HarperCollins, who took the first leap of faith on my books. I hope, and trust, this is only the beginning of our road together.

To my family, particularly my parents, who are excited for me each time as if it were my first book, and take great delight in reporting what people are saying about it (as a parent myself, I understand what a wonderful feeling it is to hear such things).

Finally, with the deepest love, to Osnat, my personal secret ingredient as a writer and everything that entails. And of course, to Rona and Uri, who bring me more joy than words can describe.

About the Author

LIAD SHOHAM is Israel's leading crime writer and a practicing attorney with degrees from Jerusalem's Hebrew University and the London School of Economics. All his crime novels (five to date) have been critically acclaimed bestsellers. He lives in Tel Aviv and is married with two children.